I0725073

THE DEATH DEALER

SENTINELS OF MAGIC BOOK 2

T.M. CROMER

PROLOGUE

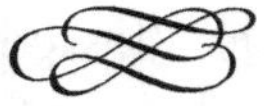

"Papa?"

"Almost ready, Sabrina," Damian called out. His voice was gravelly, packed with everything he wanted to say to her, his beloved daughter. His wild Beastie. All the mixed emotions he was experiencing at leaving her to assume his job as Aether, adding to her Oracle mantle, gathered within his chest and caused his heart to hammer uncomfortably.

Undoubtedly, she would feel them because of what she was, the power she wielded. In a short time, she'd be more powerful still. All he possessed—magic, money, and a shit-ton of responsibility—would transfer to her so he could be reborn and share a new life with his mate.

At well over five hundred years old, it was time for him to retire this body and lay it to rest.

A crack rent the air as lightning slashed across the sky, tearing through the fabric of the veil and revealing a portal to the Other-world through the opening. A woman in a shimmering white, floor-length gown guarded the entrance. Her dark hair danced on the breeze her spell had created.

The Goddess.

Understanding Damian's need to take a few precious minutes for his goodbyes, she patiently waited to help his soul transition to the next stage of its existence. After bowing his head as a sign of respect and acknowledging her presence, he turned his back to her.

His gaze swept over the tombstones surrounding the one meant for him, and he finally allowed himself to let go. To experience all the love and loss he held in check over his lifetime without allowing others to see. Isis encapsulated his emotional blast and protected those behind Beastie, who had arrived as a show of gratitude and support.

Some were descendants of his.

Others, his misfit band of Sentinels. The team had defied him at every turn but continued to have his back when it mattered most. More than once, they'd stood as a single unit with him, ready to burn the entire magical community to the ground if that was what it took to see justice done or to rescue him and each other from their many crimes against the Authority.

As those bittersweet memories flowed through him, Damian smiled. He'd loved those fuckers, the men and women who'd become his best friends. His gaze touched the granite headstone closest to him, and he squatted to run his fingers over the name etched in stone.

Trevor Michael Blane.

The Death Dealer.

Damian glanced up and met the eyes of Trevor in his latest incarnation, currently a teenager making his way in the world. Their bond was strong even now. This new version of Trevor wouldn't make the connection or understand why, and he likely wasn't familiar with the workings of rebirth yet, but one day he might recall. Sometimes people did.

And, of course, Damian would always remember his friend's story. The guy had never let him down in all the years they'd worked together. Sure, Trevor's assistance wasn't given without plenty of grumbling and a whole helluva lot of swearing whenever shit hit the fan. But without fail, he'd come through when it counted.

The man had been his own worst enemy at times, but his hadn't been an easy life back then…

CHAPTER 1

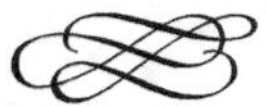

PRESENT DAY

Trevor Blane observed Soleil Stephens puttering about in her greenhouse from his spot beneath the tall pines, thirty yards away.

"Earth witches," he muttered.

How provincial they all were!

This one was no different.

She was toiling away at her workbench, scooping dirt into a pot as she planted yet another seedling. How ridiculous to use her hands and waste hours when a simple snap of her fingers would do. Watching her spend time with her plants was like watching grass grow—boring and a complete waste of his time.

She cooked like a five-star Michelin chef, though. Her cherry pie brought a smile to his lips whenever he thought about it. Four months ago, when they were all cloistered at the Aether's England estate, she and her hotter-than-hell sister Taryn made sure none of those present went hungry. Trevor still dreamed about that goddamned flaky pie crust.

"I suppose she has that going for her," he said aloud.

On the short side, Soleil possessed a full hourglass figure. Her hair was the color of the richest, darkest soil and bundled in a topknot that forever listed to one side. Stray tendrils escaped from the thick bun and curled along the nape of a graceful neck. Longer, non-strategically placed strands framed her rounded, flushed face. Like any witch, she had the ability to glamour and make herself perfect, but apparently, she preferred the form she was born with.

If Trev were being objective, he'd say she was attractive, but he preferred taller, sleeker women like Soleil's ethereal older sister, Vivian. Of course, as the wife of the Aether, she was off-limits to any man who wanted to take another breath. Damian Dethridge would smite anyone who considered hooking up with his beloved mate. And Trev had no desire to feel the pain of that sonofabitch's fury. Been there, done that.

None of his musings mattered. He was here for a job. A shitty, tedious job, but a job all the same.

When Soleil wiped her brow with her sleeve, leaving behind a smear of dirt, he cringed. Barely suppressing the desire to teleport in and scrub her face clean, he sighed his irritation. He should abandon his post. The woman rarely left her property unless she went to her nonsensical potion store, *The Elemental Shop*, to sell unsuspecting mortals her useless witchy wares. It wasn't like he needed to be here, right?

Why Trev had to stick to a timeline for this particular Death Dealer mission was a mystery. If he was going to eventually be tasked with taking her life, he might as well get it over with. He doubted he'd alter Fate's design by killing her early. The woman didn't appear to contribute to society in any worthwhile way.

A mouthwatering memory of cherry pie teased his brain.

Okay, maybe her baked delicacies were the exception. For another slice, he'd tell the Authority to go fuck themselves and protect her until his own dying day. Those delicious creations had transported him back to when his mother used to make him the best apple desserts known to man. Goddess, how he missed his mother. All these years of endless aching in his chest.

Soleil's squeal drew his attention, and he grimaced at the sight of the spilled potting soil. The poor woman was on the klutzy side, too. Why the hell had he drawn the short straw? The other Authority veterans had laughed at him when they heard of this assignment. Most were sent after the worst-of-the-worst criminals.

Not Trevor, though.

He was forced to babysit an earth elemental witch until the deities determined her time was up.

Who really knew why? He'd stopped questioning the Fates twenty-seven years ago. Going against the Authority would get you dead or, at the very least, punished. And who wanted banishment? Not him. The last time he'd braved going against his employer for the Aether and his daughter, it had earned him and his teammates shit jobs. Similar to this one.

And he hated it.

Trev appreciated the finer things in life. Wine, women, and fast cars. Not necessarily in that order. The witch in the greenhouse was another means to that end.

Like a startled deer, Soleil's head came up, and her eyes scanned the tree line where he was hidden. His inclination was to duck backward into the brush, but he was confident she couldn't see him behind his cloaking wall. She frowned her confusion and spun in a slow circle, looking for the source of her unease.

It appeared Soleil Stephens had finely tuned instincts. Finally! Something Trev could admire about her. Not that he wanted to, because liking her wasn't conducive to carrying out her assassination.

Again, the Aether came to mind. Trev prayed the man wasn't close to his sister-in-law. That was one fucker he didn't need on his ass. They'd met and worked together to end evil in the past, and he'd seen what Damian was capable of. Hopefully, he would understand that orders were orders when they came from on high. Likely not, though. Trev would need to do some fast talking.

A black-haired child chose that moment to run into the greenhouse. Cradled within the circle of her arms was a small cream-colored animal. "Aunt Soleil! Look what Summer gave me!"

"Summer? Who's Summer, Sabrina dear?"

"Cousin Alastair's daughter."

Trev straightened as his stomach dropped to his feet.

No one had told him a child would be hanging about. Especially not *Dethridge's* child. This situation just grew too sticky for his taste. If Sabrina was here, her protective father wouldn't be far behind. Not to mention, the kid scared the bejesus out of him on a regular basis. Her predictions were freaky accurate, and her abilities were like none he'd ever witnessed. At ten years old, she shouldn't be stronger than everyone he'd ever met. It wasn't natural.

The air around him crackled and snapped a mere second before the Aether appeared. The barrier created by his invisibility ring disintegrated, exposing him to Damian's steely obsidian stare.

Oh shit.

"You have one extremely short window of opportunity to tell me why you're spying on my daughter, Blane. And it had better be good."

The Aether wasn't tall or overly muscular. Damian Dethridge leaned on the side of a pretty boy. Although, at well over two hundred years old, the man would *never* be considered a boy. No one would dare call him one, either. He was the most powerful force on the planet, minus a god or goddess, and Trev would gamble he'd give any of them a run for their money if it came down to it. All in all, not a man to piss off.

"Not your daughter, Dethridge. You know I'd never hurt her. My mission is the earth witch."

"Mission? What possible *mission* could a Death Dealer have with my sister-in-law?"

Trev was sure his face turned a pukey shade of green, but he manned up and answered all the same. "The Authority sent me."

"Well, the Authority can unsend you. My extended family is off-limits."

"I can't go back until my work is completed, Dethridge. I'm already on probation. They'll kill me if I disobey."

"I'll kill you if you don't. So I suppose you need to decide which way is preferable for you to leave this world."

Frustration welled inside Trev, and he wanted to kick the tree he'd been lounging against. He needn't have shown restraint, because the Aether possessed the ability to read minds if he cared to. Still, Trev held back. Barely.

"Look, my orders are to watch her. For now. I'm not to harm her unless a command comes down from Councilwoman Vector."

Considering eyes studied him, taking his measure. They gave away nothing of Damian's feelings on the matter. "Why Soleil?"

"I don't know."

"Figure it out. *Fast*."

"I'm serious. *I don't know.* Believe me, I've taken a lot of shit for it, too."

"He's telling the truth, Papa," piped a young voice behind Trev.

"Dammit, Beastie!"

The magical slap was indicative of Damian's anger, and Trev was slammed into the thick base of the oak tree. The rough bark scraped his forearm, but he'd be damned if he whined about it in front of them.

Sabrina ignored her father's wrath and approached him. She was a pint-sized tornado and the feminine version of Damian, and those fathomless yet all-knowing eyes on a child seemed wrong. After a full minute of watching him, she smiled.

The eeriness of it traveled all the way to his toes.

"It's good to see you again, Mr. Trevor," she said cheerfully. "I—"

"Beastie, go find your mother."

"But he's going to—"

"Not another word!" Damian's sharp command rang out like a gunshot. The wildlife of the forest behind them went silent, as did Trev. Mainly because he forgot to breathe.

Sabrina's pink, heart-shaped lips thinned in irritation, and she glared at her dad.

What did it say about the size of the balls on a kid willing to go toe-to-toe with her unrelenting, all-powerful father? Solid brass cajones on that one, for sure.

"I'll just be heading out now," Trev said with a jerk of his thumb over his shoulder.

Although the Aether hadn't bothered to look at him, his chilly address locked him in place. "You'll go nowhere, Blane. Not until this is settled, and I'm sure my children are in no danger."

Sabrina faced Trev with twinkling eyes and a wide smile. "That's a good thing. You'll get to see Aunt Soleil again."

Soleil was unable to keep up with her niece whenever the child decided to teleport off without warning. The Aether had appeared about thirty yards west of her greenhouse, and Sabrina was off. Frustrated beyond measure, Soleil stomped to where the girl had reappeared behind her father.

Only then did she see the man Damian was talking to.

He had sandy-brown hair and a stern countenance. His face wasn't beautiful like Damian's, but his visage had an arresting quality. His build was that of a professional football player, but he held himself with a comfortable grace as if he was at ease in his big frame. If he walked into a room, people were sure to do a double take.

And she knew him.

Or rather, *of* him. Soleil had been unable to stop obsessing since their first meeting.

She was out of breath by the time she arrived at Damian's side, and it wasn't for the singular reason that she was out of shape. Lifting pots and soil had built her stamina, but all that went by the wayside with one glimpse of Trevor. She'd arrived in time to hear the Aether's low-voiced command and Sabrina's cheerful response. She also witnessed Trevor Blane wince.

He wasn't super excited to see Aunt Soleil, was he?

Keeping her expression blank and showing no outward sign of the turmoil she was experiencing, Soleil gave him a tight, dismissive smile. Next, she faced Damian. "I'm sorry. She's quick."

"No bother, dear Soleil. It's not the first time. My daughter and I will have a nice, long discussion about her penchant for placing herself in risky situations without permission."

Sabrina cast her eyes downward, focusing on the kitten she held. The girl was the picture of contrite. "Sorry, Papa."

Soleil didn't believe the little monster for one second, and she struggled not to laugh at the false apology. Glancing up, she caught Damian's sardonic smile, and she snorted. Not a ladylike sound by any means, and her face burned when her brother-in-law laughed.

Mortified, she pressed her palms to her hot cheeks and avoided looking at their too-observant visitor. No one was more surprised than she was when Damian wrapped an arm around her shoulders, hugged her close, and kissed her temple.

"You are beautifully unique, Soleil. Remember that, my dear," he said in a low voice.

There was a deeper meaning in his words, but she was damned if she understood what it was. However, if the Aether decreed it, she'd try like heck to adhere to it.

"I'll take Sabrina back now."

"No need. I'll escort her to Vivian," Damian said, hoisting his daughter in his arms. "Maybe my wife can figure out how to curb Beastie's impulsiveness. Goddess knows I can't, no matter how I've tried."

"Blane, we'll talk soon," he added.

With one last stern look toward their visitor, the Aether teleported away, leaving Soleil at a distinct loss as to how to extract herself from her current situation gracefully. Taking a deep breath, she faced Trevor.

His haughty-eyed stare made her squirm inside. She wasn't in any doubt about the man liking her. He definitely *did not*. Why her niece felt he'd care to meet her again was anyone's guess. If Soleil was disappointed, she refused to show it.

"I'll let you go back to whatever it was you were doing," she said as politely as she could manage. She didn't know why she paused for Trevor's response, but she did, and when it came, she cringed.

"Trust me, you'd never be able to stop me from whatever I was doing."

His arrogance rankled.

"Well, have at it, buster. I hope you have fun." In a huff, she turned and began the trek back to her greenhouse.

The contrary man trailed along behind her.

She spun back around. "Why are you following me?"

"I'm getting on with whatever it was I was doing." For the first time, he looked amused. "And I intend to have fun with it."

Soleil's stomach dropped, and she was positive she wouldn't like the answer to her next question. "What *were* you doing?"

"Observing you."

"Why?" Her heart rate kicked up, and her palms became sweaty.

"An assignment from the Authority."

Dreading his response, she ventured another "Why?"

"I'm their resident Death Dealer."

Panic took over. His mission could only mean one thing—her demise! Blackness descended, and she promptly fainted.

CHAPTER 2

Trevor wasn't quick enough to catch Soleil when she collapsed, but he was a damned sight faster when it came to stopping the blood flow from the wound on the side of her head. She'd connected with the sharp edge of a rock as she fell, and now, Trev's life was forfeit if he couldn't heal her before Dethridge found out. The Aether would assume he'd attacked her.

Irritated with his new charge, Trev lifted her into his arms, surprised it didn't feel like an effort, and teleported to her greenhouse. After placing her gently on the cushioned bench serving as a daybed, where she liked to read, he squatted next to her and smoothed the burnt-chestnut hair from her wound to examine it. It was nothing to provide the healing touch that came naturally to him.

Soleil wasn't going to suffer undue injuries on his watch. Not as long as he was forced to answer to the Aether. He could dance around anything the Authority threw at him later.

Trev heard her sharp inhale followed by a hiss of pain, but he didn't stop until the gash was sealed. He was finishing up as her lashes fluttered open, and he made the grave mistake of eye contact.

Those eyes!

Round, with milk-chocolate irises, they were large and warm, but they saw through him in an instant. Never before had a woman looked at him with trepidation or disdain—not without reason. Soleil had none.

She awoke spitting mad and shoved his hand away. Glancing wildly around, she calmed somewhat the instant she recognized her surroundings. Still, she kept a safe distance from him, with her back pressed against the greenhouse wall.

"Thank you," she said. Grudgingly, at that.

Trev almost smiled, but years of maintaining a poker face helped hide his amusement. "Death Dealers don't heal strangers without consequence. Please keep this to yourself."

Her eyes flared wider in her alarm, but she nodded her agreement.

Needing a diversion from his standard boredom, he studied her workspace. Things looked different up close. Homier instead of chaotic, as he'd first suspected. Benches and bistro tables were scattered about, tucked in alcoves thick with palms. Newly potted plants dotted a stained wooden table running the length of the greenhouse. The overall effect was rustic and charming. Sure, not his style, but nice, all the same.

"Why is a Death Dealer spying on me?" Her voice wasn't tentative, as he might've suspected, but neither was it one-hundred-percent back to normal.

Trev paused in his inspection of an orchid. If he didn't miss his guess, it was extremely rare.

"Is this a Rothschild's Slipper Orchid?" He shouldn't be surprised Soleil owned one, but he was. "These go for upwards of five thousand dollars on the black market."

Her brows shot up as astonishment lit her face, and Trev noticed for the first time that her brows were almost black. Next to her soft brown eyes and milky skin, the contrast was extraordinary. Much more interesting than the orchid beside him.

"I know what it is and where they are grown, Trevor… or, er, Mr. Blane." Her forehead crinkled delightfully in her confusion. "How do you prefer to be addressed?"

"Trevor or Blane. You can leave off the mister."

"Hmm."

Because her reaction was odd, he felt the need to question why. "What's wrong with my first name?"

"Nothing, I suppose."

He cocked his head a fraction. "What's not right with my name?"

"It's just all the Trevors I've ever met are complete assholes," she blurted, missing his shock as she warmed to the subject. "Total jocks with nothing better to do than to terrorize shy, over-weight girls in the—" The instant her diatribe caught up with her brain, her hand flew to her mouth and her skin turned the scarlet shade of the Spanish Dress rose blooming on the bush beside her.

"Seems your schoolmate has given all the rest of us Trevors a bad name," he managed with a straight face. "Should I kill him?"

Her skin turned parchment white, and she frantically shook her head.

He presented his back to hide his grin. "I don't know. I have strong standards, and the smearing of so honored a name—"

A clump of dirt hit him in the back of the head. Not hard enough to hurt, but definitely enough to get his attention. For the first time in his entire adult life, he was shocked speechless by a woman. He spun around and looked at her with new eyes.

Apprehension was in every line of Soleil's round face, and her lips were compressed as if she was attempting to hold back a plea of forgiveness. But her chin, surprisingly pointy, considering, lifted in the air, and fierce determination was reflected back at him from those expressive eyes.

"What the fuck, lady?"

"I don't want you to kill bullies named Trevor."

He crossed to where she sat with her shoulders back and her fingers woven tightly into the sofa throw she mostly rested on. Her white knuckles gave her away.

Trev allowed a small, wicked smile. "What about bullies not named Trevor?"

It sunk in he was joking, and her relief was palpable. She closed her eyes, and he wanted to beg her to open them again. The thought shook him.

"I should go." But strangely, he didn't want to. This was the most interesting day he'd had in months, and he was loath to leave. Still, she was beginning to have a bizarre effect on his equilibrium, and he'd always made it a point never to interact with potential targets. Not that she was one after today. Once the all-powerful Aether had discovered Trevor's surveillance of Soleil, the likelihood of Trev carrying through with a definitive action was nil. The man would approach the Authority directly and take matters into his own hands.

"Wait! I have a question." She lunged forward and grabbed his arm, falling into Trevor as she tangled with the blanket. Her face impacted low on his stomach, just above the waistband of his slacks, as she fell to her knees. With a gasp and a horrified glance upward, she clung to his hips, frozen like a deer in the headlights.

His reaction was shockingly different. The sight of her—flushed cheeks, mouth parted in surprise, and wild hair tumbling down around her shoulders—turned him on like nothing had in months, perhaps even longer. Of their own accord, his fingers tangled in her riot of curls. To do what? He couldn't exactly say, but when reason took over, he tilted her head back and away from his thickening dick. To do otherwise would embarrass them both.

"I should go," he repeated, not recognizing the gravelly voice as his own.

· · ·

SOLEIL GRIPPED HIS WRISTS ON EITHER SIDE OF HER FACE AND USED the strength of his arms to propel herself upwards. She hadn't missed the sliver of movement indicating he was going to urge her head toward his crotch before his reason returned. And she sure as hell wasn't certain what she'd have done had he not changed his mind and shifted her head away.

Humiliation became her closest companion.

"I'm sorry," she managed. "I'm not the most graceful of women."

"Yeah, think nothing of it."

They still had yet to release one another, and the unknown force keeping their gazes locked disturbed her on a deeper level. She shouldn't be attracted to a Death Dealer. No good would come of it. She certainly hadn't imagined his dismissive look earlier, either, and she was pretty sure he didn't care for her brand of earthy woman. Tearing her gaze away from those piercing blue eyes of his, she did a sweep of his body. Why not, when it was up close and personal?

"Like what you see?" His initial shock had apparently worn off, and he was watching her the way a cat would a mouse it intended to toy with.

"I was simply wondering if you ever left the house in anything other than dress clothes."

His mouth ticked up slightly on the left side, the only hint she'd amused him. By the time she'd blinked, his expression was once again bored. He had the nerve to glance at his watch, then say, "You have roughly twenty seconds to spit out your question. I have a schedule to keep."

"Rude."

"Fifteen seconds."

"Screw you," she snapped.

"Ten," he replied. "And wouldn't you like to?"

"Not in the least, you arrogant beast."

"Mm." He tilted up her chin and stared deep into her eyes. All signs of boredom gone. The cat had come out to play. "Shall I prove you wrong, Soleil Stephens?"

Goddess, she wanted him to, but she shook her head.

"Your loss, earth witch." He checked his watch again. "Time's up."

"No! Wait. I—"

But he was gone, and she was talking to an empty greenhouse. Disappointment and frustration ganged up and tried their best to suffocate her. She shoved them both away. Later, she'd see what Damian could tell her about Trevor Blane and why a Death Dealer might be stalking her. In the meantime, she'd do her damnedest to get her wayward desires under control.

She'd only taken two steps when she felt a foreign presence behind her. Spinning around, she raised her hands to strike. Trevor was too fast. He gripped her wrists and urged her arms out to her sides, but not in a painful way. When his rock-hard chest pressed into her breasts, Soleil did her best not to whimper at the pleasurable contact.

"I forgot something," he said in a low, seductive voice.

"Wh-what's that?"

"This."

He lowered his head to hers, pausing only long enough for her to protest if she intended to—*she had absolutely no intention of objecting*—and then he possessed her mouth like a fucking pirate of old. Soleil tugged at her wrists, trying to free her hands so she could touch him. But he held her captive as his talented tongue repeatedly delved into her mouth, wringing little mews of pleasure from her.

When he pulled away, unmistakable satisfaction was reflected in his gleaming eyes and a gloating smile she desperately wanted to smack off his face.

"I think that proves all we need to know," he said with a mocking laugh.

For some strange reason, he hadn't released her or shied away from the contact with her body. As if he'd just realized the same thing himself, he dropped her arms and stepped back.

"See you around, earth witch."

"Not if I see you first," she retorted, angry at herself for wanting a man who was clearly a jerk.

He placed a palm over his heart and sighed dramatically. "I'm wounded."

Temper stirring, Soleil balled her hands into tight fists. She hated to be mocked, and it appeared all Trevors were punkasses. And because she'd never been great at comebacks, she silently stewed in the face of his amusement.

His gaze dropped to her lips, and he shook his head slightly, as if bemused. "Who the hell knew you kissed like that?" he murmured, almost to himself.

"So maybe you're the one who would like to screw *me*," she taunted with her hands on her hips.

They both winced.

Yeah, she really needed to work on her witty rejoinders.

CHAPTER 3

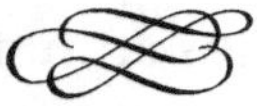

For three entire days and nights, Soleil berated herself, mentally cringing whenever she thought of the encounter with Trevor. How moronic could one woman be? Her retorts had been absolutely painful. Sometimes, she wished she had the best of her other sisters. That she was beautiful and bold like Taryn. Flirty and fun like Vivian. Cutting and confident like Josie. Trevor would be forced to take her seriously then.

She'd lain in bed, spending countless hours recalling their kiss, her body burning with remembered desire. When she wasn't wide awake, recounting every stupid word she'd said, she was tossing and turning in a fitful sleep. Her dreams were filled with Trevor's strikingly handsome face and mocking eyes.

Frustrated beyond belief, she tossed down the romance novel she was reading and rose to pace the greenhouse floor. Due to her irritation, her plants drew back, shying from contact. Never in her life had it happened, and she hated that it did now. Her plants were her babies, always to be treated with love and respect.

Working to calm her mind, if not her spirit, she inhaled and exhaled. She'd almost reached a semi Zen state when the atmosphere around her changed. She didn't need to turn around to know who stood there. His energy washed over her, making her shiver—and not from cold.

"What has you in a state, earth witch?"

"None of your business, Death Dealer." Hmm, perhaps she was channeling some of Josie's attitude after all. She spun to face him. "What do you want?"

His raised brows lowered as a wicked smile curled his lips. "You seem a little salty. Something keeping you up at night?"

Blood rushed to her face.

"No!" She denied hotly, mortified he'd guessed the truth. Her lie was too little, too late. And definitely too emphatic.

Or so his laugh clearly said.

"I repeat, what do you want, Mr. Blane?"

"Trevor. And you looked bored." He wandered to the cushioned bench and lifted the novel to peruse the back cover. "You seriously read this crap?"

She snatched it from his hand and hid it behind her back. "It's not crap! Kate Bateman is one of the best historical authors today. Her humor, her—"

Trevor shut Soleil up with his lips.

Her beloved book dropped to the ground with a muffled thud.

Sorry, Kate.

Soleil wound her arms around Trevor's neck and shifted closer, hoping he'd do something daring, like take her on that padded bench. After all, that's what Kate's dashing hero would've done. Together, they could create enough steam to obscure the windows of her greenhouse.

She was so lost in the fantasy that she nearly fell forward when he pulled away.

His brows dipped together, and his face was a mask of confusion as he focused on something behind her. She followed his line of sight, only to see fog rising from the ground, thickening the air around them.

Oops! Her fantasy had become too real.

"What the hell?" he muttered.

"The plants need humidity," she blurted. "It's on a magical timer."

Cringeworthy excuse, Soleil.

His confused expression disappeared, and he looked at her with something akin to regret.

She turned her back, not wanting to see his disgust for her take over. Never good at human interactions, she'd always lost herself in botany. And now, she wished she had a foliage-like ability to curl inward and protect herself from any outside threat.

Picking up a spray bottle, she considered using it to cool herself down, but it would be humiliating while he was watching. She misted the closest plants, moving along at a snail's pace as she inspected the dirt, stalks, and leaves. With an added burst of vitality for each one, she continued to the next and the next. All the while, silently praying he'd leave.

"Hmm."

Don't turn! Don't turn!

She turned.

He was lounging on the bench, with Kate Bateman's book in hand, flipping pages as if fully engrossed.

"'Hmm'? 'Hmm,' what? Why, 'hmm'?" She didn't bother hiding the suspicion in her voice. Surely his focus on the story was a ruse, right?

"Just that. *Hmm.*"

"One doesn't 'hmm' for no reason, Mr. Blane. One—"

"Trevor," he said without looking up.

Flip. Another page. Another eyebrow lift. Another slight twitch of his lips.

Inside, she was squirming like an earthworm on steamy pavement after a soaking rain. "Mr. Bla—"

"Trevor."

Flip. A chuckle and, this time, a small smile.

"Mr. B... uh, *Trevor*," she corrected when he cast her a sharp look. "Will you please put my book down and go away?"

A sparkle lit those startlingly blue eyes, and his smile widened into an engaging grin. "No."

Irritated to the fullest, she stormed over and ripped the book from his hand. Or tried to. His grip was too strong, and after three useless yanks, she stopped their ridiculous tug-of-war. Stuck there, with her damp, dirty fingers smearing the ink of her favorite romance novel, and Trevor's stupid, smirky face only inches from her heaving bosom... er, *breasts*... Soleil felt foolish.

Like one would a burning ember, she let go of the book and gripped her hands behind her back, sucking in a deep breath. The movement expanded her rib cage, shoved her boobs out, and drew his undivided attention to her peasant top... and what lay underneath.

All teasing left his face, and his suddenly hot gaze remained locked on her chest.

Uh-oh.

"What do you want?" she croaked.

He snorted a laugh. "That's not a question I can easily answer."

"Try."

"I want to do my job and go home." His sigh sounded regretful as he raised his gaze to meet hers.

Careful to hide her disappointment, she shrugged one shoulder. "Then go. No one wants you hanging around like a damned spook anyway."

"No?" The smallest of smiles curled Trevor's lips, and Soleil couldn't stand the arrogance of it.

"No," she snapped. "This is my sanctuary, Mr. Blane—"

"Trevor."

"—and I never asked you to invade it with your... your... your confident grin and your mocking eyes." She folded her arms over her chest, managing not to wince when she smeared her white top with soil. Faced with Trevor, who was always pristine, Soleil felt frumpy. Reminding herself she could remove the stain with magic later, she lifted her chin and glared.

"Mocking eyes?" He laughed outright. "Your Ms. Bateman has filled your head with nonsense. Modern men aren't the stuff of heroes."

Soleil had never wanted to strike someone more. Or prove him wrong. She knew she could.

"You look like you just won the blue ribbon at your local 4-H club," Trevor said with a chuckle.

"I know I appear to be a country bumpkin in your eyes, but without horticulture, the world would die off."

She'd said it stiffly, as if she was deeply offended by his comment. And perhaps he'd intended to get a little dig in. To remind them both they weren't compatible. The Soleil Stephenses of the world were all about a warm hearth with an army of brats. It wasn't for him. Trev liked the city with its art museums, culture, and vast array of women and foods. He'd grow bored in five minutes if he had to live the country life on this lost fucking island in Massachusetts.

"And real men *are* the stuff of heroes. *Damian* is a prime example of that."

He laughed. Of course she'd view Dethridge, with his courtly manners and proper speech, as the quintessential hero.

"Why are you laughing?"

Her indignation made him laugh harder. She was the epitome of an offended virgin.

"You're a jerk, you know that?"

Trev wiped his moist eyes with the tips of his fingers, trying to control himself and failing. He fell back against the pillows and hugged his stomach as he struggled to catch his breath.

A clump of hard-packed soil hit him in the chest, sobering him instantly. He stared down at the dark smudge on his previously clean white shirt, then at her, in shocked wonder. "What the actual fuck, lady? Why do you keep doing that?"

Soleil lifted her chin, but hurt lingered in her soulful eyes. "I don't like to be the brunt of someone else's humor."

"So you resort to throwing *dirt* like a two-year-old?"

Trev wouldn't have believed it possible with her previous inability to hide her feelings, but all expression dropped from her face, leaving it a blank mask. Her once-shining eyes had lost all life and were dull as she stared back at him.

And he hated it.

Hated the practiced look she wore, as if she'd had to perfect it to protect herself from bullies.

Bullies named Trevor.

But he wasn't a bully, and he didn't pull the wings off colorful little butterflies like Soleil. When exactly he'd gone from thinking her drab to colorful, he couldn't say.

"I'm sorry," he said meaningfully. "You surprised me, but I wasn't trying to be hurtful, Ms. Stephens."

"Soleil," she replied softly, licking her lips but not meeting his eyes.

Deep down, Trev understood he was forgiven for whatever slight he'd offered up.

"I wasn't trying to be hurtful, Soleil." She backed away as he rose to his feet, and he took a step toward her, then another and another until he was staring down at her bent head. "I was merely teasing you. Not trying to upset you."

"And I was just trying to tell you that you're wrong. Heroes exist in the world."

"I'll have to take your word for it. In my line of work, I've seen the worst of the worst. Nice people are hard to come by."

"You have a brother. Is he not nice?"

"Simon?" Irritation curled his lip. "How do you know my brother?"

And why the hell did she look so guilty?

"I d-don't. Not r-really." She took a step back. "I asked Damian."

Not liking the way she said the man's name, like she really *did* have a case of hero worship, Trev scowled.

She gulped.

"Why are you scared of me, earth witch?"

"You're a D-death Dealer, and you look p-pissed as hell."

Well, yeah, that might intimidate someone. "You don't have to worry about any of that… *yet*."

Eyes wide and fearful, she backed up a step.

"Oh, for the love of the Goddess! I'm not going to hurt you, Soleil." He couldn't prevent the sneer as he said, "Your hero, Damian, would wear my guts for garters if I did."

"You're jealous!" she blurted.

They both winced.

"I am *not!*"

For a moment, she looked crushed, then she crossed her arms over her ample chest and glared. "You can forget it, mister! My sister loves her husband, and he'd give you an aneurysm in a second if he even *suspected* you had the hots for her."

"*What?* Why in the world would you think I have the hots for your sister? I mean, she's sexy as hell, but—"

"Because *everyone* has the hots for my sisters. Vivian, Josie, Taryn…" She shrugged and turned away. "You just seem like the type to go after classy women."

He was, but he wouldn't confirm it and give her the win. Also, who knew when the Aether would be listening in? The last thing

Trev needed was for Dethridge to think he was after the man's wife. Because his train of thought had jumped the track, it took Trev an extra heartbeat or two to register Soleil's slumped shoulders.

In his mind, he replayed the conversation. She actually felt inferior to her siblings! Upon first seeing her, he might've believed she couldn't hold a candle to the other women, but now... Well, now he doubted he'd not notice her first should the group walk into a room together.

Approaching her, he observed the graceful line of her neck and the way the dark hairs curled into little ringlets on either side, like little sentinels guarding the silky skin there. Trev had the overwhelming urge to place his lips on the V created by her shoulder and neck, currently exposed by her peasant top.

"I'm not interested in Vivian," he said gruffly. "I can imagine a lot of people find your sisters attractive, Soleil. But you're a beautiful woman, in your own earthy way."

She spun so fast she crashed into him, and he instinctively caught her around the waist, preventing them both from falling.

Her chest rose and fell with her rapid breaths, and Trevor was damned if he could keep his eyes locked on anything but the exposed curve of her breasts not covered by material.

Christ alive!

He wanted nothing more than to bury his face in the shadowy valley created by their fullness. To cup her tits and suck her hardened nipples until she cried out and begged him to fuck her.

His gaze flew to her flushed face, locking on her pillowy cherry-red lips.

"Yeah, I'd say you're pretty fucking hot yourself, sweetheart." His voice had come out deep and growly, surprising them both. Closing his eyes, he shook his head. What the hell was this woman doing to him? He'd teased her earlier about losing sleep, but his nights had been haunted by their kiss, too. And after their second...

He needed to leave this island and go back to the city to get laid. Soon. If not, he was likely to do something totally out of character and asinine like promise Soleil the moon and stars or give her a shiny diamond ring. Trevor didn't do commitments. Things along those lines gave him hives.

"I've got to go."

CHAPTER 4

"What the hell do you mean you won't reassign me?" Trevor was on the verge of kicking puppies and making babies cry. Or crying himself. "The mark knows of my existence. She's aware I'm following her, ma'am."

"You have your orders, Blane," Councilwoman Agnes Vector snapped. "See to them."

"But—"

"We're done here."

Cold and final, the lead councilwoman of the Authority dismissed him without a second glance, and it took everything within Trev's power not to leap over the high table and strangle the witch with her dangling necklace.

Turning on his heel, Trevor stalked to the exit, only stopping when Councilwoman Mathilda Price stepped in his path. The long black robes of the Authority hid what he knew to be a high-octane body made for racy sex. Wavy golden hair, large cobalt-blue eyes, and a wide mouth set off her Margot Robbie look.

"Mattie."

"Trev." She gave him a tentative smile, and his response was a tight one of his own.

They'd been lovers for a brief time about a year ago, but he'd screwed it up with his inability to commit to her. To love fully. And she deserved far better than his sorry-ass excuses.

"If it's any consolation, I don't think the Stephens woman is your intended target," she said softly as she darted a glance toward the adjourning council members.

"What do you know?"

"I can't discuss it here, but if you'd like to meet for a drink, I'm happy to tell you."

He gave a brisk nod and, conjuring the name of a local restaurant close to where he was currently residing, slipped the note into her hand as he brought it to his lips to lightly kiss her knuckles. "See you at seven?"

"I'll be there."

"I look forward to it."

Her smile was melancholy as she shook her head. "Don't say things like that, Trev. You'll have me believing you actually care to see me again."

Jerking back in his surprise, he opened his mouth to insist that he did indeed care, but it would be a half truth. They both knew he would only allow himself to feel so much. He was a Death Dealer and was as jaded as they came.

"Until seven," he said quietly, beating a hasty retreat. Maybe he was running from his demons, or maybe from his embarrassment, but either way, he hated that he'd hurt her for no good reason other than his stunted emotional growth.

As he stormed across the courtyard to the designated teleport area for contracted staff, he came face-to-face with Fintan Sullivan, the Seer. It was on the tip of his tongue to ask what Fintan could tell him, but he decided against it. If there was anything life-altering, his friend would volunteer what he knew.

"Sullivan."

"Blane."

"Have you seen, er, uh, well, do you happen to know where Draven is?" Christ, it was always awkward asking questions of someone with psychic abilities without making them sound like a freak. Trev always stumbled over the simplest terms, much to Fintan's amusement.

"Sure, and I'm not his keeper today, I'm not. You can always text the bastard."

"I have. He's gone radio silent since the tribunal for Sabrina and Damian a few months back."

"Ah. Yeah, and he hated being pulled out of hidin' to face the Fates, as he did." The wry amusement on the Seer's face told Trev that Fintan delighted in the fact.

"He's worried it'll happen again?"

With a careless shrug and fading attention, Fintan's bright seafoam gaze turned inward.

A vision. The only reason he'd fade away so quickly was an important vision from the Sullivan ancestors.

Trevor gave him the time he needed to learn whatever it was they wanted to impart, and he kept a watchful eye on their surroundings. No one else seemed to notice Fintan had checked out or that his eyes had turned a cloudy white.

With a shudder and a gasp, his friend returned.

"Fuck me, and I hate when they do that," Fintan muttered. "I'm after thinkin' they do it deliberately, I am."

"Anything urgent, or were they giving you the lotto numbers to replenish your bank account?" Trev tried for humor, but it fell flat. Or so Fintan's glare told him.

"You can feck all the way off, yeah?"

Unable to help himself, he laughed. "Sorry, but if I had a gift like yours, I'd be a goddamned millionaire, dude."

"Sure, and I am." Fintan shot him a sharp look. "But then, so are you."

Trev grinned but kept silent. There was no way in hell he'd confirm or deny what he made.

"What do ya want me to be tellin' Draven if I'm to *see* him?"

Chuckling at the emphasis on "see," Trev said, "Just tell him to call me. I need a drinking partner and someone to talk me down from doing stupid shit."

"Well sure, and I could do that." Fintan shrugged when Trev's brows shot up. "I mean, I *could*, to be sure. But I won't." And in one of the rarest occurrences known to man, the Seer grinned and left Trevor shaking his head.

It only occurred to him after Fintan was gone to ask what exactly he'd meant. Did he mean he could tell Draven that Trev needed a friend or that he could be the friend Trev needed? And if he'd intended the answer to be the latter, then why not? Was Trev supposed to do something stupid, like seduce the earth witch?

Soleil Stephens had muddled his brain, and he needed to find a way to distance himself from her. STAT. Killing her would be impossible now, with the Aether ready to take his head off should he look at her cross-eyed, and the fact that Trevor was finding her more desirable by the day put a kink in any future plans as well. He no longer had the benefit of indifference on his side.

***

MATTIE SHOWED UP AT PRECISELY SEVEN, WEARING A STUNNINGLY simple black dress that highlighted all her luscious curves. She was built like a Vegas showgirl and could bring an unsuspecting man to his knees.

Trevor rose to greet her, dropping a quick kiss on her lips out of old habit.

She preened as she stared up at him, fluttering her lashes. For one brief moment, he toyed with the idea of using her to drive

Soleil from his mind, but Mattie's starry-eyed gaze didn't bode well for a commitment-phobe like him. He'd broken off their affair for good reason. He'd never gotten over the woman prior to her.

Shoving Deni from his mind, Trev shifted and held Mattie's chair for her to sit down. When he casually glanced up, his gaze connected with the one person he'd wished to avoid.

Soleil.

Fuck.

In a purposeful act of avoidance, she glanced at Mattie. Even from where he stood, he could see her mouth tighten and disappointment cloud her eyes. As if trying to rid herself of the feeling, she gave a little shrug and turned her attention to the man across from her.

Draven!

That sonofabitch was making time with Trevor's earth witch!

Okay, so, not *his* earth witch. Not his *anything*, really. But for fuck's sake! They'd shared a kiss only four days ago. She had some nerve dating other men this soon.

He frowned at his own idiotic thoughts and sat next to Mattie. Unfortunately, it put the other couple in his sights. If he got up and selected a different seat, he'd look like a complete tool to both Mattie and Soleil.

"She's pretty."

Trev jerked his head around to stare at Mattie. "Who?"

There was censure in her normally dancing eyes. "Don't play stupid, Trev. It doesn't suit you."

"I'm not. I…" But what could he say? He wasn't ready to admit to obsessing about a provincial woman who was clearly not his type and who was on a date with someone three times her age, who should already know better than to mess with an innocent like her.

"Who is she?" Mattie's question was oddly personal. She wasn't merely asking to know the woman's identity—that she already knew, though she might not recognize her dressed as she was. What she truly wanted to know was what Soleil meant to him. It was an answer he couldn't give.

"My mark."

"Oh! I didn't realize."

He followed her gaze to see Draven stand, speak to the server, then guide Soleil in their direction with drinks in hand. Reluctance was written all over her face, and had she been any less of a people pleaser, she might've objected. But Soleil was easily manipulated in her desire to make others happy.

Trevor and Mattie rose as the other couple reached their table.

Wordlessly, Draven leaned in and bussed Mattie's cheek. When he drew away, he placed a hand on Soleil's lower back to urge her forward. "Mattie Price, Soleil Stephens."

"How do you do?" The formality in Soleil's greeting wasn't lost on Trevor. She was ill at ease and resorting to politeness.

"It's a pleasure to meet you. I'm acquainted with your brother-in-law, Damian. How's he faring after the tribunal?" Mattie asked as she resumed her seat.

Although Trevor sat and Draven drew out a chair for her, Soleil remained standing as if she intended to bolt at her earliest opportunity.

"He's well, thank you." Again, she avoided eye contact with Trev and looked at Draven. "If you'll forgive me, I need to be going. I—"

"Why?"

All eyes turned to Trevor, and he could've bit his damned tongue off for speaking. Why couldn't he just let her go?

"I have things to do," she replied primly.

"What things? Another romance novel?" His lips quirked in a teasing smile, but the second her cheeks reddened, he knew he'd erred. "Soleil, I—"

"If you must know, I've arranged to meet with a procurer of

rare plants. I'm working with Spring Thorne to repopulate a specific species, and he may have what we need." Chin high and an embarrassed flush staining her skin, she nodded to Draven. "Thanks for dinner. I'll give you a call soon." Then she turned to Mattie. "I'll tell Damian you said hello. Good night."

Without a backward glance, she headed for the exit.

Trevor bolted after her.

Behind him, he heard the scrape of a chair and Draven say, "Well, I guess it's you and me, *cher*. What are we drinkin'?"

Knowing Mattie was in safe hands, he left to find Soleil. Belatedly, it registered that he hadn't gotten the information he needed about why he was assigned to Soleil in the first place.

Trevor cleared the door in time to see Soleil hail a cab. The damned driver went right past her to a model-thin blonde in a tight miniskirt. Soleil's shoulders slumped, but with grim determination, she shifted to hail another.

Squealing tires grabbed Trevor's attention, and he had barely enough time to reach Soleil and drag her to safety as a dark SUV with blacked-out windows jumped the curb. If he didn't know any better, he'd say it had been heading straight for her.

"That was close!"

"Yeah. Too close," he silently replied to her comment ringing in his head.

For a few precious heartbeats, they stared at each other. Thoroughly horrified.

"Did you just—"

"You heard me—"

Again, they shared a shocked look. Yep. They'd mentally connected as only a higher magical being could—with their mate. Shoving aside the implication of hearing her inside his mind, Trevor ordered her to stay put.

The SUV was long gone when he got to the street.

"Anyone get a license plate?" Soleil asked from directly behind him.

He spun back to see her speaking to the valets. Someone needed to teach her the meaning of "stay put."

"No, ma'am. Sorry," one twenty-something guy replied to her question. His companion was too busy staring at Soleil's cleavage to respond.

"Hey, buddy. Up here," Trev growled, snapping his fingers a foot above the kid's focus.

Blushing a deep cherry red, the guy looked at him and swallowed hard. "Yeah, sorry, no."

"Thank you," Soleil said with a sweet smile as she held out a twenty-dollar bill to first one valet, then the other. "I appreciate your help."

Running a hand through his hair, Trev snorted. "What help? They were useless twats," he said once the boys were out of earshot. "Disrespectful, at that," he added.

"They are young men, Mr. Blane. They're all obsessed with breasts at that age."

His gaze dropped to her impressive chest. "At any age."

Soleil rolled her eyes and walked away, but in the reflection of the restaurant windows, he could see her slight smirk. Running to catch up, he clasped her elbow and directed her toward the parking lot.

"Come on. We can teleport to your home faster than finding a ride."

"I can get home by myself, and besides, I'm in a hurry to meet the plant dealer," she protested.

"Right."

How had he forgotten?

Maybe you were too distracted by your dishy date. Her snippy thought came through, loud and clear.

Did he tell her?

Yep. It was too good an opportunity to pass up.

You do realize we can now read each other's minds, right? he told her telepathically.

Horror filled her wide milk-chocolate-colored eyes, and Trevor smiled his satisfaction. Needling her was simply too much fun.

CHAPTER 5

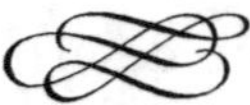

*T*revor had read her mind! And right when Soleil was feeling especially catty.

Trying to act nonchalant, as if she wasn't freaked the fuck out that he had access to her innermost thoughts, Soleil shrugged and turned her back to him.

How the hell was she supposed to block him? Wasn't it bad enough that her face was already an open book? She wanted to scream at the unfairness of it all.

"I can teach you," he said, surprising her with his serious tone.

"I have to go. The procurer—"

"Of rare plants. Yes, I know." Trevor placed his hands on her shoulders and squeezed. "Can't you reschedule, Soleil? That near miss must've shaken you up."

"I…"

How did she tell him she'd already forgotten about the SUV? The second his arm encircled her waist and he hugged her to him, reason fled, and all that remained was sensation. His steely forearm across her abdomen had created a fluttery feeling, and it was still going strong. That was to say nothing of the chaos caused by the spicy but citrusy scent of his skin enveloping her.

Bergamot, if she wasn't mistaken.

Currently, his massaging hands were causing a riot of emotions. Want. Confusion. Nervousness. Hope? The last one prodded her into action, and she stepped away from his intoxicating touch. Goddess, her body was overly warm, and it felt like she was walking through the desert with the noonday sun high overhead. Not a single oasis in sight. Sweat trickled between her breasts, and she fanned her scalding-hot face as she hurried toward the street.

"Soleil!"

He reached her right when she would have stepped into oncoming traffic.

Her distraction was great.

"Please, Mr. Blane—"

"Trevor."

"Trevor. Please, leave me alone."

"I can't," he said in a gruff voice.

Helplessly, she stared at him. Whether Trevor's confession was because of his appointment to watch over her or something deeper, Soleil didn't know. Clearly, he had an easier time keeping his thoughts to himself than she did.

"The man I'm supposed to meet is a stickler about time," she said. "It's obvious I'm not going to shake you, so let's go." Proud of herself for taking charge, she briskly walked toward the alley, praying there were no cameras to catch her teleport. She had two minutes to get to Gene Stockton, or she'd never hear from the man again.

"What's so important that you need to get to this guy within two minutes?"

"Stay out of my damned head," she snapped. "And it's the Wood's Cycad."

"The what?"

"Wood's Cycad. It's extinct in the wild, and no one knows exactly how many are grown privately. My hope is, with Spring's help, to create adult plants and replant them in their natural habitat."

"Who cares if this particular one dies—"

She spun around and shoved his chest. His forward momentum caused her to strike harder than she normally would've.

His breath whooshed from his lungs.

"Fuck!"

Trevor's curse was internal, but she heard it all the same. Taking no small satisfaction in breaking his concentration, she grinned.

"Christ, I want to kiss the hell out of your fuckable mouth." His wicked thought stunned her.

"Oh!" The shock—and something else she wouldn't explore at the moment—caused her face, as well as other parts of her anatomy, to tingle.

Color crept up his neck, and he gave her an apologetic look. "Sorry."

"No need to… um, well, yeah, I…" They probably resembled a matching pair of beefsteak tomatoes. She shook her head. "I've got to focus on wood, er, uh, Wood's…uh, Cycad. Wood's Cycad!"

A naughty smile curled his lips, and his immediate thought was filthier than the ground beneath their feet. *"You can focus on my wood. Any day of the week."*

Her breasts tightened, and her embarrassed flush was a dead giveaway. He knew very well she'd heard his bawdy reference.

"Stop it, Mr. Blane," she scolded. Presenting her back, she allowed a small smile. He was indecent to the extreme and her favorite kind of bad boy, although she'd never say it aloud.

"You don't have to," he replied. "You really need to learn to block your thoughts, babe."

"If I murder you, I no longer have to worry about it," she retorted. "Believe me, it's definitely an idea I'm toying with."

"Hmm, but sleeping with me is more prominent in your mind. I say we go with *that* action plan."

"I say there will be no action. Not now, not ever!"

"Spoilsport."

"Wood's"—she whirled and narrowed her eyes—"Cycad is too important to me. If you're going with me, hold my hands."

"I could find a more pleasurable place to touch you—"

"Shut it and hold on."

TREVOR APPRECIATED THE BECOMING FLUSH ON SOLEIL'S CHEEKS and the challenging light in her dark eyes. Call him warped, but their banter was more exciting than any he'd experienced in as long as he could remember. Why she held his interest when no one else could was puzzling, yet she did.

He'd embarrassed them both with the "fuckable mouth" comment, but Goddess above, she had the sexiest one he'd ever seen. Porn star worthy. Not that he watched a lot of porn, but he'd seen a film or two in his day. Also, Trev had tasted Soleil. Twice. Mistakes both, but ones he couldn't get out of his head.

As he held her hands, his cells amped to burning. He didn't like not knowing where he was going, and he certainly didn't love the idea of chasing a moody, elusive botanist, who was a time nazi. But Soleil had almost been run down, and Trevor couldn't help but believe the two things were related. Yes, the SUV jumping the curb might've been accidental. Yet he had the sneaking suspicion it wasn't. If someone had Soleil in their targets, he intended to find out exactly who and why. Then he'd use his considerable gifts to destroy them.

"You've been quiet since the parking lot," Soleil murmured as they walked toward one of five enormous greenhouses belonging to the man she was to meet.

"I'm wondering why anyone would want to run you down," he replied.

"It was probably an accident."

Trevor scoffed. "I don't believe in accidents or coincidences in my line of work."

"That must be a sad way to live, always suspecting people of wrongdoing."

"I didn't say that," he protested.

She simply lifted a brow.

Glancing around, he took stock of the estate. Waves crashed against the beach in the distance, and the tropical setting said they weren't anywhere close to Massachusetts anymore. "Why did you need a taxi if you were coming to a different continent?" he asked.

"I wanted to go home before the teleport. It makes me uncomfortable to pop in and out from public locations. Big Brother is always watching."

Trevor nodded. She definitely had a point. His younger brother was FBI. "What's this guy's name, anyway?"

Pausing on the pathway, she cast him an irritated look and said, "I'm sure I told you."

"No, babe, you didn't."

She frowned her confusion. "I'm almost certain..." She gave an airy wave. "No matter. His name is Gene Stockton, and he's—"

"Are you fucking kidding me?" Trev knew he was shouting, but he wanted to wring her freaking neck for putting herself in imminent danger.

"Stop yelling at me, Mr. Blane," she ordered coldly.

"Trevor," he corrected absently. He inhaled and exhaled to get his fear-for-her-induced anger under control. "Do you know who Stockton is? Did you do your homework before blindly traipsing halfway across the world for a fucking flower? We've got to—"

"Ah, Mr. Blane," came the silky smooth, albeit menacing, voice of Gene Stockton from behind them. "I don't believe you were invited to this meeting, and I'll ask that you kindly stop yelling at my lovely guest."

The sound of gunstocks hitting shoulders was loud in the sudden silence.

He'd been so wrapped up in Soleil, Trev failed to hear them approach, thereby missing the danger. He never missed the danger.

Never.

Every swear word he knew bombarded his brain, and it took all his willpower not to vocalize them. Soleil's wince indicated she was privy to those black thoughts. Good! Maybe, if they survived this encounter, she'd be cautious in the future.

Gene Stockton was little better than a mob boss. One Trevor's father had royally screwed over in the past. Had he known *he* was the man Soleil was supposed to meet, Trev would've put a stop to it. Now, he had to find a way to extract them without anyone getting shot.

"Let me handle this," Trev told her through their telepathic connection.

She ignored him, stepping forward with her hand outstretched.

"Mr. Stockton," Soleil said warmly as she shook his hand.

So warmly, in fact, that Trevor studied her face for signs of… what? Affection? Interest? That she and Stockton were lovers? No. She'd used a formal address, and she wouldn't have kissed Trevor like she had if she was involved with the other man. But he couldn't deny their dark looks complimented each other. Stockton was average height and on the beefy side. But it was difficult to tell how much of that was muscle under the white button-up shirt and slacks he wore. Based on the way the seams strained the shoulders, Trevor was leaning more toward well-built since the man's face was all chiseled angles.

"Ms. Stephens, it's a pleasure to see you again," Stockton replied equally as pleasant.

If one ignored the two bodyguards with automatic rifles, their greeting could be mistaken for an everyday, run-of-the-mill social interaction between two plant enthusiasts. But one had only to look down the metal barrel of the nearest mercenary's rifle to know this was no ordinary meeting.

"Not to put too fine a point on it, but I believe I asked you to come alone," Stockton said, his tone decidedly cooler as he cast a side glance Trevor's way.

"You did," Soleil replied with an apologetic look. "But—"

"But someone tried to run her down in front of a restaurant less than five minutes ago." Trevor narrowed his eyes, portraying pure menace. "Care to tell us what you might know about that, Stockton?"

Surprise, followed closely by concern, chased across the other man's too-handsome face, and Trev studied him carefully, searching for signs of feigned emotion. He could find none. The news of the near miss was a shock to Stockton.

Shit. That meant Soleil had a different enemy lurking on the sidelines.

"Did you tell anyone else you were coming here, Ms. Stephens?" Stockton asked with a troubled frown.

Before Trevor could stop her, she replied, "No."

"Excellent. Then you won't mind becoming my personal guests for a few days, until we can be sure you weren't followed."

Soleil blinked.

Trev swore savagely, not bothering to keep the words contained in his mind this time. Stockton grinned, and it transformed his handsome face to drop-dead gorgeous. Never had Trevor wanted to rearrange classically strong features so much as he did at that moment.

"Sorry, Stockton. We have another appointment after this

one," he lied unapologetically. He reached for Soleil, uncaring if the other men witnessed their teleport. Gene Stockton might not have magical abilities, but he certainly knew all about the witch community. Had known about it for years, in fact. The guy had made the bulk of his fortune through manipulating witches and warlocks to do his bidding.

But Trev wasn't fast enough. Stockton beat him to the punch and wrapped an arm around Soleil's waist, locking her in place.

"She's not going anywhere, Mr. Blane," he stated in frigid tones. "You're welcome to leave, but she stays."

Her dark, panic-filled eyes flared wide, and she cast a beseeching look Trevor's way.

"Stay calm, and let me do the talking," he told her through their connection.

The slightest forward motion of her head indicated her affirmative answer.

"Look, Stockton. I don't want to shit on your hospitality, but make your orchid trade, so we can get going. We're expected to meet Damian Dethridge for lunch. You know the man, I'm assuming?" He paused to let the name sink in. "He's The Aether, and Soleil's beloved brother-in-law."

Amusement curled Stockton's lips. "And you expect me to be suitably impressed by the fact, I suppose?"

"I don't expect you to be *un*impressed."

"Mr. Blane, while I can appreciate your concern for my welfare, I believe we should work together to protect Soleil's. I am, after all, very well protected on my island. My *disappearing* island."

A sinking feeling settled in Trevor's stomach, and he shifted to study his surroundings with an eye to security. Something he should've done when they first arrived instead of letting himself become distracted by Soleil's "fuckable mouth."

He was a dead man. If Stockton didn't take revenge for Trev's father, and if whoever was targeting Soleil didn't get him in the crossfire, the Aether was going to kill him. Hanging his head, Trevor inhaled a deep breath, then blew it out slowly. What the fuck had the Authority been thinking to assign him to this mission?

CHAPTER 6

During their tour of Gene Stockton's sprawling greenhouses, Soleil stole glances over her shoulder at Trevor. Had she not been so worried by his silence, she'd have enjoyed the experience. She'd erred in coming here for the alluring promise of a Wood's Cycad. Yes, they'd met, and yes, they'd transacted business before. Trevor's reaction had made it seem like Gene was the lowest sort of scoundrel, and yet he'd been nothing but kind to her in the past.

"Don't worry so much, Ms. Stephens. Your boyfriend will get over his pique," Stockton said in a low voice.

"Oh, no! No, he's not my boyfriend. He's not my anything, really," she babbled. "I'm his mission. He—"

"For fuck's sake!" Trevor's stern voice rang through her mind. *"Stop giving him information!"*

With an indignant gasp, she halted and spun to face him. "Quit yelling at me!"

"I didn't." He pinched the bridge of his nose and sighed heavily.

With a sickening dread, she met Stockton's twinkling gray eyes. Triumph lurked in their depths.

"Fated mates. How interesting," he said.

"No! We aren't fated anything," she denied hotly. "Certainly not mates. We aren't even—"

Trevor growled his displeasure.

Fed up with men in general, she threw up her hands and stalked to a table of orchids, where species of every kind greeted her. The variety of colors was splendid but did little to ease her irritation over her situation.

Trevor spoke, but his words were indistinguishable from this distance, and she refused to tune in to the buzzing inside her brain. Purposefully, she studied the flower in front of her, noting it was another rare plant, peeking up at her through the soil. A *Rhizanthella Gardneri*, also know as the Western Underground Orchid.

She felt his approach but didn't face him. Instead, concentrating on the pink, deep-red, and cream petals.

"Is that a Western Underground?" Trev asked.

Soleil looked up upon hearing the curiosity in his voice. Glancing beyond him, she saw Gene speaking with his henchmen, about twenty feet away. "I know it makes you nervous to be here. We could teleport if we're quick," she said.

"No, we can't. He informed me he's got Blockers working the island, and even if they couldn't stop us, his wards would fry us before our cells were fired up to go." Trevor met her shocked gaze. "We're stuck until either Damian comes for you or we convince him to let us go."

"We could always find a way to neutralize the Blockers and wards. You're powerful enough."

With shrewd eyes, Trevor studied her face, and she wondered what he saw.

"Intelligence," he answered with a tilt of his lips. "And loveliness."

She pressed her palm to her thudding chest. "Stop doing that. Thoughts should be private," she scolded.

"I agree, and we'll figure out a way to cut the cord of our connection once we return home." He covered her hand with his. "But until then, we're going to be one unit. Share one mind. We're going to work together to get off this fucking island and get you to safety. Got it?"

She nodded and cast a quick glance over his shoulder toward their host. "I don't want you to believe me completely foolish. I've heard the rumors about him."

"Then why did you come here?"

"The Wood's Cycad. It's worth the risk."

Their gazes locked, and after a few telling heartbeats, his dropped to her mouth. The pounding in her chest was harder and louder than a Lambeg drum, and she was positive he felt it despite her hand as a buffer.

"Mm. Some things are, I suppose," he said in agreement. After a long moment, he dropped his arm and stepped back. "We've been invited to dinner, but first, we're to be shown to our room to freshen up."

"Room? Don't you mean rooms?"

The eyes he focused on her were blazing hot, and she could swear she heard her skin sizzle from the contact.

"No, Soleil. I mean *room*." He smirked, and she had the burning desire to smack the superior look off his face.

"This place is palatial. I'm sure there are plenty of beds for you to choose from."

"Except I'm not letting you out of my sight."

"I'm in no danger from Gene. He's always been nice to me in the past. I'd fear you before him," she retorted.

Trevor stepped into her space, and she shifted backward, her butt coming in contact with the greenhouse worktable. Still, he pressed into her. The full contact of his hard body against hers scattered her brain cells to the wind. Or it would've, had there been a breeze. As it was, those useless cells dropped to her big toe, along with her stomach.

"You're afraid of me?" He sounded intrigued by the prospect, and the intensity in his probing look made Soleil swallow hard.

"A little," she admitted with some reservation.

He brushed the tip of his nose along the column of her throat, pausing below her earlobe to inhale deeply. His lips grazed the shell of her ear, and a shiver of pleasure raced through her.

"Why?" he asked huskily.

Soleil had the presence of mind to press her hands to his chest, but it seemed her fingers had a mind of their own and roamed over the hard, sculpted muscles of his pecs. "What?"

"Why are you afraid of me, Soleil?" His voice was hypnotic, drugging her and dragging out a response she'd have preferred to keep to herself.

"I've never felt with anyone the way I do with you," she confessed. "And you're a Death Dealer. You've the ability to destroy me in multiple ways."

SOLEIL'S ANSWER WAS EQUIVALENT TO A BUCKET OF ICY WATER over Trevor's head, and he stiffened.

She wasn't wrong. Trevor avoided long-term for a reason. Primarily because his touch brought death. Or prolonged exposure would, anyway. For the safety of others, he kept affairs to a limited time frame.

He straightened away from her and resolved to do better. From now on, he had to remember to keep his thoughts hidden and his hands to himself. It wouldn't do to lead her on when there could be no future for them.

"Is that what you're doing?" She asked softly, concern in her wondrous eyes. "Leading me on?"

"Fuck." Pasting on a cool smile, he softened his next words. "Please try to stay out of my head, and I'll do the same."

Her nod was slow, as if she was mulling over what he'd said. "You told me you could teach me how to block you. Will you do that?"

"Yeah. But it's late, and our *host* is champing at the bit to get inside, I think."

Soleil looked past him, and a small frown tugged her dark brows together. "He's nice. What don't you like about him? Why was your reaction so extreme earlier?"

"Let's just say he's known for his shady business dealings throughout the witch community."

"Who says?"

"What?" Trev scowled down at her. Why the hell couldn't she trust him on this one?

"You heard me. Who says? Who are the people bad-mouthing him?" She paused and smirked up at him, and damned if he wasn't distracted by that goddamned sexy mouth. "And I'm not going to trust you on this one," she stated primly. "I don't know you any more than I do him. Also, you might need a few lessons on blocking *your* thoughts, too."

With a frustrated huff, he stalked toward their warden. "If you're determined to keep us here, Stockton, have someone show us our room."

"Rooms," Soleil piped in from behind him. "We want separate rooms."

"No. We. Do. *Not!*" Trevor ground out.

Her chin jutted out, tempting him to strangle her. Or kiss her. But definitely to share a bed with her.

When she flushed, he grinned evilly, suddenly feeling lighter than he had a minute before. He'd forgotten to contain his thoughts again, and she wasn't indifferent to the sexual scenarios currently running through his mind.

Someone cleared their throat, and still, it wasn't enough to break Trevor and Soleil's staring contest. What did it say about him that her stubbornness was a total turn-on?

Without looking away from her, Trev lifted his brows challengingly and said, "Stockton, if you have adjoining rooms, we'll be grateful for your hospitality. If not, we'll require one room."

Gene Stockton's voice was highly amused when he replied, "That can be arranged."

Chin still in the air, Soleil breezed past Trevor and accepted Stockton's proffered arm.

"Thank you," he heard her say to their host.

"My pleasure, Ms. Stephens. At dinner tonight, we can discuss the reason for your visit, and tomorrow, we'll do what we can to discover who tried to harm you." Within minutes, they were outside a suite of rooms, and Stockton gestured with a wave toward the door. "I believe you'll find everything you need, and if not, I'm certain you can conjure it."

"But the Blockers—"

"Are only to prevent you from leaving. Not to curtail your magic in general."

A troubled light entered the man's gray eyes, but fled so quickly Trevor thought perhaps he'd imagined it.

"Might I have a brief word with you, Mr. Blane?"

Soleil hightailed it through the door, and Trev was left to wonder if Stockton had held him back by design or if there was a real reason. He didn't have long to wait.

"I don't trust you," Stockton stated coldly, all pretense of an affable host gone. "I don't know why you felt it necessary to trail along with Ms. Stephens, but—"

"Because as I stated, someone tried to run her down five minutes before we got here," Trev retorted. "If you believe I'm leaving her in your care without protection, you've got a screw loose."

The other man narrowed his eyes as he studied him. "Then I suggest we discover who might have an ax to grind with your lovely companion." A sly expression crossed his face. "I hope you realize you have competition for her affections. I find her a delight."

"Are you a hundred years old?" Trev sneered. "Who says things like that? 'I find her a delight,'" he mimicked with a sneer. "No wonder you live all alone on an island in the middle of the Pacific."

"You know where my home is located?" The question was soft yet deadly.

"I've always known, Stockton. You're on the Authority's radar. Have been since you went head-to-head with my father."

"Your father." Tone flat, Stockton stared at him, but his overall energy wasn't as combative. "If you'd ever like the truth of our encounter, I'm happy to tell you. But I'm going to recommend you don't believe everything you hear. Dinner's in one hour, Mr. Blane."

There was an unexpected dignity in the way Gene Stockton carried and conducted himself, and his entire vibe was puzzling. Acting on impulse, Trevor pulled out his phone and called his brother, Simon, the moment Gene was out of sight.

"Hey, Trev. Why are you calling so late? Everything okay?" Although sleepy sounding, there was a sharpness to his brother's voice. Trev calculated the time difference for the East Coast, and tapped the heel of his palm to his head. He hadn't realized so much time had passed since meeting Maddie at the restaurant.

"Everything's fine. I, uh..."

"What's going on? I recognize the hesitancy in your tone." The sounds through their connection changed, indicating Simon had put him on speakerphone.

"Si, do you remember Dad's dealings with a man named Gene Stockton?"

Evelyn Thorne-Blane, Simon's new wife, joined their conversation. "Stockton? Why does that name sound familiar?"

"His file crossed my desk once, and I passed it off to you. We suspected he was a lesser player in a money-laundering scheme," Simon replied.

"That's right. Turned out he was clean," Evelyn said.

"Clean?" Trevor rubbed the back of his neck and strolled down the hall to stare out at the inky night sky. "How the hell is that possible? I could swear Dad said he was part of Dutch's organization."

A few years ago, they'd discovered their father, Benjamin, was alive and in hiding from a mafia kingpin named Dutch. The man had been responsible for the death of their mother, Gloria, when Simon was still a child and Trevor was a young adult, freshly recruited by the Authority, like every generation before him. The Blane family members were Death Dealers, and the higher-ups liked to use them as glorified assassins for their magical causes.

Benjamin Blane, however, had different ideas.

Having infiltrated Dutch's organization and taken the lives of the kingpin's immediate family, he quit the business. Initially, the Authority tried to rehabilitate him, or, as Trevor preferred to call it, reprogram aka brainwash. But Ben had lost his nerve and refused to work with them again, sealing his fate. Trackers had been unable to find him, though, and to this day, Trevor didn't understand how. The Authority employed the best of the best.

"No," Evelyn said, drawing Trev back into their conversation. "Stockton was the only legitimate business contact Dutch had. His wife was obsessed with orchids, and Gene Stockton is a procurer of rare plants. Also, he's a helluva business man. Trades in stocks."

"In that case, why the armed guards on a disappearing island in the middle of nowhere?"

"Do you know how much some of those plants are worth on the black market?" Simon asked.

"Yeah, I forgot about that for a minute, but really, I couldn't give two shits. I just needed to know he wasn't part of Dutch's organization."

Evelyn laughed. "Well, you have your answer. Gene Stockton is legit."

"Why does he need witches on his payroll?"

"Again, that goes back to his inventory," she said. "He'd be a fool not to protect his investment."

"I suppose." Trevor sighed. "Si, do me a favor whenever you head to the office tomorrow, will you?"

"What's that?"

He explained about the incident at the restaurant. "Please pull up any video footage around seven fifteen yesterday. See if you can get a plate and a name. I need to know who's after Soleil."

After he signed off, Trevor made one last visual sweep of the grounds through the window next to where he lingered. A small figure running across the grass caught his attention, and he peered closer. The girl appeared to be a young teenager, and her hair was cropped close to her scalp. Rail thin, it looked like a strong wind could knock her over if she wasn't careful. Who was she? And why was she running around in the dark?

CHAPTER 7

Trevor exited through the terrace doors, kicked off his shoes, and followed the dirt path the girl had used. When he caught up with her, she was sitting on the sand, which was still warm from earlier in the day. Her arms were clasped around her raised legs, and her chin rested on her up-drawn knees.

"You okay?" he asked gently, noting the flimsy little-girl nightgown and worrying it would provide no protection against the brisk sea air.

"Yeah." Her gaze swept him, and she turned away dismissively. There was no real curiosity when she asked, "Who are you? Another doctor?"

"Doctor?"

"My dad keeps them coming, determined to find a cure." Her voice was flat, as if she was disillusioned by life.

Why would someone as young as she feel that way?

"I'm not a doctor. My—" What? Companion? Friend? Mark? What was Soleil to him now?

The girl watched him closely. "Your what?"

"I was just trying to figure it out. Let's go with friend." Trev shrugged and gave her a self-deprecating smile. "My friend deals in rare plants. Her dream is to repopulate extinct and endangered species across the world."

Although her gaze turned thoughtful, the girl remained mute.

"Is your dad Stockton?"

"Yes."

"I'm Trevor Blane." He squatted and held out his hand for her to shake.

"Lily Stockton."

The second she touched him, he could feel her ebbing life force. She was dying. Whatever disease she had was terminal.

Although he suspected cancer, Trev asked, "Why is your dad rotating in doctors? What's wrong with you?"

"Defective heart. But I'm not a candidate for a transplant." When he stayed silent, waiting and watchful, she grimaced. "And cancer. Rhabdomyosarcoma."

"I'm not certain what that last one is."

"It affects the soft tissue in my body. Mine is stage IV. Dad said it couldn't be treated because of my weak heart muscle."

Based on her overall energy and the trace magic he could detect throughout her aura, Lily was receiving magical infusions of a sort. Was that why Stockton had wanted Soleil to come to his estate?

With a casualness he didn't feel, Trev nodded, plopped down next to her, and stared at the waves as they reflected squiggly lights from a peek-a-boo moon.

"How long do you have, Lily?" he asked softly.

"The last doctor said a few months. That was about three weeks ago. Dad fired him. Said he didn't know his ass from a hole in the ground."

Rather than sound amused, as a normal teen might, she sounded tired.

"Your father refuses to give up hope."

"Yeah," she agreed. "It's going to be bad, though. When I'm gone, he's…" With a deep inhale, she shook her head. Trev got the impression she was frustrated more than sad.

"You want him to give up hope?" he asked.

"Yes. No! I don't know." She dumped a fistful of sand off to her side. "Why is he trying so hard when I'm going to die anyway?"

"He's your dad, kid. In my experience, there are fathers who go to the ends of the earth for their children."

Her curious gaze on his face felt like a living thing, and oddly, Trevor wanted to hide from what he knew her next question would be.

"Did your dad?" she asked.

"Nope. Mine faked his own death and disappeared on my younger brother and me. Until last year, we didn't know he was alive."

"Holy shit!"

"Don't swear," Gene Stockton's voice preceded him.

Trevor studied the man's profile as he joined them. There was no anger, merely a healthy concern for his daughter's welfare.

"Lily, it's late. You should be in bed, resting for tomorrow."

"I'm not going!"

"We've discussed this—"

Lily surged to her feet and glared at her father. Both fists were clenched tightly by her sides, and she looked as if she was using the last of her energy stores to argue the point. "I *said* I'm not going! Why can't you let me die in peace?"

"Because you're not dying on my watch," her father snapped.

But there was a haunted expression in his gaze as he stared at her.

Tears filled Lily's fierce eyes and trailed down her cheeks to drip from her jaw. "I'm tired, Daddy."

"I know, and that's why you need to rest. There's a dinner tray in your room."

She closed her eyes and shook her head in her frustration. It seemed Gene Stockton intended to willfully ignore what she was trying to relay.

"Mr. Stockton, I'd like to talk to you in private, if I may."

In an instant, rage clouded the other man's face, and in his blind fury, Stockton looked ready to pummel Trevor for no other reason than the fact he was present.

Trev kept his cool, understanding Stockton's grief and frustration for what they were. "Sir, I think you'll want to hear what I have to say."

He nodded once. "We can meet in my study after I escort Lily back to her room."

"I want to hear it, too," Lily said. "If it concerns me, I should get a say."

Summing her up and weighing his options, Trev slowly nodded. "Okay, then I say we discuss this here and now, while you're up for it."

"Daddy?" Her voice was pleading, as if she expected her father to reject the idea.

"Okay."

Trev hid a smile and turned to watch the water lap the shore as he waited for Stockton to bundle his daughter in the quilt he'd brought outside with him. Once they were settled, he cleared his throat. "Stockton, do you know what my father was? Is?"

"A warlock, or male witch."

"Yes. But do you know what ability he possesses?"

"No," Stockton admitted.

"And me? When you left me alone earlier, did you reach out to your contacts to find out what I'm capable of?"

"I did. Few knew, but one suggested you're a magical assassin."

"That's putting a grim spin on it, but it's close to accurate. Feel free to call off your investigators, Stockton. I'll share." Trevor locked gazes with him. "I'm a Death Dealer. I can kill with a single touch."

Other than the gentle crash of waves, silence reigned. Shooting a glance at Lily, Trev noticed her eyes were rounded with wonder.

"What exactly are you proposing, Blane?" Although challenging, there was an underlying wariness in the man's tone.

"The flip side of my abilities is that I can heal." Trevor let his words sink in.

Gobsmacked, both father and daughter stared at him as if he'd grown a second head.

"Normally, I'd need permission from the Author—uh, my bosses, but I doubt they'd grant it for a mortal," he told them. "So if we do this, we'll need to bring in some of my heavy-hitter friends to cloak the ceremony."

GENE STOCKTON STARED AT THE DANGEROUS WARLOCK SITTING beside his daughter. When he'd found out the man was an assassin, his first instinct was to get Trevor Blane the hell off his island. But curiosity had gotten the best of him, and he'd spied on Blane via the security cameras strategically located around the estate. He'd also shamelessly tapped the call the man made to his brother and sister-in-law and watched as the suspicion died from the man's eyes.

When Trevor caught sight of Lily outside, he hadn't appeared threatening, merely curious, so Gene had continued to observe him via a security app to see what the guy would do. Throughout their conversation, he'd listened in, appreciating Blane's frank comments and how he hadn't treated Lily as if she were a fragile flower. She hated being considered sickly.

Gene had only stepped in when his daughter swore, and his scold was a matter of habit rather than a true rebuke.

"You can heal my daughter? For good?" he asked hoarsely. His shock hadn't completely worn off, and he didn't quite know what to say. One question was prominent in his mind; what price would he be forced to pay?

"I can, and I will."

"Why would you?" Lily asked, eyes narrowed. Her suspicious nature made Gene proud as punch. As quick-witted as she was, Lily Anne Stockton would never be hoodwinked.

Blane's entire self was open and honest when he responded. "Because no one should have to suffer the way you are. Especially not a kid."

Mulling over the man's reply, Gene felt grudging respect build for him. It was the opposite of what he'd experienced for Benjamin Blane. That fucker had almost cost Gene his life.

After Dutch's wife and daughter were killed, the kingpin had shown up, prepared to torture anyone and everyone to find out the dirt on the traitor in their midst. Benjamin Blane had gone by a different name then, but it didn't take Dutch long to uncover his true identity.

Thankfully, Gene was able to convince him that he wasn't involved. Not long after Dutch left him—thankfully with digits and limbs intact—Gene decided to learn everything he could about the spy Dutch had unknowingly welcomed into his organization.

He never revealed what he'd discovered, because Dutch would've murdered the Blane boys without a second thought, just as he had their mother, Gloria. So Gene had kept whatever he uncovered in his back pocket for a rainy day. Today might be that day.

"Perhaps you should state what you expect in return, Mr. Blane," Gene said coolly. "Or, I should probably clarify, what you and your brother, Simon, expect." In his experience, most people didn't do things out of the goodness of their hearts. Especially not the FBI.

Trevor Blane shocked him again when he said, "Not a damned

thing, Stockton. I don't barter for profit. Your kid should be able to live a full and happy life."

Meeting his daughter's gaze, Gene wondered if she could see his fear mixed with hope, as he saw hers. "Lily?"

Her tired eyes contained a hint of steel. "Yes, but if it doesn't work, you have to let me go, Daddy. No more doctors. No more treatments. Okay? You let me go." When he hesitated to agree, she firmed her mouth and glared her irritation. "Promise me, or it's no."

"It could come back," he hedged.

"It's doubtful it will, but if it does, you call my number, Stockton. I'll return to help her," Trevor vowed, eyes solemn.

"And if you're not alive to help her?" The question had to be asked, and Gene hated that he had to be the one to ask it. Hated that it sounded like a subtle threat.

Fortunately, the Death Dealer didn't take it that way. "Then my brother will help her, and failing that, I'll leave instructions for another."

When Gene looked at his daughter again, she was staring at Trevor Blane with hero worship in her shimmering eyes. His fear was nothing compared to her courage. With a nod of acceptance, he shook Trevor's hand.

"Thank you."

"Thank me after it works. I still have to call in a few people to pull this off and not get found out by those in charge." Trevor glanced between them. "I'm not trying to give false hope. It can be done, *if* we aren't stopped."

"I understand."

"Good. I'll see you at dinner." The Death Dealer rose to his feet and snapped his fingers. All the sand clinging to his backside fell from him, leaving his slacks pristine.

"Neat trick," Gene said dryly.

A fleeting smile crossed Trevor's lips. "One of my favorites." To Lily, he said, "Tomorrow is going to be a trying day for you, kid. At breakfast, we need to discuss what this entails. The process won't be a walk in the park. In fact, it's going to be painful. I'll explain everything before we start, and if you change your mind, I'll understand."

"I won't, sir," she promised.

Love for his daughter swelled in Gene's heart. If he could take her illness and pain for himself, he would. His desire was for her to live a full life and experience all she'd ever dreamed possible.

"Okay. Good night."

As Trevor Blane disappeared into the inky night, Gene faced his daughter. "If you're as keyed up as I am, I'm going to suggest a kitchen raid."

Lily giggled. "Ice cream and cake?"

"You know it!"

"What about dinner?"

"I'll have a tray sent to our guests. You and I have reason to celebrate."

CHAPTER 8

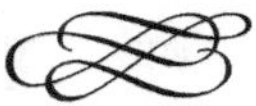

After he finished his meal, Trevor placed a call to Fintan.

"And why would ya be bringin' me into your cracked plans, ya scut?" his friend asked with his standard surly growl.

"I'm not, other than to ask you what the future holds for the girl, and for us, if we're caught."

"Sure, and the Fates could be listenin' right now. Did ya even think to cloak us before ya dialed me number?"

"I'm not an idiot, Fin."

"Pfft. That's debatable, it is. You're a feckin' eejit if you're thinkin' this won't have consequences, yeah?"

"That's why I need you. And Draven."

"And the Aether."

Trevor grimaced. "I'd rather not involve him if I can help it."

"Well, seein' as I'm sitting here in his study, you'll not have a choice."

Fuck.

Damian's smooth, albeit amused, voice came across the line. "Hello, Blane. Care to tell me why you haven't brought Soleil home yet?"

"She wants some orchid or another from Stockton."

"That takes all night to accomplish?"

"We're kind of stuck here. Blockers," Trev confessed. He winced as he heard Fintan's savage swear and Damian's cool apology to the man for letting his emotions get the better of him. "We aren't in danger," Trev hurried to say. "Stockton's private and prefers not to let people bounce in and out."

"Let me get this straight. You're telling me you intend to help the man who has trapped you, along with *my wife's sister*, on some godforsaken island?"

"Well, when you put it like that…"

"How exactly would *you* put it, Blane?"

"Probably like that. But Lily's a kid, Dethridge. I don't know why this one matters; she just does."

A long pause greeted his statement, and Trev held his breath, awaiting a response.

"All right. If Fintan can see no danger and Soleil is returned safely by tomorrow evening, I'll not interfere."

Exhaling his relief, he nodded, although the two men couldn't see him. "Good. So, you'll release Fintan and Draven to teleport here in"—he checked his watch—"seven hours?"

"If they're willing to get involved and thwart the Authority. The choice is theirs."

"Thank you, Damian."

"Don't thank me yet. When you return, we're going to discuss why you would allow Soleil to traipse halfway around the world after a bloody plant."

The situation would've been funny had it not been serious. "I've got no say in anything Soleil Stephens does, man. That's one female who does whatever the hell she wants. I'm just along for the ride."

"See that she doesn't come to any harm."

As soon as Trev signed off and sent word to Draven to call him, he padded to the connecting door to check on Soleil.

Inching it open, he peered through the crack. She was snuggled into her comforter, with the lamp still casting a soft glow over her pretty peaches-and-cream skin. A book was crushed to her chest, and it appeared she'd fallen asleep while reading another steamy historical romance by Bateman. Soleil certainly loved her romance novels.

A grin curled his mouth. As he shifted to close the door, her voice drifted to him.

"Good night, Mr. Blane."

The husky murmur shot straight to his groin. The shock was so great he jerked the door wider to stare. Oddly luminous yet heavy-lidded from sleep, her eyes were focused on him, and her soft smile caused his heart to beat faster. If she were any other woman, Trevor would believe she was purposely tempting him. Not her, though. Soleil didn't know the power she possessed. The power she gained with every minute he spent in her company.

With a fleeting frown, she blinked and eased upright. "Are you okay?"

"Yeah," he replied. The single syllable was brisk and gave away the lie.

After carefully marking the page, she set aside her book and pushed back the covers to stand. The lamplight illuminated her shapely figure through her nightgown, and Trev experienced another jolt.

He wanted to order her to get back in bed and pull the covers up to her chin, like some Regency gentleman from her silly novel, but all he could do was stare as she glided toward him. His mouth watered with the need to touch her, but he wouldn't. Couldn't. Because Soleil Stephens wasn't the type of woman a man dallied with.

Dallied?

Oh, for fuck's sake! He might as well use that ridiculous book of hers as a how-to guide to being a dastardly dull duke or overeager earl if he was going to use words like *dallied*.

She scowled, and his stomach dropped. He'd forgotten to screen his thoughts, and she'd likely received a direct line to his distaste for romance novels, in general. Although Trevor didn't know Soleil well enough to predict her pique or dismissal of trivial things like tastes, he didn't want to hurt her feelings.

But she dumbfounded him when she asked, "What makes you think I'm not okay with a dalliance?"

Her question froze him in place, and his pulse pounded harder.

"Are you?" His raspy voice revealed his desperate hope that she was.

"Perhaps." Her eyes were lighter, flirtier, and yet penetrating as she studied him. It occurred to Trevor that Soleil was a watcher of people. If asked prior to that moment, he'd have said she was a bit self-absorbed considering her plant obsession. Hell, he'd watched her for a week before he was discovered. All her attention had been focused on checking soil, misting foliage, reading books, and eating bonbons.

He grinned. He couldn't help himself. Her hair was deliciously tussled, and those previously luminous bedroom eyes of hers were narrowed, sizing him up for whatever sexual fantasies she had in mind. His hope was they were plentiful and he met the mark.

Of its own volition, his hand rose to touch her. He used his thumb to stroke her plump lower lip. "When you make up your mind, let me know, babe. Until then, you should probably get some sleep." Leaning in, he followed the gentle caress with the briefest of kisses. "Good night."

SOLEIL STOOD MOTIONLESS, PARALYZED WITH WANT. HER STOMACH filled with a thousand swirling butterflies, and their activity was so great, she felt queasy. How could one man be so certain of himself and his skills?

Yet Trevor was. His easy confidence *screamed* Bed God.

For once in her life, Soleil contemplated doing something daring. Considered stripping off her nightgown and inviting him to her bed with no expectations other than one night of bliss. Sure, he'd accurately guessed one-night stands weren't her jam, but for him, she'd make an exception.

And likely wind up with a broken heart.

But oh, it might be worth it.

"I'm okay with a dalliance," she blurted.

Trevor stopped halfway to his en suite bathroom, his spine stiffening as if touched with a hot poker. He remained that way for the longest minute, and Soleil held her breath the entire time.

Would he take her up on it?

"Not tonight," his voice echoed through her mind.

Her disappointment was keen.

His finely shaped shoulders dropped, and he faced her direction. "I want to. Never doubt it. But I don't believe you're as ready for a fling as you'd like to think you are, Soleil. You should know, I can never offer more."

"Why?"

Brows drawn together in a deep frown, he closed the distance between them. If she inhaled deeply, her breast would brush his chest. But he made no move to touch her.

"I'm not relationship material," he said, and the statement was as flat as his suddenly world-weary eyes.

"Why?" she asked again. The need to understand him was driving her to push boundaries she never would with anyone else.

"My prolonged touch is a death sentence." He sighed and ran a hand through his hair.

For a brief instant, their bodies touched from his movement, and he stepped back as if burned. "My brother's first wife died of terminal cancer. Did you know that?"

She shook her head.

"Yeah, because his touch, even with his magic bound, was toxic. Like mine. Like my father before him. Like our grandfather before that."

"But your father was married, right? And Simon has remarried Evelyn Thorne, if I'm not mistaken. He can't be too worried about her."

"True, but there's extenuating circumstances for that last one." Trevor's head cocked, and a mocking smile curled his lips. "You're discussing marriage. So not a dalliance girl, after all?"

"No!" Her skin burned, and she was sure the flush was not attractive. "I mean… I didn't say I wasn't a dalli… uh, well, you know." With a wave of her hand, she tried for worldly, but her stuttering gave her away.

His smile widened, and his hypnotic blue eyes gleamed with unholy amusement.

Soleil lifted her chin and met his bold gaze. "I'm merely pointing out that others before you have had relationships. Successful marriages. Your argument isn't valid."

"Wrong, my dear Dalli. My grandmother passed away within ten years of giving birth to my father. Her only child, by the by." His expression sobered. "My mother was a powerful witch in her own right, but she was the victim of my father's reckless decisions. As for Simon's wife, she was mortal, yes, which made her disease ten times worse. It ravaged her body until she was unrecognizable." He grimaced. "If you don't believe me, feel free to research my family tree. Whether by accident, design, or disease, a Death Dealer's bride is marked from the moment she says 'I do' and is destined to die within ten years."

Trevor crowded closer and ran the tips of his fingers down her cheek. "You deserve more than to wait for sand to trickle from an hourglass, counting down the minutes of your life."

"What about your past girlfriends and lovers? The ones you gave a time limit or sent away?" she asked him, watching the play of emotions cross his sad face. "Are they cursed?"

"Doubtful. There was only one I even considered staying with, and she left me high and dry. Maybe she was the one who got scared."

"I wouldn't get scared," she said softly. "Not if the reward was a great love."

A curtain fell over Trevor and his thoughts, blocking her from seeing behind the cool mask he now presented. "Even if I did fall in love with you, Dalli, which I won't, I don't believe in happily ever afters. I'll leave that to you and Ms. Bateman."

Stepping back, he purposely closed the connecting door in her face.

Soleil wanted to beat on it with her fists. To chew him out for assuming she was nothing but a romantic fool. But wasn't she?

One minute she was assuring him she was sophisticated enough for a dalliance, and the next, she was pleading a case for love and marriage. A sex-savvy woman seeking short-term pleasure from him wouldn't have argued the possibility of more.

"Way to make yourself look like a ninny, Lei," she muttered to herself.

As she settled under the covers, she sighed her regret. A man of Trevor Blane's experience would've definitely rocked her world.

"You can believe it, Dalli."

"Get out of my head!"

"It's free entertainment until you learn to cloak your thoughts better."

"Dick."

"Can't stop thinking about sex with me, huh?"

"I think I hate you."

But she was smiling as she turned off the light. Pausing, she frowned and glanced at the closed door.

"Mr. Blane?"

Silence greeted her.

"Mr. Blane?"

Nothing.

Then it clicked. He always refused to answer if she didn't call him by his given name.

"Trevor?"

"Yeah?"

"I thought you wanted the connecting door open to watch over me. What changed?"

"Two things."

She waited for him to continue, and his mental sigh was so forceful it was felt.

"I don't think Stockton is a threat to you," he finally said through their connection.

"And the other reason?"

"If I hear you rustling around under those sheets, I'm likely to take you up on your offer, Dalli. Then, we have a whole other problem on our hands."

She desperately wanted to ask what the problem was, but managed to refrain. Barely.

CHAPTER 9

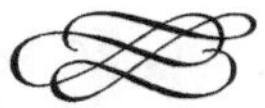

Soleil dreamed of Trevor.

Dressed to the nines in Regency garb, he presented her with a mini blood-red rosebush. His eyes were liquid pools of molten steel as they traveled the length of her body. Glancing down, she gasped.

She was dressed in nothing but a tightly cinched white corset that went from just above her hips to her breasts, and stockings tied up by frilly pink garters. Matching pink bows were placed over the nipple area. Four-inch white fuck-me heels completed the outfit, and her overall look was sexy virginal vixen. Soleil frowned down at her body but didn't have long to think about the fact her outfit was more modern-boudoir couture than Regency underwear.

In a move that stole her breath away, Trevor knelt in front of her and grinned his appreciation at seeing her bits up close and personal. His hands traveled the length of her stockinged calves, beyond her knee, pausing only when they hit the skin of her upper thigh. He groaned and pressed his forehead against her corset-clad belly as his fingers skimmed her exposed promised land, coming back wet.

With nothing left to do but enjoy her wicked fantasy, she gripped Trevor's thick sandy-brown hair and dragged his head back, meeting his hungry gaze.

"No, milord. We'll be found out. My reputation will be in ruins," she protested in a temptress's husky voice not her own.

To her eternal delight, he growled and clutched her ass cheeks, dragging her closer until his mouth was an inch away. *"Fuck your reputation!"*

His tongue swept her folds, teasing, tasting, and she pressed her pelvis into him, urging him on with hands, hips, and fevered pleas. Trevor feasted as if he were a starving man. As pleasure curled through her, a moan was ripped from her throat.

"Yes," she cried between panting breaths. "Yes!"

She shattered into a million pieces, and shudders wracked her body as her eyes rolled so far back, she would've sworn she saw behind her. When she returned to herself, she was lying on a four-poster bed, with its velvet curtains enclosing them in an intimate cocoon. Her legs were splayed wide, and between them, Trevor was kneeling, resting on his heels as he admired the view.

With purposeful movements, he disrobed and ripped at the flap of his smalls. An instant later, his member was free and cradled in his large palm. As she watched, he thumbed the pre-cum on the tip and smoothed it down the shaft. Using his other hand, he reached for her, plunging his middle finger inside her. With agonizing slowness, he eased it in and out with the same rhythmic stroke he used to pleasure himself.

Soleil had never seen anything so fucking hot in her life.

"Free your breasts," he rasped.

Hurrying to do his bidding, she snapped her fingers to loosen her corset ties, then shoved it down to expose herself to his burning gaze.

"Touch them," he ordered.

She did.

"Cup them and offer yourself to me."

Again, she complied with his demand. Arching her back, she shoved her chest forward.

"Christ, you have great tits, Dalli."

A shiver ran through her at the roughness in his voice. He was a man on the edge, ready to take her. Savagely use her in ways a woman secretly yearned to be used.

Gripping her hips, he pressed the head of his dick to her opening.

"Tell me what you want. Tell me you want me to fuck you until you scream."

"I want you to fuck me until I scream," she replied dutifully and oh-so truthfully.

"Trevor," he said. "I want you to fuck me until I scream, *Trevor.*"

Again, she did as he commanded and repeated him word for word.

A wicked light entered his eyes as they settled on her panting mouth.

"I want you to do something for me first, though." Her lips parted further in her surprise as he crawled up her body and presented his fisted cock to her. "Suck it."

"With pleasure, milord," she replied, licking her lips.

His tortured groan made her smile as she closed her mouth around him, deep-throating him with every slow, sensuous thrust of his hips. He started to draw back as if he feared losing control, and Soleil gripped his beautifully sculpted ass to hold him in place.

"Dalli," he gasped. "I'm going to come in two seconds if you keep that up."

"I don't mind," she whispered her assurance.

"No." He clasped her wrists and pinned her arms over her head. Shifting, he straddled her stomach, careful not to crush her.

Bent over her as he was, she was at his mercy, and the knowledge shined triumphantly in his burning gaze.

Still slick from her mouth, he pushed his rock-hard staff between her breasts, then back.

"Don't move." He released her wrists.

She started to shift anyway.

Taking hold of the curtain, he tore it from its mooring and wrapped it around one of the four corners of the bed. He used the remaining length to secure her in place.

"I *said*, don't move. Unless you're into spankings. Are you?"

They were both breathing hard. Challenge sparking between them.

A naughty smile curled her lips. "Do your worst, milord."

"Ah, Dalli, my worst will leave you unable to walk tomorrow."

"That's what I'm counting on."

His brows shot up, and his first thrust was ruthlessly hard as he watched her expression closely.

She countered by spreading her thighs wider and locking her ankles around his waist.

"Is that all you've got?" she taunted.

His smile was pure deviltry but quickly faded as he pumped into her in earnest, wringing grunts and groans from them both.

Cupping her breasts, he buried his face between them and thrust harder. Faster.

The slap of skin on skin filled the room, and it was music to Soleil's ears. As were all the filthy words he spouted.

He flipped her over as if she was a featherweight, then wrapped one muscular arm across her lower abdomen to hold her tight. When his finger circled her anus, she became a little nervous and shifted to get away, never having tried anal sex before.

Trevor delivered a stinging smack to her ass, immediately applying pressure and rubbing it to take away any pain. She understood, at that moment, that pain and pleasure were a double-edged sword. One could enhance the other.

"Don't move, Dalli. You're mine to do with as I please."

Molten heat flowed through her, and she was so wet for him, she squirmed.

Using her desire for lubrication, he slid his fingers up her crack and back, teasing the opening of her ass. There was something about the will-he-won't-he that drove her mad.

"I will," he whispered into the shell of her ear, causing her body to quake. "But not this time."

She shuddered, not with fear, but with anticipation there would be more nights like this.

The smile curling his mouth raised gooseflesh on her skin as he kissed her nape. Until that second, she hadn't realized he had her by the hair, with her neck angled to expose her throat to his lips. He nipped her shoulder as he thrust into her vagina, causing her to instinctively flinch back into him as he shifted forward. He plunged to the hilt, and nothing had ever felt so good. Their joining was otherworldly, and the fullness of him inside her was like nothing she'd ever experienced. It was as if their bodies were made for each other. Made for hot, animal sex.

His other hand closed over her breast, and he toyed with her nipple, lightly pinching, making her moan. Never had such need consumed her. Stars were gathering behind her lids, and she feared passing out.

He stopped moving, and she cried out in her disappointment.

With a laugh, he kissed the center of her back and shifted her for missionary style.

"No, Dalli. I'm fucking you proper."

"Yes, you are."

His mouth closed over a nipple, and when his teeth clamped over the tip, he bit down. That tiniest bit of pain enhanced her pleasure tenfold, and she screamed his name as her body convulsed with her release.

His cum felt hot within the wall of her womb, and she used her legs to hold him in place as she ground her pelvis against his.

"Fuck, yes!" she moaned. "Oh, fuck, yes."

When she came down, she found him watching her, something like awe in his eyes. With a simple snap of his fingers, she was free of her bonds.

Trevor brushed his lips over hers, then pulled back with a grin.

"I think after those screams, your reputation is in tatters, Dalli."

"We're sure to be discovered, milord," she panted.

His soft chuckle washed over her. "I underestimated you, Soleil Stephens."

"People usually do."

"Mm. I expect they do." His eyes missed nothing as they raked her face and naked body. "Yes, I expect they do."

She blinked, and he was gone.

Heart pounding, Soleil woke up and eased into a sitting position. She was back in her room, and Trevor was nowhere to be found. Yet the feeling between her legs, the dampness and the sensation of great sex, stuck with her.

Turning on the light and drawing her nightgown down her chest, she gasped, shocked to see whisker burns. Frowning, she examined her wrists. The skin was red where the material had bound her.

"What the actual fuck?" she whispered to herself.

The connecting door burst open and slammed against the wall. Trevor was there, breathing hard and looking like an enraged bull. "Did you plan that?"

"What?"

"You know damned well what!"

He'd stormed halfway into her room before jerking to a halt. His focus locking on her exposed breasts. *Jesus H!*

"My thoughts exactly!"

. . .

WITH CONCERTED EFFORT AND BECAUSE SOLEIL YANKED UP THE sheet, which was a fucking shame, Trevor tore his gaze away from her perfectly formed, porcelain-like globes, with their pebbled dusty-rose nipples, and met her wary look.

"Did we—"

"Did you—"

"How—"

"What—"

They were both at a loss.

Trevor held up a hand to stop the madness. "Look, we've got to find a solution to this mental connection. In the meantime, you have to rein in your fantasies so I can get some sleep."

"*My* fantasies? *Mine?*"

He held firm to his convictions, not allowing himself to wince at her shrieking tone.

"Yes, and—"

She threw a pillow. "You delusional bastard!"

"Wha—" A second pillow hit him in the face in rapid succession.

"Don't think for one minute I conjured that porn-star corset, silky stockings, and those damned ankle-breaking heels! None of which were historically accurate for the time, I might add. And I certainly wouldn't have created anything so revealing for myself," she said with heat.

His brows shot up. "Really? Because I remember some filthy things coming out of your mouth."

Her mortification turned her eyes positively volcanic and her skin lava red.

Trevor had a sudden desire to laugh. To tease her unmerci-fully. "'I want you to fuck me until I scream, Trevor,'" he mocked.

"I hate you."

"So you keep saying." He moved closer, drawing back the

sheet to admire her perfect tits. "But you don't. Not even a little, Dalli."

Her skin flushed, starting at those beautiful breasts and working up her neck to rest on her cheekbones.

When her lips parted, likely to blast him with some snarky comment or another, he dipped his thumb into the opening. "I can't say I was shocked by what you could do with that fabulous mouth, but damn, was I glad."

Her blush deepened, but she maintained eye contact. Challenging him to act. Goddess, he wanted to, but fantasies and real life were two different beasts.

With a tenderness foreign to him, he brushed her messy chestnut hair from her face, luxuriating in the feel for a brief second or ten. He bent at the waist until their faces were level.

"You were right."

"Of course I was." She paused and frowned. "About what?"

"I did conjure the porn-star outfit for you," he confessed before capturing her mouth with his.

Her fingers tangled in his hair, and she held him prisoner with her fierce grip, like she had in their shared dream. Trev didn't mind. He appreciated the wildcat side of her. When he pulled back, he wanted to say screw his career, screw taking the high road so she wouldn't be hurt in the long run, screw worrying about bruised hearts. He wanted to take what she innocently and willingly offered.

But he wouldn't. There was still a decent guy inside somewhere. He only had to dig deep enough to find him.

"Good night, Dalli."

CHAPTER 10

Morning dawned, and with it, so did Trev's raging hard-on. He was beginning to think he'd never sleep through the night again if Soleil was within touching distance. The situation called for a cold shower. Cursing as the arctic blast of water first flowed over him, he gritted his teeth to endure the rest as he scrubbed and rinsed.

With any luck, Draven had gotten his text and would call soon. Trev would like to heal Lily immediately, if possible. He had the Aether's blessing, of sorts, and if Fintan could see no long-term reason why Lily *should* die this soon into her life, then Trev wanted to proceed. Hopefully, none of Fintan's psychic visions would show her future self to be detrimental to another. If they did, Trevor didn't know how he'd explain it to Stockton or his daughter. He'd foolishly made a promise last night, but it was one he intended to keep.

Another excellent reminder not to get involved, he told himself.

Trevor was elbows deep into pulling a shirt over his head when a knock sounded at the connecting door. Tossing the shirt aside, he grinned and rushed to answer. Clearly, he was a sucker for Soleil's admiring gaze. What was an exposed chest between friends?

Her reaction was almost comical. First, her eyes flew wide, then her wickedly talented mouth—and here he had to remember that was last night's fantasy and not reality—dropped open. Her hands fluttered in time with her lashes as if she had a strong desire to stroke his bare skin.

"Good morning, Dalli," he said warmly. She'd yet to shift her focus, and Trevor felt it was the perfect time to flex. Stretching his arms above his head, he locked his fingers together and made his pecs dance.

Her *"ohmygoddess"* never left her lips, but he heard it through their telepathic connection all the same. It took every ounce of willpower he possessed not to laugh. He sauntered over to the bed and, bending to best display his ass to advantage in his form-hugging jeans, picked up his shirt.

A high-pitched noise came from her direction.

Glancing over his shoulder, he flexed again, showing a powerful display of muscles across his back. "Did you say something, my dear Dalli?"

Face a raging inferno, she shook her head. "Not at all. But if you're going to continue to pose, you may want to remove your pants. You can show off *all* the goods that way."

He laughed.

Unable to discern why, he had to acknowledge to himself that it made him ridiculously happy she had not only caught on, but had called him on his game. Her sigh was heartfelt as he drew his shirt down over his abs and settled the hem at his waist.

"I had that same reaction when you covered yourself with the sheet last night," he confessed.

"We're horn dogs," she concluded glumly. "Horn dogs destined to never have wild monkey sex together."

"Are you *trying* to be depressing?"

Her tinkling laughter filled him with a desire to kiss the

sound from her lips. Instead, he turned away to pick up his phone and wallet. With one last check, he noted the time.

"Fintan should be here within the next fifteen minutes. I hope he was able to reach Draven," Trev said aloud.

"What did I miss? Why are the Sentinels coming here?"

He gave a small shake of his head. "Right. I forgot to fill you in. Come on. I'll tell you as we head down to breakfast." Pausing, he frowned. "Why are you up so early, anyway?"

"Gene texted to say he wanted to show me the greenhouse on the south lawn. He's—"

"A dead man if he doesn't keep his hands to himself," Trev muttered under his breath as she rattled on about plants and the time of day they bloomed ad nauseam.

With a hand to Soleil's lower back, Trevor guided her out his door and into the hallway.

There, he found Draven leaning a shoulder against the wall, rolling his ever-present lucky coin across his knuckles.

"Good morning, *cher*." His grin was slow in coming but encompassed his entire face, and his whiskey-colored eyes sparkled with wicked delight. A rare moment for the jaded Guardian. "You're both lookin' cozier than the last time I saw you."

"Cram it, Masters," Trev growled.

"Draven!" Soleil rushed forward and flung herself into his friend's waiting arms as Trevor scowled his irritation.

"Since when did you become bosom buddies?" he asked. Although he ignored the surliness in his tone, Draven didn't, and the bastard had the nerve to laugh.

"It's like that, then? I suspected it was."

"It's like nothing," Trev snapped.

Hurt flashed across Soleil's expressive face, but she was quick to turn from him. "Have you had breakfast yet, Draven? We were heading downstairs for a bite."

The Guardian's all-encompassing gaze missed nothing as it

swept over Soleil's shoulder, bared by her peasant top. His eyes purposefully touched on the mark Trev had created in their fantasy world, and he nodded toward it. "Looks like bites were already had, *cher*."

"What?" Her gaze followed his, and color surged up her neck as she stared helplessly. "Ohmygoddess! What... how... ohmygoddess!"

"For fuck's sake! It's a hickey, Dalli, not a snake bite."

"It seems the snake slithered into a fruitful garden, *mon ami*. Who knows what else he bit, hmm?" Draven taunted.

If his looks could kill as easily as his touch, Trevor was sure the man would be lying dead on the floor.

"Shut the fuck up," he mouthed behind Soleil's trembling back. Wrapping an arm around her shoulders, he drew her close, hoping to soothe her feelings. "It's all right, babe. I'm sorry for— you're *laughing*?"

He was incredulous. She wasn't crying in the face of her embarrassment, as he'd first believed, and the tears streaming from her eyes were from mirth!

Once again, the earth witch had shocked him silent.

SOLEIL SPARED A FEW MINUTES TO CHANGE HER TOP AS TREVOR spoke with Draven about whatever it was he'd been summoned for. Her curiosity was high, but he'd tell her soon enough. One of the things she appreciated most about the Death Dealer was his blatant honesty. So far, she couldn't say he'd ever held back. From her or from himself. It seemed Trevor Blane didn't spare anyone. In his eyes, the truth was the truth and the consequences be damned.

She could get behind an attitude like his. Soleil hated games and players. Of which, Trev seemed to be neither, and she was profoundly grateful. He wasn't avoiding sex with her because of her looks or a few extra pounds. His issues ran deeper, and his hang-ups were his own, having nothing to do with her.

But she wouldn't push for more. Either he cared to explore long term or he didn't. She couldn't force him to want a relationship. He was running scared because of what he was. The reason was understandable, too. Perhaps not entirely accurate, but understandable. Allowing him space was paramount.

If there was one thing Soleil could be proud of, it was that she wouldn't chase a man for his affection. If a guy wanted to be with her and she was willing, then he'd make it happen. If he didn't put forth the effort, he wasn't worth her time. Or so she told herself repeatedly.

She only hoped Trevor wanted to put in the effort. It hurt her heart to think he might not. Yet he'd been right about the dalliance bit. It wasn't for her. For a certainty, she would become too invested after a sexual interlude with him. The idea of never having more made her sad.

Shoving her morose thoughts aside, she wandered downstairs and followed the sound of voices to the dining room. Pausing in the doorway, she studied those present.

Gene Stockton was a handsome man. Intelligence shone in his gray eyes, and he did nothing to mask his suspicions of those present. Although he possessed no magical abilities, he was a force to be reckoned with, in his own right. The man came from old money but had built an empire from selling rare plants. He also had legitimate business dealings, but Soleil desired the things he kept in his private collection.

She'd played dumb when Trevor learned Gene's name, but she'd known the truth of who he was long before. After meeting him at a botanical exhibit two years ago, she'd scryed and learned everything she could about the man. A woman couldn't be too careful.

Gene had also made his interest in her known. There had been times when she thought about accepting his offer to dinner.

After all, they shared a common passion for plants. But she hadn't felt a spark. *The* spark. The one that told her this man was the one for her. A forever partner for life.

Her gaze drifted over Draven Masters and Fintan Sullivan to settle on Trevor, who was in deep discussion with all three men.

Her spark had ignited for Trevor. Too bad he hadn't experienced the same. She supposed it frequently happened that way. There was always someone who seemed a little bit more enamored than the other in the beginning. Did those tables ever turn? She'd have to talk to Vivian and Damian to see if that was the case.

As if sensing her presence, Trevor's head half turned toward hers even though his gaze remained on the men as he finished speaking. The instant he was done, his attention shifted to her and his eyes lit with welcome.

Did he know how transfixed she became when he turned those startling baby blues her way? Shaking off the spell he effortlessly wove, she stepped into the room.

"I hope I'm not interrupting," she said. Her voice was silky smooth, bordering on polished, and a momentary self-satisfaction swept through her. Josie would be proud of the cool sophistication her always-awkward sister had pulled off.

After a quick glance at Trevor, Gene approached her and lifted her hand to kiss her knuckles. "Not at all, my dear Soleil."

True pleasure shone in his gaze, and she smiled at the welcome. "Thank you, Mr. Stockton."

"I believe we know each other well enough to dispense with formality, don't you? Please call me Gene."

"Thank you, *Gene.*"

He grinned, and inside her mind, Trevor's irritation buzzed like a pesky fly.

She lowered her voice. "Why are the big guns here? I assume you know what those two are capable of, right?"

Gene's sparkle dimmed. "Yes. We are discussing what they're able to do for my daughter's health."

"Lily? Oh, Gene! I didn't realize she was ill. Why didn't you tell me? I may have been able to help."

His smile flashed, and the look in his gray eyes warmed considerably. "I knew the moment we met that you had a generous heart. The only reason I didn't mention it is because I have witches on my payroll. None can stop the cancer. Slow it from spreading, yes. Stop it, no."

"I can," Trevor said, coming up behind him.

"But why are Draven and Fintan here?" she asked, refusing to examine why her heart beat faster when Trevor approached or why it warmed her to know he was willing to help.

"To save my ass and help prevent the Authority from discovering what I'm about to do."

Disconcerted, Soleil blinked. "You can get in trouble for healing someone?"

"Outside the line of duty to them, yes." His mouth tightened with irritation, and it didn't take a genius to know he hated the restrictions imposed on him. "But after the death of my sister-in-law, I swore I wouldn't let the Authority tie my hands again. They can go fuck themselves."

"Damn straight! What can I do to help?" she asked.

His lips twitched, and amusement lit his eyes. Although his reaction was similar to Gene's, Trevor's reached inside her, waking the sleeping butterflies in her belly. They fluttered uncontrollably as he watched her, and the urge to squirm under his steady regard was high.

"There's nothing you can do here, babe. If it's all right with Stockton, why don't you go putter around the greenhouse?"

Immediate pique sparked inside her. His indulgent tone plucked the wrong chord and made her feel like a housewife from another era being placated. It was the equivalent of patting her on the rump and telling her to get back in the kitchen, and she fucking hated it.

Trevor's brows drew together, and his general demeanor turned to one of wariness. He guessed he'd stepped in shit, but Soleil suspected he didn't know why.

"What did I say wrong?" he asked through their connection.

"If you're too dumb to know, I'm not telling you. But don't worry about me. I'll just go 'putter.'"

"Shit," he muttered as she spun on her heel to exit the room.

CHAPTER 11

Trev caught up to Soleil in the hallway and hurriedly ducked in front of her to stop her from stalking away. "I didn't mean it the way it sounded."

"Like you were telling me not to worry my pretty, empty head with manly things?" she asked with a dangerous fire in her eyes.

"Exactly like that." Knowing he owed her an apology, he trailed a finger along her temple and swept a lock of wayward hair behind her ear. "I'm sorry, Dalli. Please forgive me for coming across as a chauvinist pig. You're more than welcome to hang out. Draven's here to create a shield to block out prying deities and Fintan to predict future ramifications if I heal Lily. I honestly don't know what you can do to help."

Soleil's stance softened, but her pout didn't completely die away. "How can you cure her all by yourself? To my knowledge, it takes multiple witches to achieve something like that. Only Damian is all-powerful."

Again with the hero worship for her brother-in-law!

Trevor shoved aside his irritation. It was no skin off his back if she admired the guy more than was healthy. That was between her and her sister should Vivian catch wind of Soleil's adoration.

"A Death Dealer has the power to give and take life," he explained. "Just as we can obliterate, we can boost the health of the body's cells. It's not something the average witch can accomplish, even with help. At least, not in the long term."

"But if you heal Lily, it will stick?"

"It should, but I don't have control over the Fates."

"It seems cruel for her to be healed only to have it return," Soleil said softly.

"I have a contingency in the event it does," Trev confessed. He refused to fail. Mainly because he liked the kid.

"Then I'll go putter in the greenhouse and leave you to it," she replied with a smile.

Trevor winced. "Christ, I didn't mean for it to sound so condescending. I'm sorry."

"You already said that."

She squeezed his hand, and Trev was startled to realize that sometime during their conversation, he'd reached for hers to hold. His subconscious need to touch her had overcome his reticence to start anything between them.

Purposefully, he released her and backed away. "Stockton has breakfast laid out in the dining room if you're hungry." Internally, he cringed at the stiffness in his tone.

Her smile didn't falter as one might expect it would. Instead, it widened. "Thanks."

"Um, okay. I'll be in there." He pointed lamely behind her, weirdly unsure of himself for the first time in history.

The sparkle in her eyes spoke of her amusement.

When had the tables turned? How had she gained the upper hand? Maybe he should kiss the smirk off her face. His focus dropped to her mouth, and his sudden desire to taste her made his knees weak. What the hell was happening to him?

Her lips moved, but it took him a solid ten seconds to register she was speaking.

"What?"

"I *said*, for the record, I don't admire Damian more than what's healthy." Her exaggerated patience annoyed Trevor. "But I can recognize he's a great guy,"

"Wha—oh. Yeah. Uh."

Fuck!

He'd forgotten to shield his thoughts, and that forgetfulness was becoming a bad habit when he was around her. Screw it, he was going for the kiss. It was the only way he could scramble her thoughts and regain the upper hand. As he leaned in, he was met with her palm in his face.

"Don't even think about it," she growled. There was laughter in the sound, as if she thought his behavior was hilarious but didn't want to let on that she did.

"Why not?"

"You don't believe I'm the type to dally with."

"*You* said you were," he countered.

"Meh."

She shrugged and sauntered off.

Trev was oddly proud of her faux air of indifference. Their back-and-forth was challenging and bizarrely fun. When he'd started this gig, he thought monitoring her movements would be duller than watching paint dry. Now, he knew differently.

The thought brought him up short.

He'd forgotten his mission! How the hell had that happened? He still hadn't worked out the *why* of his job, but then again, he hadn't given it a helluva lot of consideration after the first time they kissed. His obsession for the earth witch had gotten the better of him.

"Dalli?"

She paused in her escape and glanced back at him.

Trev closed the distance.

"I forgot something," he said.

Color crept into her cheeks, but she remained quiet and watchful.

He swept her into his embrace.

"I forgot to tell you a good-morning kiss wasn't optional. It's a necessity," he murmured against her lips.

***

SOLEIL WAS STILL THINKING ABOUT THAT EARTH-TREMBLING KISS two hours later. How was it so much hotter than any they'd exchanged before? What had changed?

Maybe it was the way his burning gaze had traveled the length of her body, stripping her bare.

Maybe it was the memory of their shared fantasy.

Or maybe it was something more. Maybe they were developing an emotional bond deeper than either dared to acknowledge.

She touched her fingers to her lips and scowled as she tasted dirt.

Ick!

She dusted off her hands and shook her head. Trevor Blane could scramble her brains even when he wasn't present. Deciding her concentration was crap, Soleil left the greenhouse. She walked along the path leading to the beach, passing the thicket of hibiscus bushes that disguised an eight-foot, metal security fence. The gate was open, so she traversed the steps down to the sand and approached the shoreline.

After glancing around and only spotting a powerboat in the distance, she snapped her fingers and changed into a one-piece bathing suit. Next, she bent to wash her hands in the water. As much as she loved having her hands in soil, feeling the magic flow through her when she was wrists deep into the planting process, she despised dirt under her fingernails.

A ping sounded behind her.

Startled by the noise, she straightened and turned. The movement saved her life as a bullet tore through her upper arm, where her heart had been seconds before.

Her first instinct was to teleport, and her cells warmed. The magic was immediately aborted due to Stockton's Blockers' spell. Locked in place, Soleil ducked and curled into a tight ball, conjuring a force field the way Sabrina had taught her to do after her niece's abduction at the hands of an Arcane Devourer.

Bullet after bullet struck the shield directly in front of her face, and Soleil couldn't hold back her terrified screams.

The protective bubble held.

Two more shots were fired in rapid succession, but she remained safe.

"Thank you, Sabrina," she whispered. "Thank you, thank you, thank you!"

Although the layer of her shield was translucent, there was a faint distortion when she tried to peer out and get a location on her attacker. The muffled sound of an engine roaring to life caught her attention, and in a blink, the powerboat sped away.

Heart practically beating out through her chest, Soleil staggered to her feet, wildly checking around her for the threat.

"Let the shield hold. Please, let it hold," she prayed to the Goddess as she inched backward toward the steps leading to Gene's back lawn.

A shout from behind her had her spinning in blind panic.

Trevor's horrified expression was one she'd never forget. His gaze was focused on her ruined upper arm as he ran full-out to get to her. As soon as he was within touching distance, he reached for her—and got the shock of his life! The power of her force field knocked him on his ass. He blinked his disbelief, and his reaction would've been hilarious had Soleil not been bleeding out on the sand.

Knees weak, she dropped down.

"Don't faint," she told herself fiercely. Her pain was great, but she held on to consciousness through sheer stubbornness.

"Lower the shield!" Trevor shouted. "I can't heal you if you don't lower it."

What did it say about her cowardice that she didn't want to dissolve the one thing keeping her safe?

"You're not a coward, Dalli." His voice flitted through her mind. *"You're clever, and you thought fast on your feet."*

They locked gazes, and his tight smile reassured her.

With her uninjured arm, she waved, peeling back an opening large enough for Trevor to get to her. The second he registered the clear line of sight, he dove through and hugged her tightly to him.

"I lost years when you screamed," he said feelingly.

"How did you hear me?"

"Through our link. The others must've thought I was insane, taking off mid-sentence." After kissing her brow, he eased back to examine her arm. Frowning, he asked, "Why didn't you stop the blood flow?"

"I didn't think of it. Is it normal to feel this woozy?"

"Yes. Lie down," he ordered. With one last scan of the horizon, Trevor covered her wound with his hands.

Soleil cried out, and in her pain, she lost the ability to maintain her protective shield. "Trev!"

"It's okay, babe." He never lost concentration and continued to knit her bone. "Draven and Fintan are keeping watch, and I can see Stockton's men already scouring the beach."

Sweat beaded his brow, and it was the only indication of how hard he struggled to heal her.

"I thought this was your thing. You act like it's hard work or something," she joked weakly.

"I expended a lot of energy to help Lily."

Soleil placed a hand on his wrist. "Is this something someone else can do? Should we call Damian?" When Trevor turned his fierce glare on her, she dropped her arm. "I'll take that as a no," she muttered.

"I can fucking heal a shattered humerus, Soleil," he snapped.

"Shattered—*oh!*" Thinking what that bullet would've done to her heart had she not moved, she felt faint again.

"I won't think less of you if you pass out," Trevor said. "I can't guarantee I won't take advantage and sneak a peek at your tits, though."

His teasing brought her back from the darkness, and she sputtered a laugh. "You say the nicest things."

He grinned, and Soleil savored the gorgeous sight.

"Thank you, Trevor," she said softly.

"You don't have to—"

"I do. Not just for healing my arm but for charging to my rescue."

Turning his too-intense gaze to her, he opened his mouth to speak, but before the words could be uttered, the Guardian and Seer rushed up.

"No sign of the fecker," Fintan said with a disgusted shake of his head.

"How are ya feelin', *cher?*" Draven asked.

"Not great," she admitted, hissing a breath in as Trevor manipulated the muscles around.

Bending on one knee, Draven touched a finger to her forehead. A sensation similar to euphoria flowed through her, dulling the pain. Giddy, she giggled.

"That might've been too much with all her blood loss," Trevor remarked. "She's drunk on the magic."

"Sure, and there's worse things to be," Fintan replied with a twinkle in his eye. "There's nothing so grand as a pretty *cailín* laughin'."

Soleil sighed and smiled up at him. "I'm not at all sure what you just said, Mr. Sullivan, but I could listen to you talk all day and never get tired of it."

For the first time since she'd met him, she witnessed Fintan grin. "Maybe I'll be entertainin' ya with me stories while you're abed, yeah?"

"Not likely," Trevor growled as he rose with her in his arms.

He staggered, but when Draven reached for her, Trevor cut him off with a shake of his head. "Back off."

"You're weak from all the healin', *mon ami*. Let someone help you for a change."

Soleil, equalling out from the magical infusion and seeing the wisdom in the Guardian's words, cupped Trevor's jaw. She waited until he met her gaze before speaking.

"No one is questioning your strength, Trevor. But you said it yourself. You've expended a lot of energy to heal Lily and now me. Please let someone help you."

Seconds ticked by, and sweat trickled from his brow. Right when Soleil thought he might dig in, he closed his eyes and nodded.

CHAPTER 12

Trevor sat beside Soleil's bed as she slept.

Thank the Goddess she'd thought to create the protective bubble. He assumed she'd learned the trick from the Oracle, and it likely saved her life. Other than to say "assault rifles are the devil" before falling asleep, Soleil didn't discuss her ordeal. The image of her riddled with bullets made his gut churn. He'd meant what he said to her about her fast thinking.

"How is she?"

Trev glanced up to see Gene Stockton hovering in the doorway and grimaced. "She's fine, but she'll probably be jumpy for a while until we find the fucker who shot her."

"I can't understand why anyone would want to. She's one of the kindest people I've ever met."

Stockton shuffled closer to the bed and gazed down at Soleil. His brows were drawn together as he pondered over what she might have done to deserve an enemy of this magnitude. Likely, Trev wore the same look.

"She has a simple life, from what I can tell," Trev replied. "Plants. Her family's shop. Hell, she even cares for the homeless three times a week. I'm as stumped as you why anyone would target her."

"But they are. You said it yourself." Stockton's expression was grim as he met Trevor's eyes. "Someone tried to run her down outside the restaurant, and today, they shot her. Thankfully, they were a piss-poor shot."

"Actually, she conjured a protective shell. Spent bullets littered the sand around her." After scrubbing his face with his hands, Trevor shook his head. "I don't get it, but I think this is why I was assigned to her."

"Like a guardian angel? I thought you were a magical assassin."

"Yeah. Mostly, I am. But maybe this time, I'm supposed to be on hand to heal her for whatever the Fates have planned."

Stockton made a face, then eyed her thoughtfully. "I don't buy it. If she leads such a simple life, what could they possibly need her for?"

"Repopulating the earth with all your black-market plants?"

Gene laughed. "Perhaps, but she isn't the only earth witch working on the project. She and Spring Thorne have created a collective to restore endangered or extinct plants. Wildlife, too, if I'm not mistaken."

"Christ. Let's hope they don't get it in their heads to Jurassic Park the planet." Trev muffled a yawn with his palm.

"Why don't you try to rest? I can watch over her until she wakes."

His brows shot up. "That's like leaving a cat with a mouse, man. Not going to happen."

Stockton chuckled. "As much as I'd love to seduce her, she only has eyes for you, Mr. Blane. You're a fool if you can't see it."

"I see it. But a relationship with me will find her dead within ten years." Despite how much he might wish differently.

"Looks like she'll be dead sooner without you around,"

Stockton said. "Ah, I can see you hadn't thought of that. You saved her life today."

"She saved her own life. I only healed her arm." Trev shrugged. "If not me, she'd have called her brother-in-law."

"Do you think you should contact him anyway? It could be these attempts weren't the first ones, but our mysterious villain is incompetent."

"Confession?" When Stockton nodded, Trevor continued. "I'm afraid of her brother-in-law. He's ancient, all-powerful, and scary as fuck when he loses his temper. And I have the feeling he might let loose with his anger if he finds out she's on some rando's hit list."

A half smile twisted Gene Stockton's lips. "Better to have as many people looking out for her as possible, though. She's too beautiful a person to succumb to a bullet or the bumper of an SUV, no?"

Trev shot him a sharp glance. "Did I mention it was an SUV?"

"You didn't. She did. You were too preoccupied watching her to notice what she was saying last night at dinner." He approached and held out his hand for Trevor to shake. "I'm not your enemy, and I'm certainly not Soleil's. You saved my daughter today, and I'd lay down my life for either of you."

Rising to his feet, Trevor accepted the offer of friendship. "I meant what I said. If Lily's cancer comes back, contact me. Before I go, I'll give you a list of names as a backup. They can all get the job done."

"I owe you."

"No. I don't hold markers. I have a lot of Karma to fix on my father's behalf."

"You realize Benjamin's sins aren't yours, Blane? Tell me you understand that."

Trevor didn't reply. Instead, he shifted to face Soleil's bed and stared down at her, noting her pale complexion and how her eyes shifted beneath closed lids, indicating she was in a dream state.

"I have my own sins, Stockton. My hands aren't clean, and they're too dirty for the likes of her." He swallowed down the self-pity trying to choke him. "But maybe someday, I can be worthy again."

"You're worthy now, whether you believe it or not, *cher*," Draven said as he joined them. "You've played the hero many times in the last months."

"You're wrong. I did what I was told."

The air shifted, growing heavier, and Damian stepped from the shadows.

Gene Stockton's face was pure shock.

"The brother-in-law," Trev muttered in an aside to him. Louder, he said, "Gene Stockton, Damian Dethridge."

The Aether gave a half nod and offered up a suave smile. "Mr. Stockton, I presume? I apologize for popping in unannounced, but it's come to my attention that Soleil was injured. I—"

From behind him, Sabrina ran through a fold in the fabric of space he'd created and straight for Trevor. "I told him Aunt Lei needed us."

"Dammit, Beastie!" Damian's growled irritation created a thick atmosphere. "When will you do as instructed?"

"It's safe, Papa," the girl replied, unrepentant.

"That is not the point, and you bloody well know it."

"You shouldn't swear," she said pertly. Dimples appeared as she grinned at Trev. "I wanted to tell you something, Mr. Blane."

"*No!*" He practically shouted. With a wary glance at her father, Trevor shook his head. "Sorry. The last time she imparted information, my brain nearly exploded inside my head."

Damian's stern expression disappeared, and wry humor lit his face. It was clear his daughter was a miniature version of him. Hands down, the guy would win the title of Sexiest Man Alive for the next two hundred years running. Like him, his daughter would grow to be a great beauty, with her black hair and obsidian eyes. She was already the loveliest child he'd ever seen.

The *scariest*, considering the power she wielded, but the loveliest, all the same.

"We got off topic." Draven smiled down at Sabrina and tousled her curls. "I was just tellin' your friend he was worthy of Soleil's affections, *ma petite amie*. What do you think of that?"

Trevor growled Draven's name as a warning.

Unperturbed, the Guardian shrugged, and his eyes, usually lifeless and uncaring, twinkled with intent. Was his plan to matchmake? Why?

"He's right, you know," Damian said as he came to stand beside the bed. Reaching out, he grasped Soleil's hand and felt her pulse, then gently tucked her arm at her side. Seemingly satisfied she was okay, he faced Trevor. "You rid the world of Loman O'Connor and helped rescue an island of prisoners in the process, Blane. You assisted me in protecting an estate full of people. You kept death at bay for Josie, then helped in the retrieval of my daughter. Now, you've become Soleil's protector." Damian cocked his head and studied him. "How is it you don't believe you're hero material?"

"Because I'm not," he snapped.

"Someone needs a nap," Sabrina declared loudly into the void Trevor's irritable reply had left. Pointing behind her raised hand in his direction, she added, "It's not me."

"I can see your gesture, kid," Trevor said with a snort.

"I know." She shrugged and climbed up on the end of the mattress by Soleil's feet to watch her aunt sleep. "When can I meet Lily?"

Gene, who had been silent during the entire exchange, likely from shock, sputtered back to life. "You know my daughter's name?"

"I'm the Oracle. I know everything, Mr. Stockton."

Sabrina wasn't trying to be cheeky; she was merely stating a fact. The girl could see the past, present, and future. Not just what had been or would be but all the possibilities in between. Of course, all that was in addition to her continuously forming Aether abilities.

Stockton shot Trevor a questioning glance, to which he nodded in answer.

It shriveled his balls to get close to Sabrina, knowing she possessed the power to bring him low with a single touch of her finger, but he squatted by her side. "Why do you want to meet Lily, kid?"

"I can't see her future."

Gene sucked in a breath as Trevor swore.

"But I healed her," he protested, suddenly livid at the unfairness of life. Why shouldn't Lily have a full life like anyone else?

"Beastie didn't mean your plan didn't work, Blane. Only that the Fates haven't gotten wind of Lily's recovery and mapped out a future for her yet," Damian said in a kind voice. Nicer than he needed to be since Trev was practically yelling at his daughter. Thankfully, the Aether read intent, and his wasn't to harm Sabrina. Otherwise, he'd be dead already.

"Gotcha." Still out of sorts, Trev ran his hands through his hair. The desire to escape was building inside him, and he needed to get away. "Okay, since all of you are here to watch over Soleil, I think I'll go take that nap, after all."

Damian's tone was highly amused as he said, "Pleasant dreams."

CHAPTER 13

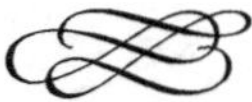

With all the mayhem, both Trevor and Soleil felt we should honor tradition and skip Chapter 13. One can never be too careful, and they're going to need all the luck they possess to discover the threat to Soleil's life.

Might I suggest a bathroom break and a restocking of snack supplies for the remainder of this story?

CHAPTER 14

*A*s soon as Trevor was alone, he peeled off his blood-soaked clothes and jumped in the shower. Under the scalding deluge, he could think clearly again. One thing was for sure, someone had it out for Soleil. The first incident could be brushed off as an accident or a drunk, if one were inclined to lean that way. But the second attack would've riddled her body with bullets had she been an ordinary mortal.

He had a mystery to solve, then he could get the fuck out of Soleil's life and on with his own. It was necessary for his emotional stability to get it done quickly. Every minute spent in her company endeared her to him a little more, and he couldn't risk his heart. Couldn't risk hers, either.

"Trevor?"

Her voice echoed in his head, and he wanted to weep at how uncertain she sounded.

"Yeah, Dalli. I'm here. Sorry for the thought dump. I assumed you were sleeping and didn't block you."

"You're not responsible for me. Please don't stick around out of any heroic need to save the day."

"Why the hell would you say something like that?" His frustration with the situation ratcheted up five notches.

"Because it's true."

Turning, he saw her on the other side of the glass enclosure. With her arms folded across her stomach, she appeared unsure of her welcome. Trevor didn't try to hide his nakedness. She'd seen it all in their hot-as-fuck fantasy, and she had to know that if she entered the bathroom while the water was running, she was likely to stumble upon him in the buff.

"You shouldn't be here, Dalli." He grew hard under her steady stare, and she wasn't even looking down, merely meeting his searching gaze.

"Every minute endears you to me a little more, too," she confessed.

He closed his eyes and hung his head. How the hell did he fight against something they both wanted? Even if it was for her own good in the long run, he was only human. He didn't possess a superman strength, allowing him to hold her at a distance.

Trevor jerked when her arms encircled him, but he didn't lift his lids or pull away. The press of her naked breasts on his chest was pure heaven, and he could stay in that moment forever.

"This will lead nowhere," he warned. "Your heart is too precious to risk on someone like me."

"Duly noted."

He met her sweet chocolaty eyes and couldn't look away. Her expression shifted the instant she realized he was putty in her hands, and the quiet confidence she exuded defeated his stubborn need to protect her from his eventual departure from her life.

"Why can't you be the strong one?" he whispered achingly. "I could accept no."

Soleil tenderly trailed her fingers along his jaw, maintaining eye contact. "A fulfilling life is about the sum total of our experiences, Trevor. I want that. There's a madman after me—and yes, I agree with your reasoning on that front—and I could die tomorrow."

His denial rose up swift and fierce, but she held up a hand to forestall him.

"It's the truth, and we both know it. Why not live for today? Why worry about a future we have no control over? Ten years. One year. One day. What matters is right now." She smiled, and he was lost. "I want whatever time we can have, and I promise I won't regret a single second of it when you walk away."

"That's the problem, Dalli. I'm not sure I can anymore." His voice was severe, but it didn't deter her. He didn't want it to. Whatever she had planned when she stepped into his bathroom, he hoped she'd see it through to the end.

"Good." Her tone was smug, and Trevor was contrarily joyful about his defeat.

"Are the others waiting on you?" he asked with a nod in the direction of her room.

"No. They left me to 'sleep' and went off to discuss security."

"You were *pretending*?"

"Not the entire time." She grinned, and the wickedness in her smile spoke to his inner devil.

"Well, look at you, Soleil Dalliance Stephens," he drawled. "What a sneaky wench you turned out to be!"

Her husky laugh shot straight to his dick right along with her hand.

CHAPTER 15

"He's fallin' for her."

Damian turned from the window and met the Guardian's concerned eyes. "I'm aware."

"You're not worried about her continued health, Aether?"

"I am, but not in the way you imagine."

Draven gave him a curious look. "You're not readin' my thoughts. How do you know what I'm imaginin'?"

As he opened his mouth to respond, it occurred to him the other man must be able to feel him poking around his mind. Damian frowned. No one, other than the strongest of their kind, could sense him. His best friends, Alastair and Castor, yes, because he didn't try to hide his trespass. His daughter, too. But few should be able to recognize the intrusion for what it was. "First you. How did you know I wasn't privy to your thoughts?"

"I can feel you, and others if they try." Draven nodded toward Sabrina, who was across the room, happily chatting Gene Stockton's ear off as the man nodded and smiled. One father with the patience of a saint could recognize another.

"When you do it, there's a sense of heaviness. It's similar to a threatenin' headache."

Having never experienced the sensation, Damian considered the Guardian's description. Other than Beastie, no one had the ability to read his thoughts without his express permission. Not even higher beings, like deities or the Fates, dared attempt it. He wasn't opposed to slapping back with his magic.

"Fair enough. In answer to *your* question, I went on the assumption you were referring to the Blane family's supposed curse."

"Supposed?"

"There's no such thing. Not for them, anyway. If it were real, then anyone he cares about or who spends time in his vicinity would be at risk. I'd never take a chance with my daughter's health."

Draven ran a poker chip across his knuckles, causing it to disappear at his pinky, then reappear at his thumb to start the motion all over again. The gesture was absent-minded and habitual, stemming from years of game play. He shrugged, never breaking the speed of the traveling chip. "You're assumin' he cares about your girl, Aether. Perhaps he's only humorin' the both of you."

Levity laced Draven's comment, and Damian didn't take offense where none was intended. "It's true we have a tendency to impose ourselves on people in certain situations. I'll give you that." He smiled in response to the other man's quicksilver grin. "But either way, if such a curse existed, I'd know about it."

"I've been friends with him awhile. I've seen the bad luck his family seems to have. Hell, Simon was bound, and he *still* put off enough power for his first wife to contract cancer."

"True. But a Death Dealer also has the power to heal, and no mandate from the Authority or Fates will stop them should they wish to save a family member or loved one."

"You're forgettin' Simon's wife died."

"I'm not. Her passing was tragic, but the reason was the binding of Simon's powers, not the existence of them. And I'm responsible. No one and nothing else."

"You?" Draven asked sharply. His dark-blond brows dipped as his expression darkened, turning forbidding.

"It's a long story, but I consumed his power when he was a boy at his father's bequest. I regret helping Benjamin, but I wasn't in possession of the truth at the time."

"It doesn't negate the fact his wife died."

Damian suppressed a grimace. "It doesn't, but don't forget the Fates may have had a hand in it. It's possible their intent was to prod Simon in a direction he might not have taken while still married to Tiffany."

Draven stared at him with intelligent eyes as he considered his reply. With a slow nod, he said, "You don't believe Soleil's goin' to be affected by Trevor's magic."

"I don't. Should she become ill, I'll step in," he promised. "My sister-in-law *will* have a long and healthy life. Which brings us to the next part of our conversation. I want to know who is trying to kill her."

"I was with her at the restaurant prior to Trevor and her runnin' off. I detected no threat inside."

Unless a magical being of Draven Masters's caliber was expecting an attack, he wouldn't be alerted to danger. He'd need to keep his senses open, which would be draining for most.

"Did you purposely scan the room while there?" Damian asked.

"It's a habit I've developed over the years. When you've been in hidin' or taken part in Wild West poker games with temperamental outlaws, you develop eyes in the back of your head."

"Understandable. But perhaps you should keep better company."

Another quicksilver grin flashed on the Guardian's rugged, unshaven face. "Perhaps I should, *mon ami*. Perhaps I should."

"Why do I feel like your last comment was directed at me?" Damian mused aloud, causing the other man to chuckle.

"Because it was?"

They shared a laugh before Damian sobered. "So what do you think, Masters? Who could possibly have it in for Soleil? She possesses the loveliest heart of anyone I know."

The Guardian squinted as he considered the problem. "Whoever's behind it is certainly incompetent, no?"

"Mm."

"What about your girl? Can she not tell you who's responsible?" Draven paused his hand movement and pocketed the chip. "Or Fintan."

"I'll ask, but if Beastie knows, she usually volunteers the information well before I've had a chance to inquire."

Draven's normally disillusioned eyes were lit with affection as he cast a glance Sabrina's way. "You may act put-upon, but you're blessed, *cher*, and you damned well know it."

"I've never denied my good fortune." Damian observed his daughter's animated face. With elfin features, she was adorable, but the promise of great beauty was there, if one looked close. The time was fast approaching for him to explain to her the power she wielded. To stress the importance of putting up walls with strangers and maintaining balance in all things.

"I don't know if I thanked you properly for the coin or for helping us out of a sticky situation with the Authority, but I owe you a debt of gratitude, Masters. You need only tell me what you want, and I'll see it's done."

"I believe your daughter paid your debt." The Guardian's gaze lingered on Sabrina, and his expression turned haunted. "Is she always right?"

"She sees multiple outcomes and analyzes the visions to determine the one most likely to happen. But her predictions aren't foolproof, if that's what you're asking."

Draven met his eyes. "She once told me the soul can come back if it wants to."

"You must know about reincarnation."

"Yes, but she insinuated Brooke Ellis was…" He inhaled deeply. "I need to know if Brooke was my wife."

"Would it matter if she was? She'll have no memory of her previous life, and it might prove disappointing for you that she doesn't." Damian wasn't trying to be unkind, but expectations led to heartache.

"So I should go it alone until it's my time?" Sadness, regret, and loneliness were rolled together, creating the sizeable emotion in Draven's voice. "And what about her? Will she ever find her great love if I leave her to her fate?"

"I've always coached Beastie not to reveal what she knows. It could alter the outcome. But if it were me, and Vivian was the one who'd returned, I would want to know."

The Guardian's eyes were tormented, as if he'd heard what Damian said but was afraid he'd interpreted the comment wrong. Afraid to believe.

"Ask her, Masters," he urged. "Tell her I said it's okay for her to reveal if Brooke Ellis and Jolene are one and the same and if pursuing a relationship will bring you the happiness you seek."

"Just like that, friend?"

"Just like that."

Damian watched the Guardian walk away. The other man's stride was slow and stiff, as if Draven fought himself and was losing the battle with his need to discover the truth.

"Sure, and you're gettin' soft, Aether."

He didn't turn to look at Fintan. "Mr. Sullivan. So glad you could finally join us."

"Is it a romantic ya are, then?"

"You're not going to let it be, are you?" With a sigh, he faced the Seer. Fintan appeared decades younger than his years. With a lion's mane of hair, beefy build, and hard features, he looked half-wild. Acted it, too. "Perhaps I believe everyone should be happy. Including your surly ass."

The man didn't grin, but his sea-green eyes filled with wry humor. "I'll not be after rainbows shootin' out me arse. That's for the likes of him." His expression darkened. "Besides, the woman I'm fated to love will be bringin' my downfall along with her. I'll be avoidin' *that* feckin' trouble, I will."

"If it's fated…" Damian let the sentence dangle, knowing full well it would get under his skin.

"I'll thank ya to be shuttin' yer mouth and not cursin' me, yeah?"

He smiled as Fintan stalked off to acquire a drink.

Ever since the tribunal, Damian's ability to see the near future had been restored. Unlike Fintan, who received visions from his ancestors, and Beastie, who saw the past, present, and future outcomes of every situation for every person, his power was more basic in nature. He could discern things as they pertained to him and those close to him, but only within a two to five year span. Which was well enough. The Fates were always spinning their wheel and pulling their threads. The future was fluid, always evolving based on their whims.

Damian sobered. As hard as he tried, Fintan would have a difficult time avoiding Taryn or the destiny lying in wait for them. If the Seer saw his downfall at her hand, the event was farther down the road than Damian was privy to. But after the sadness attached to the lives they'd both led, Fintan and Taryn should be allowed to grasp whatever happiness they could.

With a shrug and a sip of his brandy, Damian shrugged off his melancholy.

One problem at a time. And the primary one was Soleil and who might have it out for her.

CHAPTER 16

"So, who do you think has it out for me?" Soleil asked.

Trevor almost swallowed his tongue. "How the hell can you be so blasé about it?"

"Honestly?"

He nodded, but realizing she couldn't see him with her head resting on his chest, he said, "I can't wait to hear this."

Soleil sighed. "I believe it's a case of mistaken identity."

Her reasoning escaped him, and he told her as much.

"Think about it, Trevor. I don't go anywhere or do anything other than to a novelty shop in my small town and grow plants. By your own words, I putter around a greenhouse all day."

"Dalli—"

"Let me finish." She rolled toward him, and the feel of her full breasts against his chest distracted him. So much that he almost missed her next words. "I think the incident at the restaurant was an isolated accident."

Weaving his fingers in her thick dark curls, he held her still as he stole a kiss. "And the shooting? Seems to me you were the only one on that beach, babe. They took aim."

"What if whoever it was believed I was Gene's girlfriend or someone important to him? Maybe it had to do with revenge on him for some reason."

As much as Trev hated to admit it, she had a point. "Okay. Let's assume you're right, and I'm not saying you are because my gut is telling me differently. But suppose it *is* a case of mistaken identity. You're still not safe here. Please, let's get your plant from Stockton and get the fuck off this island."

"I can do that." Her grin was too charming for his liking or his peace of mind.

He stroked his fingertips along her healed arm. "Are you in pain?"

"No. I'm okay, Trevor. Truly."

"When I think about what might've happened had you not created that bubble..." Suppressing a grimace along with his shudder, he stared moodily into her worried eyes.

"Are *you* okay?" she asked. "It seems you care awfully much about—"

"I don't," he stated coldly. "Don't mistake anything I do for caring, Dalli. It's a surefire way to get your heart broken."

"I only meant—"

Feeling exposed, like his innermost feelings were on display, he pulled away and sat up, presenting his back to her. "I have to meet the others to discuss a second healing session for Lily."

"Trevor."

"*What?*" He winced at his waspish tone. "Sorry. I..." But what could he say? He couldn't care about her. She was his mark, and when the time came for him to tell the Authority to stuff it up their ass, she'd be someone else's. The thought created such pain in his gut that he sat on the floor beside the bed and drew up his knees.

"Trevor!" Soleil was beside him in an instant, cradling his face between her palms and staring at him with her large, worried eyes.

After tugging her hands down, he grudgingly acknowledged her concern. "I'm fine."

"You're not. You're pale and sweaty." Her lips thinned into a straight line, and she looked like she wanted to be anywhere but there. Inhaling deeply, she said, "Tell me why the Authority has it out for me. Maybe we can—"

"Stay out of my head."

"But you—"

"For fuck's sake, Soleil! Leave it alone!"

The hurt on her face was crushing. Shutting his lids over tired eyes, he reared back and smacked his head on the mattress's edge, doing it a second and third time for good measure.

She drew away, mentally and physically.

"Dalli—"

"No, you're right. Caring—for either of us—is off the table."

He fucking hated her icy expression. "It's not like that. I…"

But it was.

"You should've left me to my fate on the beach, Trevor."

A snap of her fingers clothed her in couture and applied model-perfect makeup. Her hair was swept up in a sleek ponytail, resting high on her head. The neatest he'd ever seen it. Come to think of it, he didn't care for the form-fitting dress or high heels she'd conjured. The overall look made her appear like just another desperate woman striving for perfection.

But it wasn't *her*.

Not his Dalli.

"What… Where… Why…" He scrambled to his feet. "Why are you decked out?"

She followed his gaze to her breasts and gave them a boost with her hands, positioning them higher and causing an abundance of cleavage above the U-shape opening. As she smoothed her palms down her waist and hips, she shot him a challenging glare, glamouring her body into runway-ready.

"Isn't this what you're used to, Trevor? Incomparable women like Mattie Price."

"Stop it." He didn't care for how sick her pretense made him. There was nothing she needed to prove, and she was as beautiful as ten Matties. "You don't need to do this for me, Dalli. You're perfect the way you are."

"Oh, this isn't for *you*. We both know you're not interested after our single hit-it-and-quit-it encounter. This is for *me*. And perhaps Gene."

Trevor jumped up and pressed his nose to hers.

"I'll kill him," he warned with a growl. "Believe me. I'm capable."

"Not with Damian and the others present, you won't."

She smirked. Fucking smirked like she had the upper hand! And perhaps she did. It annoyed him when he couldn't read her intent.

"How did you block me?" he demanded.

"Maybe our interlude changed the Fates' design, and we aren't meant to be mates, after all." She gave a dismissive sniff. With a careless shrug, she pivoted and minced her way toward the door. Halfway there, she tripped over air, barely catching herself from face-planting on the antique Persian carpet.

He laughed.

That would teach her to pretend to be someone she wasn't!

"You're a punkass, Trevor Blane!" Her exposed skin flushed a ripe berry shade.

A tchotchke sailed by his head and landed on the bed.

He laughed harder.

When he had his humor under control, he tsked and said, "When we leave here, I'll take you to a ballpark, and you can practice your aim. Maybe next time, you can hit the side of a barn."

Her narrowed eyes promised retribution.

It came faster than expected.

. . .

RECENTLY, AS SOLEIL AND SPRING TOILED AWAY IN THE THORNE greenhouse, her friend told her about when she'd filled Knox Carlyle's mouth with dirt during one of their fights. Without giving it further thought or Trevor any warning, Soleil did the same to him.

His rage gave the phrase "spitting mad" a whole new meaning. As she watched him gag, sputter, and spit, she exchanged her heels for flats and offered him a middle-finger wave as she sailed out the door. It felt damned good to get the upper hand for a change. To win in their battle of wits.

"You haven't won anything, Dalli."

"Get out of my head!"

"Looks like the Fates prefer us together, after all, so maybe I'll hang out in here a bit."

His irritating voice sounded way too smug for her taste. Picturing Gene naked, she envisioned a long, thick penis.

"For the love of—! That's just plain disgusting, Soleil Stephens. I threw up in my mouth!"

She giggled but sobered quickly. Sure, she'd scored one against him, but beating him in one battle didn't win the entire war. Halting mid-stride, she pressed the flat of her hand to her chest. Were they at war? Why did it have to be that way at all? She'd only ever wanted peace in her life.

The truth was, she liked Trevor Blane. More than she should. Yet he repeatedly shoved her away. It boiled down to one thing: he didn't want to care about her, so he wouldn't. At least she had one rocking sexual encounter to remember him by. From their first kiss, she'd known their joining would be epic, and it was. Hopefully, as time passed, she wouldn't compare all other men to him. Maybe her memory would fade, and she'd find her soulmate. A man to love her as she was. One who was perfect for her and so sweet it gave a person cavities to see them together.

Closing her eyes, she sighed. Wishful thinking was all well and good, but it was pointless at present. A consultation with Damian was in order, and finding out why the Authority would assign a Death Dealer to watch her was paramount. What had she done to deserve to die? Was her aim to repopulate dying or extinct plants all that terrible? Was she really so horrible that she needed to be extinguished?

Large, warm hands encircled her shoulders, and she jumped.

"Trevor!" she gasped. "What the fuck?"

"I felt your freak-out building." He turned her to face him. "It's going to be okay, Dalli. No one is going to hurt you."

"You can't assure my safety. Hell, you're the one they sent to do me in."

"About that, I'm not sure they did." With a dark frown, his eyes trailed across her face, up to her ponytail, and back down to grimace at her cleavage. "Can you change back into you, please?"

"No." She knocked his hands from her shoulders. "Explain your reasoning."

"You're pretending to be someone you aren't—"

"Not *that*. The reason why you aren't sure the Authority sent you to kill me."

He scowled.

She glared.

The corner of his mouth ticked up as his irritation melted away. His was a face she could watch all day and never tire of.

"Same," he murmured as his gaze flitted about, touching her every feature until it finally landed on her gloss-coated lips.

"Same? Oh!"

Ah, her thought about watching him. She was flattered to think he might find her as fascinating, but not so gratified that it was only when she'd layered on face paint he'd found it so.

"The makeup has nothing to do with how lovely you are,

Dalli." Using his fingertips, he traced the lines of her face, ending with her nose. "It's hard to believe I ever thought you were provincial or plain. Or that I've only known you a short time when it feels like I've known you forever."

She sucked in a breath. With careful precision, she blanked her thoughts and expression. It wouldn't do to let him know how easily he could weave the seductive spell over her or how fast she could succumb.

"There are people I meet and think the same thing about," she said with a tight smile. "Similar personalities and a strange familiarity are all it is."

Drawing away, she headed toward the stairs. He dropped into place beside her, matching her stride. "Maybe, but you can't discount the attraction we feel."

"I can't. But I can certainly ignore it." She stopped and waited until he retraced his steps back to her. When they were facing one another, she shook her head. "You're hot and cold, Trevor. You don't know what you want or why you want it. No one is ever going to tell you what to do because you'll rebel."

"That's not true." His indignation scraped along her nerve endings.

"It is. You hate your chosen career path, the fact you're alone without a partner to love, and you resent having to babysit me."

"Dalli—"

"Zip it." Seeing the wariness in his expression tugged at her heartstrings. "Let me finish. None of it's a bad thing, and I'm not criticizing you. I'm stating the obvious." His uncomfortableness built, and hers did to feel it. What the hell did it mean that they were now sensing each other's stronger emotions? "Trevor, you won't let yourself care because you believe you're cursed. There's no such thing. You've bought into a made-up notion. Witches are the worst with that crap, and they fall prey to superstition and what might be nothing more than coincidence."

"There is no such thing as coincidence in my line of work."

"Circumstance, then."

"You don't know what you're talking about." The gruffness in his tone was born from his hurt and the convictions he'd clung to his entire adult life.

"I *do* know. I've seen enough of it throughout the rainforest tribes. People cling to what they believe—good or bad—and become dogmatic. You're convinced there's a time limit on love for anyone with the last name Blane. It's just not true."

"Christ, Dalli! It must be nice to live in your perfect world, where nothing bad happens, and everything is roses. Or, in your case, orchids. But it's not the case in the *real* world."

His scorn stung, but she lifted her chin.

"I've experienced your *real world*, Trevor. My parents died when I was young. My sisters, Josie and Taryn, are constantly at each other's throats because Josie took it upon herself to protect us by sleeping with Morcant. I was almost run down, and today, I was shot." She inhaled deeply and looked him dead in the eye. "I'm falling hard for a guy who is a complete coward when it comes to love. It's not all orchids, babe. Far from it, if you ask me."

CHAPTER 17

*A*s Trevor sat down the length of the table from Soleil, he tried his best to concentrate on what Lily Stockton was jabbering about. Yet his mind returned again and again to Soleil's scathing retort.

"I'm falling hard for a guy who is a complete coward when it comes to love."

He snuck a glance her way.

She'd refused to drop the glamour entirely. Only going so far as to return her body to its original form, but her make-up leant to her supermodel good looks. Had he first seen her this way, he'd have never thought her plain, and he'd likely have tried to get her into bed within minutes of meeting her, believing she would know the score. Gorgeous, full-of-themselves women usually did. Hell, his last lover wrote the book on manipulating men with her beauty.

Deni.

She'd disappeared without a trace, and the best Trackers had been unable to locate her. Seven glorious months they'd spent together, making love and plans. Laughing over the most ridiculous things. But she'd left him. No explanation. No note. Only the diamond ring he'd bought, intending to propose to her. There it sat, seemingly gaudy in its black velvet box placed strategically at the center of the kitchen island, with nothing around it. Not even a fucking fruit bowl.

She'd discovered it in his sock drawer, and the message was clear. Trevor would always be alone. An island unto himself, with no one and nothing to cling to. Two years later, her defection still stung. Closure would've helped. That and not laying his fucking heart at her feet for her to stomp on after he'd told her all his deepest, darkest secrets. Was one damned discussion to say why she was leaving too much to ask?

"Trevor."

Soleil's worried voice echoed in his mind, dragging him from the past. Her flawless brows were drawn together in her concern.

"Who's Deni?" she asked.

"No one I intend to discuss with you."

Her frown dropped away, and her eyes cooled. The milk chocolate color darkened, telling of her unhappy state, and she gave a slight nod, acknowledging his rudeness.

"Understood. Sorry for the intrusion. It won't happen again."

Her tone was one he didn't recognize from her, and it grated on his last nerve. Trevor also wanted to rip off the fucking fake mask she wore.

Soleil wasn't that person.

She wasn't Deni.

But she looked like her, or rather, this made-up version of her did.

His fingers went numb, and when his soup spoon clattered to the bowl, Soleil flinched. From his oddball reaction or the loud sound, he couldn't tell, but it stood to reason she'd be jumpy from the shooting earlier. He should be considerate of her PTSD, but he was suffering a shock of his own.

How had he not recognized their resemblance before? There

had been many times he'd seen Deni's chestnut hair pulled up in a messy knot, high on her head, setting off her graceful neck. Many times, he'd seen her tinkering in the kitchen as she whipped up one of her delicious creations, looking for all the world just as delectable.

Cherry pie.

It had been Deni's favorite.

Trevor stared at Soleil in horror, and she stared right back, equally as horrified.

Were his burgeoning feelings for her an echo of the past?

"Mr. Blane?"

Lily's concerned voice penetrated the chaos of his mind, and he inched his head in her direction, though his gaze remained locked with Soleil's.

Without a doubt, she'd been privy to his thought dump, and she was hurt by what she'd seen.

"I'm sorry, Dalli," he whispered through their connection.

Her eyes dropped to her bowl, and with a dignity he would never have associated with her, she placed her spoon beside the dish and picked up the napkin to dab her lips. Finally, she glanced up, and there was pity in the look she gave him.

"For what, Trevor? Being in love with another provincial earth elemental? That's what she was, wasn't she? That's why you hold witches like me in such contempt."

"I don't!"

"Maybe not as much anymore, but you did when you first met me. If you're honest with yourself, you'll admit it."

But he couldn't be honest with himself. Not in a room with six other people, all looking between them with varying degrees of curiosity or amusement.

"Mr. Blane, are you okay?" Lily asked.

"Trevor," he corrected, his focus locked on Soleil. "And I'm fine, Lily. I need to discuss something with Soleil. If you give me a half hour, we'll begin the second phase of your healing."

"Sure."

Her voice sounded small, and it caught his attention. "You okay, kid?"

"Yeah." She shrugged, not meeting his eyes.

"She's crushing on you. Seems to be a freaky power you hold over women. Don't worry. She'll get over it. I imagine we all do," Soleil said.

Trevor disliked the cattiness in her response. *"Knock it off. She's a kid, and she's dealing with cancer of the heart."*

She never responded and, instead, shifted to look at Damian, who watched her closely. Whatever she saw made her mouth tighten with displeasure.

"If you'll excuse me." Soleil rose to her feet and cast those present a polite smile that didn't reach her eyes. "I think I'll go rest for a bit. Today took a lot out of me."

Stockton was first on his feet, drawing out her chair. "Are you okay, Lei? Should I call a doctor?"

She softened what previously felt like a brittle smile for him. "Between Damian, Mr. Masters, and Mr. Blane, we have the strongest healers available, Gene. I'm fine. Really. Just tired."

"Lei? Since when did he start calling you Lei?" Trevor demanded through their link.

She winced.

"If you're up to walking the gardens after dinner, I'd love to show you my recent acquisitions," Gene offered.

Trevor had had enough. *"Tell him you're not available and be done with it, Dalli! The poor bastard is pining away for you."*

The only indication she'd heard him was the stiffening of her shoulders.

"That'll be lovely, Gene." She had the nerve to lean in and kiss the fucker's cheek. "Thank you."

"My father likes her," Lily said to Trevor. "I think you have competition for your girlfriend."

"She's not my girlfriend, kid." Although his tone was snappish, it didn't seem to bother her.

"Dad said you were locked in your bedroom with her."

The superiority in her voice irritated him to no end. "You shouldn't believe everything you hear. Besides, kids your age shouldn't know about sex, and guys my age shouldn't discuss anything *remotely* like sex with children."

"One, I'm not a child. Two, I never said it was for sex, just that you were locked in your bedroom. And three, I know about sex. I don't live in a bubble, dude." She wrinkled her nose in disgust. "But yeah, talking about it with a guy old enough to be my dad is gross."

"He's a helluva lot older!" Trev retorted like the child he accused her of being. The comparison thoroughly annoyed him. "He's fucking ancient."

"I'm fifty-two," Gene said dryly as he approached. "Hardly ancient. Only three years older than *you*, if I'm not mistaken."

Trevor shoved back his chair and stood. "This conversation took a turn for the worse. I'm out."

Lily giggled, and Gene chuckled as Trev grimaced.

"I need to find Dalli," he muttered.

"Dalli? I thought her name was Soleil?" Lily's confusion would've been adorable had Trevor been in any sort of indulgent mood.

"Inside joke." He gave Gene a sour look. "One only a close *friend* is privy to."

Stockton smirked, damn him.

Trev was really beginning to despise smirkers.

First Soleil, now Stockton. There was no end to the *smirkiness* going around.

"Do you still love her?" Soleil wanted to punch herself for asking the question the second Trevor walked into her bedroom. What the fuck was she thinking? She'd seen his reaction to the memory at the table. She'd heard his thoughts about the engagement ring.

"No."

"Pfft."

"Why ask if you won't take my word for it?" His tone was waspish.

She cast him a sharp glance in the vanity mirror. When he met her gaze with a challenging one, she knew he was spoiling for a fight.

Well, let him! Engaging in battle was entirely up to her, and she had no intention of giving him the satisfaction of a knock-down-drag-out. With a careless shrug, she lifted the cleansing wipe and scrubbed the makeup off her skin.

Another glance in his direction showed his expression softening.

"It was a long time ago, Dalli."

"I heard. But two years is a mere drop in a bucket of time for a Death Dealer, isn't it?"

In the mirror, she saw Trevor's approach. He stopped shy of touching her, but Soleil could feel the heat of him at her back. His energy was dynamic and far-reaching.

"You shouldn't lead Stockton on."

She snorted. "Please don't talk about leading people on. Not you."

"I haven't. We discussed it before you stepped into the shower with me."

"True. But then don't behave like you care at other times. Rein in the pretended jealousy act."

"It's not pretend," he said as he eased her hair from its mooring and spread it over her shoulders. Threading his fingers through the strands, he massaged her tender scalp. She closed her lids in bliss. "I *am* jealous. Of every look, every innocent touch, every smile you send his way. I want to use my ability to murder him slowly. Feel his soul disintegrate under my hands."

Her eyes flew wide, and with her heart pounding out of her chest, she met his intent gaze in the mirror.

"I won't. Not unless he hurts you or breaks your heart, Dalli. So if you"—his jaw clenched, but he powered on—"if you decide to be with him, let him know he needs to treasure what he has."

Trevor's image grew blurry, and Soleil blinked away the forming tears. Clearing her throat, she shifted forward and dislodged his hands.

"Sure. I can do that," she said, rummaging for another face wipe.

"I wish it could be me," he said in a low, aching voice.

"If you wished it, you could make it so, Trevor." She hardened her tone and her heart. "You're your own worst enemy in the love department. Not your supposed family curse."

He dropped his arms and stepped back, his face a cool mask. "Believe what you want, but I know the truth."

"Sure you do. Men always know what's best for women, don't they?" Soleil didn't try to disguise her mocking tone.

"What do you want from me?" he snapped. "A white picket fence and a dozen babies?"

"Yes, all women are looking for a man to impregnate them." She rolled her eyes and shot him a look filled with disgust. "What's wrong with a normal relationship? Someone to love you and who you love in return?"

"Do you think I can wipe all the blood of the past from my hands with a few pretty words? Killers like me don't settle down to a normal life, Dalli. The Authority won't let us. And when we try, someone else pays the price. Those we *love*."

She faced him and gripped his hands.

"You're not the killer you think you are, Trevor Blane." He tried to draw away, but she held on tight. "I've spoken to Damian. I know—"

"When?"

"When what?"

"When did you speak to Damian? Not while you've been here. You haven't had time."

"Well, no. It was before. When I first… when we…" She pressed her lips together and inhaled, digging up the courage to confess she'd been fascinated with him from day one. "I asked him after you dispatched Morcant. When things settled after Sabrina's abduction and tribunal."

Trevor frowned. His darkening expression fed her nervousness.

"Is he the reason I was tasked with watching you? Was this all a setup?" he demanded.

"No!" She released his hands quicker than she would a shriveled earthworm. "I thought you were hot and asked what your deal was. That's all."

Trevor remained quiet and watchful as if he were weighing her honesty.

"You don't have to believe *me*, but you must admit Damian has too much integrity to set you up. Do you honestly believe a man so omnipotent would lower himself to play matchmaker?"

A smile kicked up the corners of Trevor's mouth. "No, I don't."

She sighed her relief, but her stress returned as she considered their situation. "But the Authority *did* send you for a reason, and we need to discover what it is."

The door burst open, and her brother-in-law loomed in the doorway. The skin was tight around his obsidian eyes, and his full mouth was pulled down and thin with displeasure.

Soleil's stomach flipped. "Damian! What's going on? Is my sister okay? Sabrina? Nate?"

"They're fine. It's Spring Thorne. There's been an attempt on her life."

CHAPTER 18

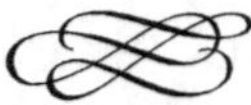

"Tell us what you know," Soleil said once she was seated on the bed next to Trevor.

His fingers were woven through hers, and his tight grip on her hand bordered uncomfortable. Yet she needed the support and didn't intend to complain. She saw Damian's gaze sweep over them, noting their closeness, but he didn't appear smug or make any comment. He was merely cataloging the moment and nothing more.

"Alastair called. Spring's greenhouse was blown up about ten minutes ago."

Soleil struggled against the urge to vomit. "And Spring? How badly was she hurt?"

"She wasn't."

"Thank the Goddess! Maybe next time you can lead with that." After taking a deep breath and expelling it again, she jumped to her feet, prepared to call Spring. But Trevor had yet to release her, and Soleil stumbled, falling into him. His arms closed around her, and he hugged her tightly as he buried his face in her hair. With her limbs pinned to her sides, she shot Damian a help-

129

less look. Other than a fleeting smile, he didn't help her escape Trevor's crushing hold.

"Let him have a moment." Damian's gentle voice flitted through her mind, startling her.

She understood he had the ability to read another's thoughts, but she hadn't realized he could implant them, too.

"When necessary," he said aloud.

"It's freaky," she muttered.

"But you and Blane have been holding conversations for days."

"Well, yeah…" Speaking of him. "Uh, Trevor. I've never been particularly claustrophobic, but I'm getting there." She wiggled her fingers and squirmed on his lap.

"Yeah, sorry." He loosened his grip enough for her to move her arms, but he didn't release her, and Soleil felt awkward under Damian's observant gaze. "That could've been yours," Trevor said gruffly. "The greenhouse. It could've been yours had you been home."

"What? Why would anyone want to blow me up?"

But someone *had* shot at her and tried to run her down. The three incidents weren't a coincidence.

"Remember what I said about coincidence?" Trevor guided her chin around for her to meet his piercing blue eyes.

"There's no such thing in your line of work."

"Exactly. Glad you were paying attention." His lips quirked as if he was trying to tease, but the worried lines bracketing his mouth never left him.

"Okay." She inhaled a deep breath and released it. "What we know is both Spring and I have been targeted. That narrows down the reason to one of our replanting collaborations, but not the party responsible."

Damian's brows shot up, and he gave her a half smile with his approving nod. "Which one, and why, do you suppose?"

"The new rainforest project is the one we've devoted our

attention to lately. We've met with resistance from those tasked with stripping the land, but from what I can tell, they have no pull or resources to stage any of these attacks." Facts were missing, and not having all the pieces for the puzzle bothered Soleil. The few absent details were vital to determining who might be targeting Spring and her. "Did Alastair have any ideas?"

"None, but his security team is on it. I don't care much for the odds of the people responsible. Alastair doesn't suffer attacks on his family."

"I should say not!" She eased out of Trevor's grasp and rose. "I'll give Spring a call and see if the two of us can come up with a list of suspects."

"Good idea," Damian encouraged. "But please remain within the walls of Mr. Stockton's residence until I've had a chance to speak with him about security and wards."

"Of course."

"I think it's tied to the Authority," Trevor stated as his gaze transitioned from her to Damian and back. "Why else would they send me?"

"You said, 'they,' but it's possible only one person was involved, right?" Soleil asked, glancing between the men. "Does the Authority always have checks and balances and multiple weighins on a decision like, say, oh, I don't know, hiring a Death Dealer to assassinate a random earth witch?"

Damian's mouth twitched, and the fine lines beside his eyes crinkled. "There are indeed checks and balances. However, council members have been known to go rogue, like in the case of Buttagier." He shrugged. "Although, I suppose it could be argued the Fates were aware of his motives and moves."

"Why do you ask?" Trevor leaned back against the headboard and cocked one knee to the side as he crossed his ankle under his straight leg. His casual pose was sexy as hell, and he looked right at home on her bed. So much so that she had difficulty remembering what she'd asked in the first place.

"You asked if it was possible only one person was involved," he added helpfully, but the gleam in his eye was a telltale sign he'd accessed her unfiltered thoughts.

"Right." Face warm, she left them to cross to the open window. A cooling ocean breeze swept through when she needed it most. The airflow wasn't random, and she supposed she had one of the men to thank for its crisp rush over her skin. "If more than one person were involved, I'd believe your assignment had nothing to do with our project." She turned. "But a sixth sense is telling me it does. And yet I can't see an entire organization getting behind killing two witches who are doing nothing but bettering the environment."

"Unless they don't want the environment bettered." Damian watched her with considering eyes as if he was putting all the puzzle pieces in place.

"There is that," she agreed. "But why wouldn't they? What do they stand to gain if we fail?"

"You said you ran up against resistance on the planting site?" Trevor asked. "Explain what happened, please."

"It was a bunch of workers with machinery clearing the land. Spring and I had a stand-in and refused to let them destroy the area we recently regenerated."

"Two women against how many men? Are you…" He choked off the rest of what he'd intended to say, but she heard it through their connection.

"No, Trevor. I'm not crazy." Soleil rested her hands on her hips and gave him the stink eye. "For your information, Spring doesn't go anywhere without Knox trailing her. We also had her brother-in-law Cooper Carlyle helping out." When he would've spoken, she narrowed her eyes. "We're fully capable of taking care of ourselves in any situation."

"Not from what I've seen," he muttered.

She dropped her arms, balling her hands into fists, and stepped toward him. Damian was quick to intercept her.

"Trevor knows you're capable, Soleil," he said soothingly. "His reaction is extreme and demeaning to you but still normal for a man worried about the woman he loves."

She caught what he'd said, but she doubted Trevor had.

"What I do, or who I do it with, is none of your business," she said, peering at him around Damian's shoulder. "You can keep your snarky comments to yourself. As a reminder, *you* weren't the one to save me today. Sabrina did, by teaching me to use her cloaking shield. So put that in your pipe and smoke it!"

Her brother-in-law looked like he was struggling to keep his laughter at bay, and she gave him a quelling glance.

"You, too."

Feeling exceptionally proud for standing up to them, she breezed by Damian, swiped her phone off the nightstand, and swept out the door into the hallway like a regal Regency heroine. Her imagined victory was short-lived. The call to Spring woke her up to the fact that the threat was real.

———

"You don't need to say it." Trevor closed his eyes and sighed heavily as he rested against the headboard. "I was an ass."

"As long as I don't need to say it," Damian replied dryly.

"She's maddening."

"The same could be said of you."

"But my issues aren't life or death," Trev protested, straightening and meeting the Aether's assessing gaze.

"It could be argued they are." Crossing to the bench seat by the window, Damian drew up his slacks and sank down. The elegance of the man was enviable. His brother, Simon, had that same effortless grace Trevor worked hard to achieve.

"How do you figure?"

"Your insistence that you're cursed."

Disappointment keen, Trevor grimaced. "Soleil's been talking."

"No. Draven and I have. Soleil is a closed book if you don't take into account her expressive face." Damian narrowed his eyes as if trying to find the right way to say whatever was on his mind. "You walk through life waiting for the other shoe to drop, Blane. That's no way to live."

"And you don't?" Trevor scoffed. "You're a king expecting to be toppled from his throne at any moment. How heavy is the crown you wear when it comes at the expense of your family, Dethridge?"

"Valid point. However, I'm not afraid to love or procreate, even knowing there will always be someone coveting what we possess." He sighed heavily. "I'm well aware there are constant threats or challenges I must answer and put down. We were both there for the Morcant incident."

"Exactly. Your wife was murdered."

"But we revived her." Damian didn't look as if he'd recovered from the incident, and the memory of Vivian's death still haunted Trevor, too. "You helped me. Without you, I wouldn't have my family. That's why I want to repay you. Why I want you to seek out love. Don't fear it."

"They die," Trevor snapped. "All of them! They die."

"Not Simon. Not your father."

"My father might as well be dead. He abandoned us a long time ago."

"Fair. But the person you love most in the world is still with you. And I believe Soleil could be another column to help support your foundation."

"I wouldn't be able to handle it if she were to die because of me, Damian." Trev opened himself up, allowing the Aether to feel his overwhelming fear and worry. "Now do you understand?"

"She's my sister by marriage. Do you honestly believe I'd allow anything to happen to her? Why do you think I'm here?"

"What about ten years from now?"

"If I'm alive, I'll be there, too. And twenty and thirty years." Compassion transformed Damian's visage from reserved to caring. "There are never any guarantees, Blane. You know that more than anyone. But I'll make you the same promise I made your brother. Should Soleil need healing due to the bleeding off of your power, I'll see it's done."

"I don't want her to suffer. Ever."

"She won't. No more than she would if she were with another."

Jealousy unfurled within Trevor at the idea of her with someone else. Just as it had earlier when he'd suggested the possibility to her. He tried to be altruistic for her benefit, but the selfish part of him would happily murder any man she chose.

"Your jealousy speaks for itself," Damian said with a half smile.

"I want her to be happy, but I don't want to see her with someone else."

"You're fated mates, Blane. It's normal for you to feel bonded to her in the way you do."

"This is some bullshit," Trev muttered.

After a full minute of tense silence, the Aether cocked his head and gave him a considering look. "Is there another reason you don't want to be with her? Do you feel she's not good enough for you?"

"I might've mistakenly believed that when I was first assigned to watch her. But no. It's the reverse. I'm not good enough for her."

"Why?"

"The lives I've taken have tainted me."

Damian stood and approached the door. "From day one, you refused to hurt anyone undeserving, Trevor. You've gone so far as to heal others without permission. Lily Stockton is an example." The man's look was determined as if he desperately wanted to impart truth on him, and Trev listened with an open mind. "I don't believe it's a secret to Soleil or you that Gene is romantically interested in her. They share common interests. Yet you are willing to heal his daughter without any reward or guarantee he won't end up with your girl. What is that if not selflessness?"

"I'm no saint, Dethridge."

"I never said you were. I'm merely saying you're a good man. A deserving one."

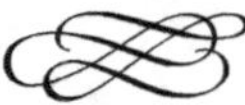

CHAPTER 19

*T*revor played what the Aether had said over in his mind. Before Damian left, he'd repeated what Soleil said.

There was no curse.

Circumstances and poor decisions had led to the loss Trev associated with Simon and his family. If that were the case, why was the weight of the past so fucking heavy?

He went in search of Soleil and found her gazing out at the beach from the hallway window. As he approached, she turned.

"Spring is livid, and rightfully so!" Temper added a steely edge to her statement. "Years' worth of work has been destroyed. Those plants were her babies."

Trevor remained silent. Likely, Soleil would've felt the same had it been her workplace. Her devastation would be complete.

"You probably think we're foolish to look at plants like—"

He cupped her jaw and bent to meet her fiery gaze. "Let me stop you right there, Dalli. I don't think either of you is foolish. Especially not over a loss of that magnitude. A lot of hard work and magical energy went into your projects. I'd be furious if it were me."

Her shoulders sagged, and sadness tugged down the corners of her mouth. "I feel so bad for her."

"Me, too." Trev drew Soleil into his embrace, offering comfort. "We'll find who's responsible, and they'll pay for their evilness. After, you and I can help her restore whatever we can."

"You mean that, don't you? You'll help her?"

"Of course."

"Thank you. You're such a good person."

He snorted. "Don't get carried away, Dalli. I'm no saint."

For a moment, she tightened her arms, and he could sense she wanted to argue the point, but she didn't. "I keep coming back to the rainforest project, but I can't connect the dots."

"It boils down to greed and corruption. Whoever has the most to gain by stopping you."

Her head shot up and nailed him in the chin. "Oof! Sorry." Her first action was to rub his chin, though her head must've been sore from the blow. But such was Soleil. Trevor was learning that she always put others above herself.

"I'm fine, Dalli." He brushed his nose against hers. "It takes more than a hard head to break my jaw."

She grinned at his teasing, then sobered almost immediately. "You said it was whoever has the most to gain. We've been fighting big pharma forever. Those corporations will go out of business if individuals can extract what they need from nature."

"I agree. Yet how did they find you and Spring? Thorne Manor and the surrounding land are well hidden. It's difficult to believe big pharma henchmen can find her place or get past the wards. Same for you."

She nodded slowly. "Magical means were used to find us."

"Yes. We need to find the connection between the two."

"We make a good team," she said with a triumphant smile.

As desperately as he wanted to agree, he held back, afraid to give her encouragement until he'd exorcised his demons.

"Sorry. I didn't mean to make it sound like anything but investigative teamwork." She drew away, and Trevor missed the feel of her in his arms.

"I didn't take it any other way, Dalli," he assured her. "I'm trying not to be overly sensitive to your innocent remarks."

"Good." She ran her palm down the buttoned seam of his shirt as if attempting to smooth the already wrinkle-free material. "That's good."

Trevor caught her hand and pressed it to his heart. "I want to tell you about Deni."

She tried to tug away, but he tightened his grip. "You don't have to, Trevor. I understand you love her."

"Loved. Past tense. She left me, Dalli, and I had to come to terms with it long ago."

"But if she hadn't, you'd be married by now."

"Maybe. Maybe not." He shrugged and tangled his fingers in her thick mass of hair. When she tipped her head back into his hands, he massaged her scalp and thought about the problems Deni and he had faced. Whatever came to mind, he allowed Soleil to see. "She didn't love me enough to stay and resolve whatever was wrong in our relationship. What did that say about our long-term success?"

"I can't speak for her, and I certainly don't know you well enough to comment on your past relationships or how you are as a person. But from what I can tell, you're determined and loyal. You deserve the same."

"Maybe I let my insecurities show." He met her desire-laden eyes and dropped his gaze to her parted lips. "Standing here with you, I'm not sorry she left."

Trevor lowered his head, hesitating for a heartbeat for her to meet him halfway, and then he claimed her mouth. His languid exploration wasn't to fire passion, although he felt it—and hers.

The kiss was more about his need to connect with her. To show her what he couldn't put into words: how much he cared, how precious she'd become to him, and the budding hope he felt for what could be a beautiful future between them.

She fisted her hands in his hair and held on tight as if she feared he'd change his mind and leave her stranded, alone in the hallway. Backing her against the wall, he pressed the full length of his arousal into her.

"I want you, Dalli. That's not in question," he said between nibbles along her jaw. "You've bewitched me to the point I want to cast aside my fears and take a chance." Capturing her earlobe with his teeth, he lightly bit down before straightening to look at her passion-flushed face. "After neutralizing the threat to you and Spring, we'll revisit this. All right?"

She frowned. "This, sex? Or this, us?"

He grinned. "Both."

"Oh."

"You seem disappointed."

"Only because I want the sex right now."

He barked a laugh and pressed a quick, hard kiss to her mouth. "I love your honesty."

"I don't know how to be any other way," she said in a vulnerable voice. "I know I'm not your normal type, Trevor. I get it. But I can't stop what I feel for you. What's growing. I mean, I *will*. I'll learn to if it's not what you want. I'll prune that shit off at the base. But—"

"I love the way you are, Dalli." He stroked her petal-soft cheek. "Whatever type I had before is no longer what I desire to have in my life. And I don't want you to shut your feelings down. I want them to continue to grow until they consume us both. Like mine are."

"Why the sudden about-face?"

He could read her distrust and readily acknowledged to himself it was warranted. "After speaking with you and Damian,

I've concluded that life is full of risks. I don't want to miss out because I fear losing you. If I do that, I've already lost."

Her sunny smile warmed the cold places of his soul. "I love that you're willing to try."

"It's scary as fuck," he admitted.

"I know. For me, too." As she traced his lips with her fingertips, her look became thoughtful. "If whoever is after me succeeds, it's not because of your supposed curse, Trevor. It has nothing to do with you and everything to do with whatever I stumbled into. Please tell me you understand and won't take it to heart."

"They won't succeed," he promised grimly.

"But if they *do*, it's not on you."

"If they do, I'll be inconsolable, Dalli." He pressed his forehead to hers and closed his eyes. "Thoroughly destroyed."

"You haven't known me long enough to feel that way."

"And yet, I do. You've wormed your way into my heart."

TREVOR WAS SAYING EVERYTHING SOLEIL WANTED TO HEAR, YET SHE didn't trust what he felt was real.

"Is this a transference of your feelings for Deni?" she dared ask. He jerked back as if struck. The dismay on his face hurt her, but she had to point out the possibility. "You loved her, Trevor, and I look like her. You thought the same exact thing yourself at lunch."

"I'll admit the delayed realization that you resembled each other was shocking," he said with a nod. "But I can discern the differences between you."

"Differences like what?" Goddess, she hated to pry, but her need to assure herself she wasn't sloppy seconds was vital.

"You're not," he said darkly.

"Not—Oh!" For a second, she'd forgotten he could see her doubts. The mind-reading thing was problematic.

"And it won't remain a problem because you'll learn to cloak your thoughts." Glancing down, he clasped her hand and brought it to his lips to kiss her knuckles. "The first major difference between you is your raw honesty, Dalli. I appreciate it more than you know."

She nodded but remained silent, waiting for him to elaborate.

"The second is your sunny disposition. Hindsight has shown me how temperamental Deni was. She always expected others to elevate her moods." He shrugged and looked out the window, not releasing her. "I never wanted to admit it, but living with her was hard sometimes. Never knowing what I'd get when I came home from a job. Initially, she was happy to see me, but in later months, she was often demanding, wanting to know where and who I'd been with."

"She didn't trust you?"

"I think that was a huge part, but I didn't understand it. Never, in the seven months we were together, did I give her a reason to believe I was unfaithful or a liar."

"No. If anything, you're brutally honest," Soleil agreed.

He shot her a sharp side glance, swiftly analyzing her response. Her openness spoke for itself.

"Thanks," he replied with a wry smile. "Yes, you're similar in looks, but you're in no way like her. Other than your ability to bake a mean pie."

She laughed. "You're saying you only love me for my baked goods?"

"No. I'm saying I love you for your beautiful soul, Dalli."

As the truth of his words washed over her, she sucked in a breath. "Trevor. You don't know me. You can't possibly love me."

"I know you," he said. "Your heart is full, yet you continually make room for more things and people. You care for everything and everyone around you at the expense of your own comfort." He ticked off the facts using his fingers. "I know you're obsessed with Kate Bateman's steamy historical novels. You'd also rather be in a greenhouse, with your hands in soil, than anywhere else on earth."

"Wrong."

His brows snapped together. "What?"

"I love my greenhouse, without a doubt. But I wouldn't rather be there. I'd rather be in your bed," she said with a saucy grin and a poke of his chest.

He matched her grin and raised her a wicked chuckle. "Fair. But to continue—"

"You don't need to. You've got the main points correct."

Ignoring her, he drew her against him and said, "I know you have a pure soul but a bawdy laugh that turns a man's head and makes him rock hard. Or maybe that's just me."

"It feels like you, for sure." She delighted in his groan as she rubbed her hand up and down the length of him through his jeans.

"Don't start what you can't finish, Dalli," he warned.

"Who said I can't?"

"I have to be in the dining room in two minutes."

"Can you get off in that amount of time?" she asked curiously as she continued to stroke him.

"If you continue to do that, I can." With a sigh, he eased her hand away. "But then I'd have no energy left to heal Lily."

Soleil smiled as she tucked her arms behind her back. "Far be it for me to suck all your energy from you."

"Jesus! Don't say suck, or it's never going down."

CHAPTER 20

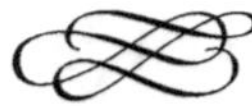

As Trevor left to meet the Stocktons, Soleil lay on her bed and thought about the situation she found herself in. She desperately wanted to talk to her sisters to get their take on what was happening. Taryn was practical and would provide valuable insight. Vivian was clever and able to create a sound plan of attack. And Josie was worldly. She'd think of angles the rest of them wouldn't.

Strange, but in the two days she'd been away, she missed home.

A knock pulled her from her musing.

"Come in."

She wasn't sure who she'd expected, but the Seer wasn't it. "Fintan!"

"I've a short window while the Fates are blocked, so I'll be thankin' ya to keep quiet and listen, yeah?"

Frowning, she nodded and sat up.

"You're not to trust Trevor Blane."

"What?" Her stomach plummeted two floors and burrowed underground.

"Ach, sure, and I've stepped into it, I have. I'm after tellin' ya to be careful what you say to him. The Authority is always listenin' in. They want him to fail, they do."

"I don't understand."

"Ya will. But the person ya seek is close to the Death Dealer."

"Who is it?"

"Jaysus! If I feckin' ken the answer, I'd be sharin' now, wouldn't I?" he growled. "This guessin' isn't all craic, to be sure."

"Do you come with subtitles and a dictionary?"

His unexpected laugh made her appreciate him in a whole new light. Fintan Sullivan was beautiful when humor lit his face. His sea-foam-green eyes were bright, and his grin engaging. Set off by a lion's mane of hair in varying shades of gold and light browns, he was truly handsome. Not a pretty boy like Damian or rugged like Draven. But beautiful in an Italian sculpture way. Chiseled and defined.

"I forget others can't readily decipher what I'm sayin'," he said in a less heavily accented voice. "But if I discover anythin' to help ya, I'll be passin' it along."

"Okay, but to clarify, I'm not to discuss with Trevor anything I find out about my attempted murders? He knows the person responsible and is in bed with them?"

"Aye to the first two and no to the third. He's not in bed with anyone but you, love, and he's happier for it, yeah."

He winked, and Soleil blinked at what she suspected was a rare gesture.

Fintan glanced at his watch and scowled. All humor disappeared from his face. "Time's up. Feck all."

"Fintan?"

He glanced over his shoulder.

"Thank you."

With a smile, he was gone, leaving her to make sense of everything he'd said.

His prime warning was not to let Trevor in on anything she

discovered. But that was easier said than done. For one, they shared every stinking thought running through their brains. Or she did, anyway. For two, he wouldn't relent until whoever was responsible was found. For three, he was sticking to her like glue.

Except for right now, a little voice said.

Soleil grabbed her phone and shot a text to Spring.

"Can Knox suppress the wards here on the island?"

Her friend responded less than a minute later.

"Yes and no. The best we can do is create a portal for you to step through if you need to leave right away."

"I do."

"One sec."

Three dots appeared, disappeared, then reappeared again. As she waited for Spring to offer up a solution to break through Stockton's Blockers and leave this place, she kept an eye on the door. All she needed was for Trevor or Damian to show up as she tried to make good her escape. She felt terrible for lying to her brother-in-law. He wouldn't be too pleased with her after she promised not to leave.

"Okay, here's what you do. Create a protection circle and conjure five red candles for the pentagram points."

She did as instructed.

"What's next?"

"Speak this spell aloud."

She laughed when she read what Spring had sent.

"Seriously?"

"It's a room-joining spell. I didn't make it up."

"I'd be embarrassed for you if you had."

"You want me to send my husband to rescue you or not?"

"Apologies."

"Speak the spell. I can thump you on the head when you get here."

Again, Soleil laughed.

The spoken words worked their magic as soon as they left her mouth. With each one, she felt the pressure build, pushing against the Blockers' power and expanding it out. Their wards popped like an overinflated balloon, and Soleil felt freedom of movement come with it.

In another instant, a rip appeared in the fabric of space between Thorne Manor and the island. Knox was visible on the other side, and he smiled as he held out his hand. Right when she would've taken it, the room spun, and a kaleidoscope of images of places she'd never been flashed across the opening to Thorne Manor. The last thing she saw was Knox's gobsmacked expression before the gateway settled on a new location.

Rough-handed men reached across and dragged her through a portal, and her terror was complete as she glanced into the faces of what looked to be a private militia.

"Good of you to join us, Ms. Stephens. We need to talk."

She stared at the woman in horror. It was like looking into a mirror—a very distorted, funhouse mirror reflecting a skinny version of herself, but a mirror all the same.

"Deni, I presume?" she asked with a casualness she didn't feel.

Doubts about Trevor and his true feelings swarmed her mind. How was it possible he didn't still hold feelings for this super-svelte lady-in-charge Deni? She was everything Soleil secretly wished she could be. Physically, at least.

A gloating smirk appeared on the perfect face across from her. "I see Trevor has told you about me."

"He said you were a bitch." Not entirely true, but Soleil took her opportunities where they presented themselves.

A granite-hard look settled on Deni's visage, and her voice was brittle as she said, "It's irrelevant. I'm here for a different reason."

"Dare I ask? It can't be good if you're reaching through portals to abduct people."

"You don't want to know your fate?"

"Based on the attempts on my life, I can hazard a guess." Soleil refused to let fear rule her. Knox knew what had happened, and he would inform the others in short order. When Damian found her, there would be hell to pay—for their enemies *and* her.

"Smart woman. I can see why Trevor might be attracted to you as a second choice," Deni said, but she couldn't hide her snideness.

"Second? I think he breathed a sigh of relief when you left the ring and disappeared. You did him a favor."

"Your smart mouth is going to find you in trouble," Deni warned.

Soleil waved a hand around her, causing the militia to raise their weapons and step forward.

"Settle down, fellas. I was about to make a point." To Deni, she said, "You don't consider this trouble?"

Reluctant amusement filled the other woman's brown eyes. "For you, I suppose it is."

"Do you worry what will happen when the Aether comes knocking?" Soleil watched her closely, gratified to see a flash of unease. "You know he will, right?"

***

"What the hell was that pop?" Gene asked.

Trevor didn't dare look up. If he were to become distracted, Lily's healing would be compromised. "Dethridge?"

"Your wards were annihilated, Mr. Stockton." There was no worry in Damian's voice, per se, but his tension thickened the air.

A sinking feeling started in the pit of Trevor's stomach. "Please check on Soleil."

"I fully intend to." With a brisk nod, Damian teleported away as Trevor refocused his attention on the remaining cancer within Lily's heart muscle. The mutated cells were particularly stubborn, clinging to the healthy tissue and refusing to give up their hold. He visualized new growth as he worked, starting from the nucleus and building outward. With each new cell he created, he eased it into position, replacing the old. Most worked, but there were those refusing to budge.

If he kept at it any longer, he would be depleted. Lily would need one more session within the next twenty-four hours, but in the meantime, she required rest.

Trevor stepped back and gestured to Draven. "Will you put her to sleep?"

"But she slept for most of the day," Gene said. His worry showed in his face, voice, and actions as he gripped his daughter's hand. Love shone from his concerned gray eyes, and he stroked back her sweaty hair. "Is she going to be okay? Did you get it all?"

"Not all of it. There are a handful of stubborn cells that'll take longer to dislodge. But we're ninety percent there, Stockton. I promise I won't quit until she's healed."

"How much more of this can she take?"

Trev shared a look with Fintan, silently asking what he saw for her outcome.

The Seer placed a hand on her shoulder, and his eyes went opaque as the visions swept over him. Fintan's process took less than ten seconds, and he stepped away with a confident expression.

"Aye, she'll be grand."

Shoulders sagging in his relief, Gene shook Fintan's hand, then turned to Trevor. "Thank you, Blane. Whatever Soleil wants from the greenhouse is hers. Let her know that, won't you?"

"I'm not doing this for payment. She wouldn't want me to, either."

"Nevertheless, I'm beyond grateful for your intervention on Lily's behalf. I need to gift you both with *something*."

"Just allow your daughter to live a full life when this is over. Don't be a helicopter dad, always reminding her she was once sick."

"Wise counsel." Gene smiled. "I can do that."

"Good." Trevor held up his hands when the man offered his to shake. "I would, but they're on fire. Like a nuclear reactor cooling down. I wouldn't want you to get burned."

Stockton glanced at Trev's palms and grimaced at the blood-red skin. "I had no idea! Is this safe for you?"

"I appreciate the concern, but this is what I do." He smiled. "I'll be fine in a few minutes, but recovery time is essential to build up for her next session."

"I understand." Gene turned back to Draven to ask him about the sleep spell, leaving him and Fintan alone.

"I've got to go find Soleil," Trev told his friend.

"She's gone."

"Gone? What the fuck do you mean, she's *gone*?" Not waiting for an answer, he shot toward the door.

When he arrived at Soleil's room, he found Damian conversing with Knox Carlyle. Neither man looked thrilled.

"Where is she?"

CHAPTER 21

"Where the fuck is she?"

Trevor's heart produced whole-body vibrations, and the relentless pounding threatened to break through his chest wall. His gut churned, and acid gnawed away his stomach lining.

"She was reaching for my hand when the portal malfunctioned. I rushed through, but she was gone," Knox said, bemused. He glanced around as if he still couldn't believe what had happened.

Shaking his head, Trevor stared at Knox. "What do you mean a portal? What about the Blockers? Stockton had them in place, didn't he?" He faced Damian. "Didn't he put them back up after you walked through?"

"He never lowered them for me. Arriving is not an issue for this island."

The Aether roamed the room, his head cocked as if listening. To what, Trevor didn't know, but he wouldn't have heard anything over his thudding pulse anyway.

"What are you searching for?"

151

"A magical signature." Damian waved his hand. *"Ostendo!"*

The daylight disappeared, and a hidden gateway to another location became visible, with a teal ribbon of light crisscrossing the person-sized opening.

"There's your doorway to whoever took Soleil," he stated matter-of-factly.

"How do you know?" Trev asked.

"It's unique to this room."

With a frown, Knox squatted and studied the edges of the criss-cross pattern. "You don't believe this was created when Soleil and I tried to circumvent the Blockers?"

"No." Damian pointed to the light source. "It's brighter on the backside and folds in on itself as it clings to this opening. If I had to guess, they're leaving this open to either return her or in hopes someone follows." He met Trevor's eyes. "I suspect you."

"But why? Why would they want me to follow her?"

"If your supposition was correct, and a council member from the Authority is behind this, they intend to kill two birds with one stone, as it were. They take Soleil, knowing you'll chase after her, and through her, they'll attempt to control you."

"Still not understanding the why of it, Dethridge."

"You don't need to. They have a reason, and we'll figure it out soon enough." His eyes swept Trevor's hands. "Where's the tanzanite ring we created for you when we went after Morcant?"

"Back at my apartment. It seemed silly to wear it after the danger had passed."

Damian held up his hand and showed his pinky ring. "My recommendation would be to get used to it. It's how our team can connect without worrying about cell service."

"Our team?" Trev asked.

"Your team?" Knox asked.

With a roll of his eyes, Damian waved a hand and restored light to the room. The portal remained highlighted, and Trevor was suitably impressed by the trick.

"Yes, our team of Sentinels, Blane. You're all under my protection, and I owe each of you a debt of gratitude to be paid at a time of my choosing."

"I could give a shit about payback other than to find Soleil," he said impatiently. "Do I walk through the portal, or what?"

"It depends on how worried you are about your skin. I'd test it first." Knox crossed to the nightstand and picked up Soleil's romance novel, preparing to throw it at the opening.

"Wait!" Trev replaced the book in Knox's hand with a vase. "She's still reading that one."

The other two men exchanged an amused glance.

"Fuck off," he muttered. "Throw the damned vase."

"Stockton might have a fit if you use that particular one," Damian said with an arched brow as he closely studied the object in Knox's grasp. "It's priceless."

"Oh, for fuck's sake!" Trevor stalked across the room and picked up a decorative pillow. "Will this work?"

"I don't see why not," Damian replied. His lips were twitching as if he struggled not to laugh. The urge to hurl it at him was strong. Instead, he tossed the pillow into the center of the teal web.

It caught fire.

With a snap of his fingers, the Aether extinguished it.

"I'd worry about your skin as well as the rest of your person if I were you," Knox said with a sigh. "That shit's going to Kentucky fry your chicken, dude."

Rage was born of Trevor's worry and inability to help Soleil. "Enough with the fucking jokes. She's on the other side of whatever this damned wall is, probably terrified and fighting for her life if she isn't de—dea—" He couldn't voice it aloud. Him, a Death Dealer whose job it was to take life, and he couldn't say the simple word.

He dropped to his ass on the floor and wrapped his arms around his knees as he struggled to draw a breath. The silence in the room was oppressive and crushed his chest, adding to his struggles. They suspected what he did.

"I'm sorry," he croaked. "I'm… I…"

Damian placed a hand on his head. "Sleep, son."

Darkness obscured his vision, and he fought the spell as long as possible.

"Soleil," he murmured as he pitched sideways.

"Was knocking him out helpful? Don't we need him to get the girl?" Knox asked as Damian placed a hand under Trevor's back and lifted him, letting his magic do the work.

"He was spiraling and useless to us until we have a better grasp of the situation."

"I'm laying odds the guy's going to be on a rampage when you finally wake him." Knox checked his watch. "I have to get back to Spring. I don't trust that whoever did this isn't after her."

"Go. And summon me if you need assistance. I'll consult with Masters and Sullivan before sending the Guardian to you to protect your wife."

"Did you forget I have a god's powers?"

"No. But if you feel confident in guarding her, I'll keep him with me."

Knox considered the situation. "Send him if your Seer thinks I need him. Otherwise, we're good."

"Did Alastair discover anything in the meantime?"

"Not before all of this. I don't know if he did since I've been here, but I'll have him contact you."

"Fair enough. Thank you, Mr. Carlyle," Damian said.

"Knox, and you're welcome, sir." They shook hands. "Please keep me posted."

"Certainly."

After Knox left, Damian considered the problem. He wasn't

surprised in the least when the door opened and his daughter peeked her head inside.

"Hello, Beastie."

"Hello, Papa."

His lips curled as she stepped to the bed and flicked Trevor's ear. "Did you think my spell wasn't foolproof, my love?"

She giggled. "No. But he's fighting it."

"I imagine he is. He's worried about your aunt."

"He loves her."

"That's the impression I got." Damian tugged one of Sabrina's black curls. "Go ahead and tell me what you intend to reveal so we can help Soleil."

"They want to make Uncle Trevor do things he doesn't want to."

"Uncle Trevor, is it?" he asked dryly. "Be careful about throwing the moniker around until it's time."

"Yes, Papa."

He studied her contrite, pixie-like countenance, admiring the fact she could keep a straight face while lying. Deciding that correcting her for the lie wasn't a battle he would win, he disregarded it. "Who's they, and why keep Soleil alive when they tried so desperately to kill her before?" he asked instead.

"They want to make him stay. Be a Death Dealer forever."

"The 'they' part of this is the Authority, no doubt?"

She nodded, and the grim expression on his child wasn't a sight he loved.

"I see. Do you have a name for me, Beastie?"

"Councilwoman Vector and Uncle Trevor's girlfriend."

"*Girlfriend?*" If he were two-timing Soleil, Damian would fry his ass.

"She looks like Aunt Soleil, Papa, but not as pretty."

"She means Deni," Trevor rasped from the bed.

"Ah, the elusive Deni who mysteriously disappeared from

your life," Damian replied, turning to face him. "You revived faster than I expected."

"Healing abilities, remember?" Trevor grimaced as he sat up and clutched his head. "What did you do to me?"

"The magical equivalent of a sleeping pill. It'll wear off soon enough."

"Soon enough to find Soleil, or did you intend to be the savior of the day?"

"Oh, no. I'm leaving the hero mantle for you to wear." Damian winked at his daughter. "What do you think, Beastie? Will he look good in tights and a cape?"

She clapped a hand over her mouth to suppress her giggles. Despite the direness of the situation, he took a few precious moments to absorb the sound and catalog the memory for a future date. When one lived as long as an Aether, it was important to remember the good times.

"You sure Deni's involved, kid?" Trevor asked, expression forbidding.

Both Damian and Sabrina knew the scowl wasn't for her. If it had been, Trevor would be rueing his birth.

She nodded and crossed to him. "I'm sorry, Uncle Trevor. She's not a nice person."

Although he narrowed his eyes on the "Uncle" bit, he never responded to the name. He nodded as he said, "Thanks for letting me know. I'll keep it in mind when I confront her."

"Choose her."

A BAT TO THE FOREHEAD WOULDN'T HAVE STUNNED TREVOR AS much as Damian's kid telling him to choose Deni over Soleil, especially after the girl called him Uncle. "Excuse me?"

"She wants you to choose her over Aunt Soleil. So you have to pick her." Sabrina shrugged as if it were a given.

"Otherwise?"

The girl sought her father's permission, and Trevor followed her gaze to Damian, who shook his head.

"If she knows, I need to also, Dethridge. Soleil's life could depend on it."

The Aether weighed his strict no-revealing-potential-outcomes rule against what he knew to be right as Trev waited impatiently for him to decide.

"The future is fluid, Blane," Damian finally said. "It's ever-changing. If she tells you what she suspects, but it alters between now and the moment it's expected to happen, you could misstep and make things worse."

The explanation made perfect sense, but it was no less frustrating to hear. "Fine. I'll play it by ear."

"It sounds like the only certainty is that you should stroke your ex-girlfriend's ego."

Trev conjured a cup of coffee and a glass of water, using one to chase the other. Hopefully, the fatigue leftover from Damian's sleeping spell would wear off soon. He couldn't go into this with a clouded mind, or he'd put Soleil at risk.

"Can anyone tell me how to find her? My Trackers weren't able to do that over the last two years."

"We'll call in Masters. Between the four of us, we can neutralize and rip open the portal."

Pausing between sips of coffee, Trev raised a brow. "Four?"

"You, Draven, Sabrina, and myself." Damian tapped his daughter's nose with a doting father's smile.

"That works." Trevor calculated their odds. "It's doubtful there's anything stronger than two Aethers and a Guardian."

"It would be if you added Ronan and Dubheasa," Sabrina piped in, referring to the two Guardians who watched over her and her brother, Nate.

"Do we need them?" It's not that Trevor didn't like Ronan and Dubheasa—he absolutely did, going so far as to consider them friends of a sort—but if they needed that much firepower to break through a portal, things were worse than he suspected.

"No," she said. "But three Guardians are stronger than one."

"Thanks for the math lesson, kid."

"You're welcome."

Trevor hid a grin behind a sip of coffee. Sabrina Dethridge was a cheeky devil, and they all knew it. She was their future Oracle, and to a man or woman, every Sentinel who served Damian in the past would lay down their life for her. For the entire Dethridge family, if it came to it—and it almost had.

"Okay, I'm caffeinated, and my magical hangover has lessened. Let's plot this thing out. I want Soleil back where she's safe."

Damian and Sabrina smiled their approval. Their favor was a good thing if they were all going to be related by marriage someday. Trev hadn't thought to ever go there with Soleil because of his curse, but if their long-term relationship was inevitable, he'd accept his fate and be happy for whatever time they had together.

CHAPTER 22

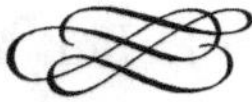

"He'll remain with the Authority, Mother," Deni told the petite, smart-dressed blonde. "Trust me. No one knows Trevor Blane as well as I do."

The smug way she'd said it, along with the superior look she shot in her direction, made Soleil want to rip Trevor's ex's head off her shoulders and use her dried-out skull as a chalice to drink aged whiskey.

Bitch.

"I understand you *believe* you do, darling, but it's been over two years since you've last seen him," Deni's mother said. "People change."

"Not Trevor."

Yes, Trevor, Soleil wanted to shout. Did the skank truly think he would sit around and pine away for her forever?

But hadn't Soleil herself had a similar thought? Hadn't she worried she couldn't compare to the other woman the second he saw her again? Wasn't there a small part of her that believed he'd take one look at Deni and ask, "Soleil, who?"

159

"Wear this." Deni's mother handed her a small vial of what appeared to be perfume. "It's charmed."

"I can lure him on my own," Deni snapped. "He bought me an engagement ring, for fuck's sake."

"Tone, Denillia."

"I apologize." But her cold brown eyes said differently.

The mother-daughter duo's tension practically crackled in the air, and Soleil hoped to use it to her advantage. If she could drive a wedge between the women, she might stand a chance of surviving.

The bold blonde's beady gaze landed on her. "Does she know?"

"No. From what I can tell, she's nothing but a bimbo. Certainly Trevor can't see anything worthwhile in her. She's a chunk, dirty three-quarters of the day, and clueless as to how he's using her."

Soleil desperately wanted to take exception to Deni's criticism and tell that human menstrual cramp to eat shit and die, but for now, she needed to play along. Maybe they'd underestimate her one too many times, and she'd find a way to turn the tables.

A large, invisible hand squeezed her shoulder, and she almost came out of her bonds.

You're not a bimbo, Dalli, and your body is perfect," Trevor growled through their connection.

The cavalry had arrived.

Soleil closed her eyes against the threatening tears. Yes, she was relieved he was here, but she hadn't realized how much it hurt to be disparaged in front of him. He'd heard and was trying to make her feel better, which somehow made it worse.

"Not as perfect as hers," she said as casually as she could.

"Meh. She's scrawny. I've had better."

She barely managed to suppress a laugh. It was no wonder she loved him.

"I love you, too, Dalli. Hold on to that knowledge, and don't forget it as this plays out, okay?"

"You know something I don't?"

"Yes."

She waited, but he didn't share. *"What took you so long to get here?"*

"I'd have been here hours ago, but the Aether slipped me a magical Mickey. I had to fight the effects."

"Damian did that?"

"To calm me down, I think." His fingers tightened. *"I was out of my mind when I found out you were abducted."*

"I'm sorry I didn't tell you I was going." How did she say she took off because she felt insecure since Fintan told her not to trust Trevor?

"He did what?!"

Having forgotten to cloak her thoughts, she winced and sucked in a breath as Trevor's outraged voice echoed in her head. Unfortunately, her action caught the attention of the women.

"Why did you do that?" Deni demanded, striding forward and double-checking her ties.

Soleil said the first thing that came to mind. "I have to go to the bathroom. I've been holding it forever, and I can't anymore."

It wasn't necessarily untrue. She'd been sitting for hours, and nature was banging on the door of her bladder.

"Too bad."

"Rude much?" Soleil muttered.

"You can wet your pants for all I care," Deni said with a sneer. "That should endear you to Trevor."

The scathing laugh did it, and Soleil kicked the bitch's spindly shin.

"Suck a bag of dicks!" she shouted as Deni bent and hopped on one leg.

"Nice one, Dalli. I need to remember that particular comeback."

If she knew where he was, she'd shoot him a glare. *"It's the best I could come up with under the circumstances."*

"It's not horrib—"

Deni's palm connected with her cheek, and the Mike Tyson-worthy slap snapped Soleil's head to the side. Her jaw immediately began to ache like a bitch, and a burning started below the surface of her skin, throbbing outward.

"I'm going to eviscerate her!" Trevor growled.

The air around them stilled, and Deni seemed to sense the threat. She frowned in confusion and shot a worried glance at her mother.

"Did you feel that?"

"Yes." The blonde woman tossed the perfume bottle to Deni. "Put it on. Quickly. When Trevor Blane walks through that portal, I want him to be on his knees and begging."

"I told you. I don't need it to snare him, Mother," Deni snapped as she dropped into the chair beside Soleil. "Now, cast a glamour to make me appear tied."

"So that's their game," he muttered.

"Who else is here, Trev?" Soleil asked him.

"Draven and Fintan."

"Uh, about Fintan."

"He said he'll explain later." Trevor's fingers brushed Soleil's cheek, and she wanted to lean into his hand but resisted the urge. The cooling sensation took the sting away, and the thrumming pain in her jaw eased. *"I've left the mark for show, Dalli. If you need to, pretend it's tender."*

"Since you're cloaked, can't you sidle up to that toe wart and obliterate her?"

"I could, but Damian wants more information from Councilwoman Vector first."

"Who's that?"

"The older blonde."

"That's Deni's mother. Are you saying she's the Authority coun-cilperson who sent you after me?"

"That's what I'm saying, sweetheart." His voice inside her head was grim. *"Whatever this is, it goes farther back than you."*

"I'm sorry, Trevor."

He stroked Soleil's cheek a second time. *"I'm going to show myself. Act surprised."*

It had taken no time for Damian and his Sentinels to defuse the burn-up-on-contact element of the portal, allowing a cloaked Trevor, Fintan, and Draven access to the room.

Trev had arrived in time to hear Deni's insulting comments to Soleil, and he'd wanted to rip her a new asshole. Until she'd struck Dalli, he'd intended to let her live. Now, she'd be lucky to.

Positioning himself by the portal, he muttered the words to uncloak himself, pretending to stumble forward as if he'd just entered. A fireworks show behind him made it look like he'd diffused the spell across the opening by crossing through.

With a faux check of the room, his gaze touched on Soleil—who acted surprisingly well, all things considered—and then settled on Deni. His mouth dropped open in fake shock as he rounded his eyes.

"Deni?" he croaked. "Oh, God, Deni! Are you hurt?" He took two steps toward her before he halted and faced Agnes Vector. "You!"

Satisfaction for a job well done curled inside him when she smoothed down her hair and smiled. "Welcome, Mr. Blane."

"What's going on, Councilwoman Vector?" His gaze touched on his two loves, past and present, lingering longer on Deni for effect before he once again addressed the head bitch in charge. "Why are they tied?"

Her beady eyes narrowed as she considered him.

Had he overplayed his role? He could do one of two things: act complacent, as if he would go along with her plans, or become belligerent, which was more believable for his personality.

"Start talking," he ordered. Lifting his hand, he conjured fire and shaped it into a ball. He added an extra element to paralyze her as the flames ate her black soul: his special fire-of-hell touch to make a villain's journey to nothingness torturous. If it got to the point where Trev had to step in and take a life, his victim deserved what they got.

"We, the Authority and myself, need assurances, Death Dealer," she said coolly. Gesturing to Soleil and Deni, she continued. "They're our guarantee, although we only intend to keep one alive to assure your compliance. The other will act as a warning to you and those who seek to defy their contract."

His stomach dipped before he remembered Damian wouldn't let anything happen to Soleil. "What assurances?"

"That you'll continue to do your job."

"Haven't I always?"

"Yes, but not without grumbling and a lot of stops and starts." She strode to her daughter on sensible heels and caressed a lock of chestnut hair. "Take Denillia here. If we hadn't removed her from your life two years ago, you'd have quit the business when we needed you the most." Vector's wide, toothy smile put a T-Rex to shame. "But by taking her off the playing field, you became angry and uncaring. You did what was required without argument."

"Only for those deserving of death," he corrected. "I don't kill innocents."

"But how can you tell who is deserving or not?" she taunted. "*We* are the ones who feed you information, Blane. We are the puppet masters."

"The Authority or you, as my handler?" he asked coldly.

"Does it matter?"

"Tell me you're going to off that smug-ass hemorrhoid, Trev. Please."

He did his damnedest not to look at Soleil and laugh, but his mouth twitched. To combat the urge, he compressed his lips.

"So, which one lives, Mr. Blane?" she asked tauntingly. "Or should I make the choice more interesting?"

"I'm not likin' the sound of that, cher," Draven said grimly, using the psychic link created by their tanzanite rings.

"Me, either."

"Bring them in," she called out.

A door opened on either side of the room. The two men, held at gunpoint, were forcefully shoved forward into the light.

Trevor almost lost his shit. "What's the meaning of this, Vector?"

"I'll let you save two, Mr. Blane. But only if you contract with us for the rest of your days. Oh, and there will be no more balking when we assign you a case. You'll kill who we want, when we want, regardless of whether they're 'innocent' or not. Got it?"

Trev swore, then and there, he was going to tear out her cruel, beady eyes and feed them to her on a platter. Across the distance, he locked gazes with Simon. The raw fury on his face spoke to his mindset. "Is Evelyn okay, Si?"

"I don't know." Simon's response was rough. Having lost one wife, his brother wouldn't be able to handle it if he returned home to discover Evelyn was harmed. He'd go nuclear.

"Fintan?"

"She's grand."

"It takes a lot to kill a Thorne witch, bro," Trev told Simon, hoping the underlying message would be received. The torment in his brother's eyes lessened, but his anger remained.

"His rage could come in handy," Soleil said.

"Yeah, Dalli, that's what I'm counting on if it comes down to a battle."

Benjamin Blane rolled his shoulders and shifted forward. "I'm going to make this situation easier for everyone."

Catching and holding his breath, Trevor waited for the other turd to drop.

His father's regretful gaze touched on him before locking on Agnes. "I'll take Trevor's place. I'll be the assassin you require."

"Sorry, but no," she replied with an airy wave. "You can't be trusted, Benjamin. Your boys will do."

Her slip didn't go unnoticed by either Simon or him. She wanted them both under her thumb.

"There are three Death Dealers in one room, Agnes," Ben scoffed. "Do you really believe we can't take down you and your crew without breaking a sweat?"

Trevor wanted to scream at him to shut the fuck up, but his father was a pro at escaping sticky situations, so he remained quiet, hoping like hell Ben knew what he was doing.

"Take this one, for instance," he said, gesturing behind him with a toss of his head.

Blood oozed from the man's nose. The vessels in the guard's eyes turned an unnerving shade of red before exploding and causing his eyes to weep blood. A moment later, he was in a heap on the floor.

"Fuck me!" Fintan shuffled closer to Trevor. *"Sure, and did you know you could do that party trick, man?"*

"No. But it's useful."

"Kill them all!" Agnes shouted as her shock wore off. She dove for an exit, only to run into an invisible wall known as the Guardian. A cry was wrung from her lips as Draven gripped her hair to halt her flight. The air around him shimmered, revealing him.

"Councilwoman Vector, why would you leave when things are about to get interestin'?" he asked.

Fintan disposed of his invisibility cloak. "Aye, and I'm not appreciatin' that you gave up our advantage, Masters, I'm not," he growled.

"Get over yourself, Sullivan." Draven grinned cheerfully. "There's fun to be had in seein' the fear in your enemy's eyes when they realize they're in deep shit."

The cocking of a gun ended the banter.

CHAPTER 23

"Guard, stand down." Brooke Ellis stepped from the shadows. "Mr. Masters, let Councilwoman Vector go and do it now."

Draven swore long and loud before a mulish expression settled on his rough-hewn face.

"Now, Mr. Masters," she demanded.

"Can't do that, *cher.*"

"I've orders to bring Councilwoman Vector and the Death Dealers to the committee. You're not to stand in my way, Guardian."

"And you intend to shoot me, *mon cœur?*" he asked in a soft, almost tender, voice. The excitement in his whisky-colored gaze was peculiar, considering the situation.

"Knock off the endearments, and I will if I must. Release Councilwoman Vector to my care, and no one has to get hurt."

Draven's smile bordered proud as if the Captain of the Red Guard had done an exceptional act by standing up to him. And perhaps she had. Who, in their right mind, would go against a man only a smidgeon less powerful than the Aether?

"Where is Damian?" Soleil asked Trev, reading his mind.

"Waiting and watching the entire scene play out. Probably eating popcorn because this part just got juicy."

"What am I missing?"

"I promise to fill you in later, Dalli."

"Uh, Trevor?"

He glanced in her direction only to see her watching Deni.

"She's about to make a move."

He frowned. *"She's tied. How can you tell?"*

"Her bonds are a glamour, to hide that she's free, but I can feel the energy shift."

"Keep an eye on her, Dalli."

Dismissing the problem of Deni for the moment, Trevor shot Captain Ellis a practiced smile. "You have a problem, Brooke. May I call you Brooke?" At her cold stare, he continued. "My father, you may know him as Benjamin Blane, isn't likely to be taken alive. He doesn't play well with others. Also, my brother, Simon, the other person dear Agnes had abducted, is FBI. This won't end well if he's not returned home immediately."

"The FBI knows better than to involve themselves in Authority affairs," she stated briskly.

"No. I mean, it's not going to end well when I lose my shit because he's not returned home immediately," Trev said in a patently false pleasant tone. As she watched him, he let his friendly persona drop and showed her the ruthless Death Dealer people feared. "Simon's recruitment into the Authority is, and has always been, off the table, Captain Ellis."

Ben approached her, and Trevor had to credit the woman for not backing down in the face of a man who could explode another's brain without breaking a sweat.

"If the Authority wants a reminder about why my son is off limits, they need only ask me," Ben said, raspy and rude.

At least he was sticking up for Simon, whereas he'd never stuck up for Trevor.

Brooke stared the entire room of people down as she cocked her head and listened to whatever her supervisors were feeding through her communications earpiece. She gestured to him. "Trevor Blane, you've been recalled. You have exactly one hour to show yourself in committee chambers." To Ben, she said, "Your presence is requested, sir. As a show of faith, they'll let Simon go."

"I'll be there," his dad replied with a side look at Trev. "We both will."

Trevor wanted to rush and check that Simon was all right, but his brother was a grown man, and if he was hurt in the abduction process, he'd have said. Mainly Trev suspected he wanted to hurry home to check on Evelyn because, despite Fintan's assurances, Simon wouldn't have peace of mind without knowing she was doing well and had suffered no side effects from the intrusion.

"You have this under control, Trev?"

"I do," he lied, praying it turned out to be true.

With a nod for him, Simon teleported away.

Next, the guards filed out, led by Brooke, who guided Councilwoman Vector toward the exit. Agnes didn't spare a glance for Deni as they left. What did it say about her parenting skills when she couldn't be bothered to check on her daughter's welfare? More telling, Deni didn't seem to notice. Her gaze was focused on Trevor, and when she saw him watching her, she flashed a come-hither smile. His mind recoiled, but he didn't allow his distaste to show. Instead, he smiled tenderly as if she held the moon and stars.

Walking to her first, he gazed down at her in wonder. How had he ever fallen for her lies? He was a fool for not researching her past and uncovering the connection between Agnes and her. Having heard the bulk of her conversation with her mother, he felt like a dupe. Seven months she'd played him, nurturing his feelings until he was prepared to propose and then crushing his hopes by disappearing without a word, leaving only the boxed ring as a rejection.

She was a consummate actress, and he needed to keep that knowledge alive so he wasn't swayed when she tried to worm her way into his good graces. And she would. If only to know she could.

"I see you were able to untie yourself. Clever," he said, giving her a warm smile. "But then you always were."

Deni preened under his supposed praise and cast a gloating look toward Soleil. Never had Trevor wanted to strike someone weaker than him, but he did now.

"I'll do it for you," Soleil offered, causing him to bite his lip to stem a bark of laughter.

"You'll get your chance, Dalli," he assured her.

Fintan untied Soleil as Trevor pretended to ignore her. Inside, the desire to kiss away the pain of her chaffed wrists was strong.

"I'm fine, Trevor," she informed him.

"Even one scratch on your delicate skin bothers me. Let me bask in my anger over their treatment of you a little longer, okay?"

"Bask away."

Again, he fought another laugh.

Deni rose and placed a palm over his heart. "I've missed you, my love."

"Gag." Soleil didn't bother to keep her snark between them.

A wave of dizziness swept him, and Trevor inhaled sharply as the world around him spun.

"Trevor!" Deni cried as he swayed.

AN OVERPOWERING WHIFF OF FLORAL FRAGRANCE WAFTED SOLEIL'S way, and she immediately understood why Trevor had reacted strangely.

"She's wearing a magical perfume," she told him. *"You have to find a way to block the smell."*

"I'm okay," he said, but then scrubbed his hands over his face as if he were struggling to stay awake.

Fintan, Draven, and Ben distanced themselves from Deni, and Soleil assumed Trevor relayed the info about the enchantment she was weaving.

"Fintan should've placed a ring in your hand, Dalli. Put it on."

She did, and her mind was flooded with the rapid-fire telepathy between the men.

"How do you plan to block her magic?" Draven asked.

"I don't know." Trevor placed his hand over Deni's and grinned down at her.

Soleil crossed her arms over her chest and glared. *"What the actual fuck? Why are you catering to her? Lock her ass up!"*

"Can't. The Oracle said to choose her. There has to be something big brewing if I have to pretend to be in love with her."

Because it would be odd if she didn't comment on their closeness, Soleil cleared her throat angrily. "What the hell? I'm standing right here."

"You were always second best, girl," Deni said smugly. The woman edged closer, pressing her body to his and wrapping her arms around his neck. "It's *me* Trevor loves."

"If you kiss her, we're done," Soleil told him, meaning it. She didn't give two shits what her niece suggested he do. Watching him kiss another woman in front of her would be a memory she'd never get out of her head.

"Don't be like that, Dalli. We're on a mission."

"You might be. But I'll rip out your entrails and hang them from the London Tower," she vowed. *"See if I don't."*

"I adore your spirit, cher!" Draven said.

"Oh, shit, she's going in!" Trevor shot Soleil a panicked glance. *"I'm—"*

"Mm," Deni moaned, covering his mouth with hers.

She acted like the mere contact of lip on lip fired her passions and was the best thing since lemon cake. Granted, not much beat lemon cake—or lemon anything. But Trevor did, and Douche-Drop Deni knew it.

"I think I threw up in my mouth," Soleil muttered as she turned away.

"I know I did," Benjamin replied with a desert-dry tone, startling her. She'd forgotten he'd lingered.

"Sure, and didn't we all?" Fintan added.

"Is this why he isn't to be trusted," she asked him in a low voice, purposely concentrating on only Fintan and hoping Trevor didn't pick up on her thoughts.

His light eyes settled on her, and he nodded. "Among other things. I'm after warnin' ya to be prepared, but ken it isn't him, yeah?"

"I don't know what any of that means."

She glanced over her shoulder to see Deni grin and reach for his crotch. At the same time, Trevor dodged her seeking hand and grabbed her wrist.

"Not in front of an audience, my love," he said, flashing a grin. "There's time for that when we're alone."

"Skank bitch needs a lesson in manners!" Soleil growled.

Draven stopped her forward charge with a hand on her arm. *"All isn't what it seems, cher."*

"How can you say that? They're mauling each other!"

"Dalli, remember what you do to me with a single kiss? She leaves me flat as a pancake."

Soleil's gaze dropped to the front of his jeans, and she registered his lack of erection. *"Doesn't mean I have to like it,"* she muttered through their link.

"I'm not asking you to. Just know I don't either. I'm aware of what she is and what her particular games are. Trust me."

She shot a look at Fintan. He'd said not to. What was she to do?

"Trust me, Dalli," Trevor urged. *"I love you."*

Her heart swelled, and happiness bubbled inside, but she

didn't reply, choosing to remain wary and alert.

When Ho Heidi Ho dove back for another kiss, Soleil shut her eyes and allowed her inner Spring Thorne to emerge. Connecting with the soil from a nearby potted plant, she mentally apologized for stealing its nutrients even as she removed the dirt and envisioned stuffing it in Deni's mouth.

A muffled screech and spitting was Soleil's reward, and she lifted her lids to see her nemesis turn blotchy and ugly with rage.

Beside her, the men laughed, and it appeared as if Trevor was struggling to hold it together, too. But Deni was incensed. The woman produced the perfume bottle and smashed it at Trevor's feet. His expression arrested, then went blank as if his thoughts were no longer his own.

"Trevor?"

He didn't respond or look Soleil's way.

"Trevor, answer me!"

His gaze remained locked on Deni, who leaned in and whispered in his ear. With a single nod, he turned from her and approached Soleil.

"She's a nobody, Trevor," Deni scoffed. "Nothing."

With a sweet smile, he wrapped a hand around Soleil's throat and squeezed.

Fintan and Draven shouted his name, jumping on him in their attempt to wrestle him away. But his one-handed grip was superhuman in strength. Unbreakable.

Trevor's Death Dealer magic swirled around them, and from the corner of her eye, she noticed Fintan swipe a wrist under his nose and gaze at his blood-soaked sleeve in horror.

"Back away!" she shouted at the others. No way would she allow them to die on her behalf. *"Trevor! Trevor, stop! Please, stop!"* she screamed within the confines of her mind, attempting to pry his fingers away from her neck. *"Babe, please!"*

Yet it was as if their link were severed, and he couldn't hear her.

But she heard him.

"Obliterate."

Spots danced before her eyes, and she frantically struggled against his hold, clawing at his hand in a desperate attempt to escape. It wasn't the strangulation that would be her undoing. No, the thing she needed to worry about was already wrapping its magic around her soul, breaking it down with the intent to crush. Obliterating.

CHAPTER 24

The atmosphere around her turned into a sparking, snapping live wire of energy an instant before time froze. The only two unmoving were Trevor and Deni, yet Soleil couldn't break his hold. The highlight? Whoever had used their ability to halt time encapsulated Trevor's killing magic and suspended her soul's extinction.

"Now, Ben!" she heard Damian shout.

Benjamin, along with her brother-in-law, rushed to where Trevor held Soleil in his death embrace. The lack of air was burning her lungs, and dancing black dots filled her vision. If they didn't separate Trevor and her soon, she would die.

Her knees grew weak.

"Restore her, Ben. I'll call the Healer to help you while I take care of Trevor."

She wanted to plead with Damian not to hurt him. To tell him that Trevor hadn't known what he was doing and Deni's compulsion spell had caused this. But she knew there would be a price to pay for this day's work.

In a flash, Trevor's hand was gone from her throat, and Ben

had her cradled in the circle of his arms. With one palm pressed to her chest, he performed whatever magical trick it was Death Dealers possessed to reverse the damage his son had wrought.

Burning began deep within her cells, and it felt like someone had poured acid on her organs. A scream was wrenched from her soul, but it never left her damaged trachea. She attempted to shove him away, but he held fast. What the hell were these Blane men made of? Granite? What made them impossible to dislodge?

Tears streamed from her eyes as she silently implored Ben to stop the torture and end her suffering. His eyes lacked the warmth of his son's as they stared at her with dispassion. Here was a jaded man who was only doing as ordered, with no care one way or another if she lived other than the consequence he faced from the Aether should he fail.

In another instant, the Healer, Jordan Brothers, knelt next to her, and the pressure of his hands on her throat made her wince. His kind eyes and friendly smile, along with his spattering of assurances, eased her worry.

Oxygen filled her lungs, and she greedily sucked it in as if she'd been underwater for an hour. Great gasping gulps provided the life-giving air she needed. The bruised feeling in her throat eased with every second the Healer continued his ministrations.

Still, the inferno within her cells raged. With her newly healed throat, she screamed, threatening to undo Jordan's repair and shatter the eardrums of those closest to her. Her horrific noise was nothing compared to Trevor's, and when she heard his cry, her instinct was to get to him. To help in any way she could.

"Damian, no! Please. Don't hurt him," she sobbed. *"Please!"*

"Hush, girl," Ben ordered, not unkindly. "All will be well."

"He's your son! Damian's killing him!"

An amused twinkle entered his flat blue eyes. "He's not. He's only taking away what no longer serves."

His magic.

Trevor would hate that.

"No!" She struggled harder, intending to stop it.

"All will be well, child. Trust the process." Ben drew back his power in slow increments.

He didn't release her to assist his son, and the knowledge she was weak as a newborn kitten was torturous. Soleil's entire body throbbed, and she experienced a freaky sense of discombobulation. Like her physical and spiritual selves were trying to reconnect but were unable to.

Touching a hand to her head, she said, "I feel weird."

"It's a side effect. You'll recover well enough, and if you don't, I'll be back for a second infusion."

A loud pop echoed off the walls, and time restarted with a resounding bang.

"What the fuck?" Deni stared down at Sabrina, who held an uncapped bottle in her hands. "Who are—" Eyes widening in horror, she shifted her gaze to Damian and Trevor, then continued on, meeting Soleil's hate-filled glare.

Trevor bucked under the magic-removal procedure and shouted his agony, drawing everyone's notice. His painful cry ripped Soleil's heart from her chest, and her tears began again in earnest.

"Please help him, Ben," she whispered.

"I am."

She shifted to meet his gaze and saw genuine concern for his son but resignation, too.

"He'll hate everyone after this," she predicted.

"Perhaps, but I'm betting not."

When Damian climbed to his feet, Deni's instinctive need to save herself kicked in, and she turned to run.

Alexander Castor stepped into her path with his beefy arms crossed over a muscular t-shirt-clad chest.

"Going somewhere?" he asked, grin menacing. His platinum hair was mussed and fell over one of his two raised brows, and challenge lined his breathtaking face.

Facing a six-feet-six Greek god descendant had to be daunting, but Deni, crafty bitch she was, put her hand on her hip and cocked it in that I-can-have-whatever-I-want-if-I-demand-it-with-a-smile way that hot-as-fuck women understood from birth.

"Well, hello, gorgeous!" Her voice was nothing short of a purr.

Castor's grin widened.

"I fucking hate her," Soleil muttered as Ben stroked back her sweat-drenched hair and Jordan held a glass to her lips, containing an herbal concoction that smelled like ass.

"Ditto," Ben replied. "Now be a good girl and guzzle that nasty shit so I'm not subjected to the odor any longer."

"Stop, or I'll fall in love with you." She found herself liking the curmudgeon. "What will it look like if I dump your son for his irritable father? People will question my sanity."

A grin flashed across his face, and the soul-weary light lifted from his tired eyes. "That's incentive for me to keep going."

"Flatterer." She gagged and sputtered as she downed the drink. "Fucking hell! That's worse than Trevor trying to kill me."

Gasps sounded around her.

She wrinkled her nose. "Too soon?"

"Yeah." Ben's lips twitched. "Much too soon."

Trevor groaned, rolled onto his side, and focused on her. *"What the fuck happened?"*

"I told you not to kiss her."

"So you decided to sic Damian on me?" He swiped the back of his wrist across his forehead. *"Just tell me you're okay, and we can discuss this later. After."*

A shudder swept through her. She wasn't sure she could relive the experience, even if it were only a retelling.

His gaze sharpened. *"Dalli?"*

"I'm fine, Trevor. We'll talk when this is over." Avoiding him, she concentrated on Sabrina, who watched Deni curiously as if the woman were a specimen under a microscope.

Her niece faced her direction. "She's not a nice person."

"We've already gathered as much, child." Ben eased Soleil into Jordan's arms and climbed to his feet. "What needs to be done?"

"We can't kill her. The Authority will be mad at us."

An irritable expression crossed his countenance.

Soleil rolled to her knees and latched on to Jordan's arm, at the ready for when she swayed. After he helped her to stand, he assisted her in crossing to Sabrina. "What about me? Isn't it self-defense or something?"

Her niece giggled, and Ben gave her an approving grin.

"To hell with Trevor," he said. "Run away with me."

Stretching up on tiptoe, she kissed his cheek. "You say the nicest things."

"I can't chase after you both right now, but when I can, there will be hell to pay." Trevor sat up and glared their way without any actual heat. "Count on it."

Soleil covered Sabrina's ears.

"Damn, now he's making me hot," she quipped. "I'm going to need you boys to duke it out."

His growl made both Ben and her grin.

"He never did like to share his toys," his father replied with a rusty bark of laughter.

"He still doesn't," Trevor assured him.

"All's fair in love and war, buddy," she retorted snidely, not quite over what had happened. "You kissed Skankzilla."

"You're getting better at those comebacks, Dalli."

She grinned. How could she help it? Who didn't love a man who appreciated snark?

Draven checked his watch. "Your hour is almost up, my friends. I'm not opposed to a second visit by the lovely Brooke Ellis, but she's liable to arrive trigger-happy." The Guardian narrowed his eyes when Sabrina opened her mouth. "Don't say it, *ma petite amie.*"

"Papa said I'm not allowed to tell what I know." Her offended sniff added to the humor of the situation.

Hanging his head, Trevor grunted. "I'm not sure I can stand, much less teleport to the Authority."

"I'll take you." Ben approached him and held out a hand. "We're in this together, son."

Disbelief and something akin to hope flashed across Trevor's wary face. "Why now?"

"I've always had your back, Trevor. You were too stubborn to see it."

"No, Dad, you didn't. Simon was the golden child." He held up a hand. "Not that I'm complaining. Or hell, maybe I am, but I love him and wouldn't steal whatever you felt for him. I wish you'd have worried about me a little more, though."

Ben squatted and gripped Trevor's shoulder. "I *always* worried about you, son. Why do you think the Authority allowed you the freedom to pick and choose your marks? I picked up the slack."

Trevor paled.

"What?" He glanced at Damian. "Is that true?"

The Aether nodded.

"I thought you were in hiding all these years." Trevor looked devastated, and Soleil desperately wanted to hug him. Wanted to tell him it would all be okay. But she couldn't. Their family dynamic was wildly different from hers, and healing belonged to them.

Ben shrugged. "I was, for the most part. There were other Death Dealers they could utilize for the easy jobs. Not many can do what I do, though."

"That whole kill-a-guy-without-touching-him thing?" Soleil glanced at the blood stain on the floor left by Agnes Vector's guard.

"That, and other things."

"You're a scary dude," she said with the utmost respect.

His grin flashed, and she saw a hint of Trevor's standard charm in it.

"Sure, and you'll be back to work after today, yeah?" Fintan said to Ben. "They'll be after a Death Dealer to replace Trevor."

The other shoe just dropped, and Trev's expressions ran the gauntlet from confused to shocked to outraged. He lifted his arm with his hand flat, palm turned to the ceiling. His concentration was great, but no magical weapon formed.

"I'm powerless?" His eyes held betrayal. "Completely? How am I supposed to defend Soleil? Or anyone else, for that matter?"

"You were the one she needed defending from, *cher*," Draven said. His tone was surprisingly gentle.

Where Trevor found the energy to leap to his feet, she'd never know, but he did. Weaving and bobbing, he approached her and raised a hand toward her face.

Her flinch was involuntary.

"Dalli." His voice was ragged and filled with an aching regret. "What happened?"

"We can discuss it later." With a tight smile, she wrapped her arms around her middle and nodded toward Draven. "You've got to go."

"Fuck the Authority. You're more important." His eyes drank her up, and she felt his desperate desire to touch her. When she stepped backward, he swore savagely.

"I'll be here when you get back. We'll talk. Swear."

CHAPTER 25

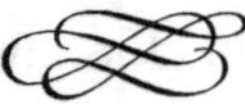

revor didn't remember anything after Deni dropped the perfume bottle, but it must've been horrific based on Soleil's reaction to his touch. Although she'd been trying to keep the mood light concerning her trauma, her haunted eyes were breaking his fucking heart. How was he supposed to leave her in this state? For what? To have the Authority slap his hand? They could dole out their punishment later.

"Go, Trevor," she said in a low voice.

"I can't leave you, Dalli." His voice cracked like a distraught teenage boy's, but he ignored the fact they had an audience. "I love you, and I need to make this right. Whatever it was I did."

"You tried to kill her, son," Ben said.

"No, he tried to erase her," Damian corrected in a frosty voice.

The blood drained from Trevor's head, and he felt dizzy. The confirmation was in Soleil's tragic eyes. But not a single tear escaped the lids where they brimmed, and her expression was resolute. "You should go."

Yet he couldn't look away from her beloved face. In the

183

furthest reaches of his soul, he knew if he left her, she'd find a way to keep him at arm's length forever.

"No," he rasped out. "No, Dalli, I'm not leaving you."

"Trev—"

The shuffle of booted feet drowned her out.

His hour had run out.

Rough hands gripped his arms and drew his wrists behind his back. The crisp snap of a shackle clicking into place followed a rattle of chains.

"No!" Soleil flung herself at the closest Red Guard, shoving him away from Trevor. The ground trembled under her rage. "Get off him, asshole!"

The guard made the grave mistake of striking her.

Trev launched himself at the fuckwit and wrapped the dangling chain around his neck. He might not have his abilities, but he had a good amount of muscle—even as weak as they were —and a burning need for revenge.

"Oh, for fuck's sake!"

The Aether's explosive temper slapped everyone back, except his daughter. Gasps echoed throughout the room, and a few unfamiliar with the sting hissed in a breath.

"Release him, Blane." When Trev hesitated, Damian narrowed his eyes. *"Now."*

The chain dropped, and he shoved the fucker away, watching dispassionately as the man gripped his throat and fell to the ground before meeting the Aether's gaze. "Happy?"

"Not in the slightest. But at least the Authority won't make me kill you for your impulsive actions."

Soleil sucked in a breath and gripped Trevor's free wrist. His one consolation was that she'd momentarily forgotten her repulsion to his touch.

She whipped around and frowned up at him. *"You don't repulse me!"*

Her outrage flooded his brain, and he winced.

"Well, you're something," he grumbled aloud.

Gripping his face between her palms, she dragged his head down and planted her mouth over his. A single swipe of her tongue over his lips urged him to open to her. To taste. To appreciate what might be their last moments if Agnes Vector sweet-talked her way around the Council.

"She won't," Soleil murmured, drawing back. "I'll go with you as a witness."

"You going to give them hell, Dalli?" he asked with an appreciative grin. "You're good at that."

Her chin came up at the same time her cheeks flushed becomingly. "I am rather, aren't I?"

"The best."

"Don't mock me."

"Wouldn't dream of it," he assured her. Focusing all his attention on their telepathic ability, he asked, *Are you okay? Like truly okay? When I think of what Damian said...*

She leaned into him and allowed him to hold her. God, he needed to, so much.

Yes. He arrived in time to stop you. Your father reversed the damage, and Jordan healed my throat.

Throat? What are you saying? I tried to strangle you?

I'm positive Deni compelled you with enchanted perfume. Soleil shuddered with remembered horror, and that emotion traveled throughout his body, becoming his own. *You only had one solitary thought, Trev.*

He picked the word from her mind. *Obliterate.*

It now made sense why Damian ripped away his abilities. After what had happened, Trevor wasn't sorry for the loss. The idea of hurting her ever again was unimaginable, and he'd rather die than cause her a moment's pain.

Jesus, Dalli! I don't know how to apologize for this. The magnitude... Words failed him.

It sank in the people around them were arguing, or more

accurately, Draven and Captain Ellis were. She was giving him what for, and the Guardian grinned down at her furious face.

"Those two should boink and get it over with."

Trevor sputtered a laugh as he gave Soleil an incredulous look. "Who says words like boink?"

"I didn't *say* it!" she retorted.

"You thought it, and with our link, it's much the same thing."

"Link?" Deni, who had been unnaturally quiet and watchful until that moment, glared at the two of them. "You're fated mates?"

Her disbelief was insulting.

Soleil thought so, too, and lifted her fisted hand to flip Deni the bird. "Fuck all the way off, Skankzilla!"

Trevor about busted a gut laughing when she promptly apologized to Sabrina for her language.

"Don't ever say things like that, sweetie. It's not nice."

"Uncle Trevor likes it."

He stopped laughing. "You've got to stop calling me that, kid."

The girl's elfin face turned sly. "Don't you want to be Aunt Soleil's boyfriend?"

She'd neatly trapped him.

"Checkmate, kid. Checkmate."

With a quick curtsy, she faced her father. "I don't want to go to the Council meeting, Papa. May I go back to Lily's house?"

"Not alone, Beastie. *Never* alone. And I have to be present at the meeting."

"Uncle Alex can take me."

They all turned to view Castor, holding up a wall with his broad shoulders and studying his nails.

"Nope."

"Please, Uncle Alex?"

"Sorry, Brina, my love. You'll need to call Ronan. Isn't he supposed to be your Guardian?" He jerked a thumb toward Deni. "I've got a prisoner to transport."

Draven abandoned toying with Brooke and held out his hand to Sabrina. "I'll watch over her. Lily will be recoverin' and need company." He winked at the girl. "We'll teach her Texas Hold'em, but no cheatin'."

"But you taught—"

He clapped a hand over her mouth. "Do you want a Guardian or not, *cher*? Your father doesn't need to know I'm a bad influence."

"He already does." Damian's tone was droll, and he shook his head in resignation.

The Captain of the Red Guard visibly melted as her gaze locked on the roughened gambler holding the hand of the beautiful child. Trevor was sure he saw cartoon heart eyes pop out of Brooke's face.

Soleil's hand settled on his lower back. *"Yep, I noticed her reaction, too. She's going to lead him on a merry chase."*

"Or maybe I'll lead her on one, eh?" Draven lifted a challenging brow when he looked at Brooke.

She blushed, and Trev suppressed his chuckle. They had more serious things to consider.

Addressing her, he lifted his wrist, causing the chain to rattle. "Can we dispense with the magical shackles? I would've shown for my hearing, but the timing was shit."

"No one said it was a hearing, Mr. Blane."

"No one said it wasn't, and we both know whenever the Red Guard is sent after Sentinels, a hearing ensues," he countered. He turned to where his father should be and realized Ben was missing. Disappointment settled in his chest. Once more, Dear Ol' Dad disappeared and left him holding the bag and facing the consequences by himself.

Trev approached Brooke. "Let's get this farce over with."

After a moment spent studying his face, she snapped her fingers and held out a hand. The man he tried to murder for backhanding Soleil produced a key with a grudging glance at Trevor.

"Johnson, you're relieved of duty." Brooke's tone was as chilly as the look in her midnight-blue eyes.

"But—"

"Did I stutter?" Her coldness could cause frostbite in under five seconds.

"No, Captain."

"Tomorrow morning, seven a.m. sharp, you'll report to my office. Understood?"

"Yes, Captain."

"Get out of my sight." She waited for his nod, then unlocked the single shackle around Trevor's wrist. "Let's go, Mr. Blane."

***

SOLEIL DRESSED WITH CARE FOR THE TRIAL. SHE TAMED HER HAIR AS best she could, adding a glamour to the mix to enhance the color of her eyes and give them a popular smoky look. For her lashes, she swiped on a thickening mascara but gave it a magical boost to separate and lengthen them. She was surprisingly happy with the look and earned a wolf whistle from Josie when she entered the room.

"You're a sexy beast. Those Authority members won't know what hit them."

"Don't make fun of me, Josie. Not today."

Her sister frowned, not bothering to hide her troubled air.

"Lei, I understand why you'd think I might be, considering the Morgan/Morcant situation, but that was an act." She gathered Soleil's hands in hers. "I love you and only want what's best for you. And you're beautiful. The makeup gives you that extra va-va-voom, but you don't need it."

Soleil stared, thrown by the honesty radiating from her. "I don't know what to say."

"Say that we can begin patching up our relationship. That moving forward, you'll believe me when I say complimentary things because they're all true. Say you forgive me for being a total shit."

"If you say it was an act, I believe you, Josie." She kissed her cheek. "Thank you."

Smoothing her hands down her Ecru-colored dress, she let out a shaky breath. "Be honest, does this make me look—"

"Don't say it." Josie turned her toward the full-length mirror. "You're wonderfully full-figured. Your boobs are enviable, and those hips… Girl, you've got it going *on*! Add a little shimmy to your steps, and men will fall at your feet."

Soleil laughed.

Hugging her from behind, Josie pressed a cheek against hers. "Love looks good on you."

And in an instant, she was thoroughly stressed again.

"It all happened so fast, and I'm not sure I believe in fated mates. I mean, I want to, but how can someone who looks like him love me, Josie? He's gorgeous and could have anyone he wants."

"He wants you, Lei. Why do you feel undeserving?"

"How can it last? He lost his powers because of me. Resentment will set in."

"I don't have an answer." She stepped back. "You know I'm not a role model for a healthy relationship. Maybe Viv can help."

After delivering a tender smile, her oldest sister and caregiver for most of her growing-up years glided toward the door.

"Josie?"

Her hair flowed in a perfect arch as she spun back. "Yeah?"

"You're a great role model. You kept us together after Mom and Dad died. Made sure our shop ran smoothly, even when you pretended you didn't want to be bothered with it." Soleil smiled at her arrested expression. "You have always been readily available for advice or to go toe-to-toe with teachers or those in charge, all on our behalf."

She rushed over and hugged her sister tightly. "It didn't go unnoticed. And I love you, too."

"Thank you. I needed that today." Josie returned her embrace.

"Do you want to talk about it?"

"No. Just feeling my age and perhaps a little lonely." She smoothed the fabric at Soleil's shoulders. "Knock 'em dead at that trial today. And hurry, or you'll be late."

Soleil arrived with two minutes to spare. She'd never seen the Authority's main chamber, but it seemed similar in style to that of the Witches' Council, though larger in scale. Twelve members gathered around a thirteen-person, U-shaped wooden table. It took up the entire raised dais and had aged oak panels with each of their last names engraved on the front.

She surmised that an appointment was for life, and the surname would magically change to another member's when a new member took their place. The place behind Councilwoman Vector's nameplate was missing.

Good.

That mad cow needed to be removed from office.

From his seat behind the defendant's table, Trevor glanced over his shoulder and met her gaze with a warm one of his own. A small smile teased his lips, and it became apparent he'd heard her unspoken insult.

"I adore you, Dalli," he mouthed.

Overcome by his lack of embarrassment in a packed room, tears welled in her eyes. Although the building moisture blurred her vision, his frown was deep enough to see.

"I'll never be embarrassed by you, Soleil Stephens. Do you hear me? Your beauty eclipses everyone in this fucking place."

"I'm glad you think so," she replied.

"I don't think. I know." His face softened. *"Not only are you sexy as hell, you've got an incredibly lovely soul. Everyone who meets you is*

blessed by the encounter, Dalli. And for me, who you chose to give your heart to, I'm doubly so."

Before she could respond, Mattie Price stood up.

"This meeting is called to order!" she intoned.

A gavel banged, and Trevor paused a beat to press home his point before turning away.

Beside him, Damian stood, looking dapper in his Dior navy blue suit with a thin black turtleneck underneath in place of a standard shirt and tie. One hand was tucked in his pants pocket, as if he was attending a casual event and having a friendly conversation. No worry lined his perfect visage.

"Stop drooling over him," Trevor admonished.

"He's hot as fuck. What can I say? But I'm only interested in doing the nasty with you. Pay attention to the trial."

Damian half turned to cast her an amused look. His obsidian eyes were twinkling as he winked at her.

Shit!

She'd forgotten his ability to read minds when it concerned him. As hot as her skin felt, her face had to be as dark as a Cymbidium Royal Red orchid.

Trevor snorted. Damn his hide!

A commotion in the hall had all heads turning toward the doors.

CHAPTER 26

Councilwoman Vector entered through the double doors as if she owned the place. The smug look she shot Trevor's way didn't bode well. Behind her was a contingent of four Red Guards, but they didn't appear to be worried about her escape. Indeed, they seemed to be her escort, as if she were their leader.

A slight frown caused Trevor's brows to dip, and he leaned in to murmur to Damian. Soleil couldn't determine what he'd said, but her brother-in-law stilled, becoming watchful. Or as watchful as a man accustomed to hiding his expression could be.

As Agnes approached the head councils' bench, she waved a hand to muffle what she had to say for the witnesses and viewers, then gestured madly toward Trevor as she spoke, passionate in whatever point she was trying to make. Whispered conversations exploded throughout the chamber as Mattie and Agnes exchanged indiscernible heated words. Those left in the dark were speculating on the outcome.

"Trevor?"

"I don't know, Dalli. It's muted for me, too."

Unable to suffer the suspense a second longer, Soleil rose and inched her way by those seated in the main aisleway. All conversation stopped as she swept open the fence gate.

"I'd like to speak."

Trevor swore savagely. "Stop her, Dethridge."

"I'd like to hear what she has to say," Damian replied. "You should, too."

"She'll make it worse. She doesn't know the Authority like we do."

Hiding her hurt as best she could, Soleil continued until she reached the bench.

Mattie showed concern as her gaze swept along the Council and then settled on her. "This is highly irregular, Ms. Stephens."

"I imagine it is. But so is having a Death Dealer assigned to stalk you, as was done to me."

"Ouch," Trev muttered.

She ignored him. "So is having multiple assassination attempts, as was done to me. And so was being used to manipulate Trevor Blane to do Agnes Vector's bidding." Soleil crossed her arms and glared at the Councilwoman next to her. "Your veiled conversation is objectionable when an innocent man is on trial."

"If you believe Trevor Blane is innocent, girl, you've been brainwashed," Agnes retorted with a derisive snort. "He's annihilated people for money and is far from pure."

"People *you* sent him to kill!" Soleil dropped her arms and balled her hands into fists. The urge to strike the blackhearted Beelzebub was strong.

"They were assignments." The woman shook her head as if Soleil were a dimwit. "Sit down, girl. You're wasting everyone's time."

"Then, if they were assignments, any payment was blood money from the Authority, wasn't it?" she pointed out. When everyone seemed unconcerned, Soleil said, "I'd like to make it known that Councilwoman Vector abducted me." Standing firm, Soleil tipped her head sideways to indicate Agnes. "She aborted my intended teleport and tied me to a chair to—"

"We know, Ms. Stephens. It was sanctioned."

Her jaw dropped as she stared at the man who had spoken. Shifting her gaze to his name, she added Councilman Melvin Glen to her shit list.

"Sanctioned?" Damian cut in. He must've sensed she was ready to take up the Death Dealer mantle for herself and wipe the floor with these asshats. "Are you saying that you sanctioned abduction and attempted murder of witches trying to restore the earth's resources? Would you care to explain why, Councilman Glen?"

"No one said anything about attempted murder," he protested with a wary glance toward the Aether. "Only the abduction."

The temperature of the room dropped ten degrees as Damian approached. "Abduction. Of my wife's sister."

Melvin paled. His mouth opened and closed repeatedly as he searched for a legitimate excuse to appease them, and his guilty gaze locked with Agnes's.

"Perhaps abduction is a strong word, Aether," Soleil said, reasserting herself yet making mention of his goddess-gifted power. He compressed his lips, and her impression was one of him fighting a grin. Weaving her arm through his and leaning into him to show the strength of their familial relationship, she sent a sweeping smile to those along the curved table. "Wouldn't you say?" As they began to nod frantically, she shot Damian a frowning pout. "What has *me* salty is Councilwoman Vector's collusion with her daughter and the threat to my life. Not to mention the mind games they played with Trevor over the last— how many years, Mr. Blane?"

"*It's Trevor.*" Rising from his seat, he continued aloud, "And—"

"Not you. Your father." She turned and gestured to Benjamin, having felt him walk into the room. Exactly how she was unsure, but she'd picked up a vibration unique to him. Later, when all this crap was settled, she'd ask them about it.

"His entire life," Benjamin growled. "Just like the Authority does with all the power players."

Melvin had the gall to protest, earning himself a severe look from Damian.

"You'd be a fool to deny it, Glen." Ben scoffed and shook his head. "But it wouldn't be the first time you were."

Anger clouded the Councilman's ruddy face, and his dark eyes snapped with frustration at being unable to defend his actions in front of a roomful of observers. This mockery of a trial wasn't going his way.

"Thanks to you, Dalli," Trev said through their link.

"They've taken enough from you," she returned coolly, still smarting because he'd believed she would fuck this up for him.

Damian squeezed her hand, then detangled her arm from his. Crossing to Benjamin, he offered a handshake. "Glad you could make it, Ben."

"Wouldn't have missed it." His pointed stare was for Trevor. "My son needed me."

Trevor's deeper emotions were a mixed bag, and Soleil felt every single one, from his doubt to his gratitude for his father's timely arrival to his worry for her.

"I had to make a stop first," Ben said, half turning toward the door.

Alastair Thorne entered. As always, he was impeccably dressed and spoiling for a confrontation with authority. Spring, Knox, Evelyn, and Simon followed. No one in their group looked thrilled to be there. Next, the Sentinels under Damian's care lined up along the walls at the back of the observation area. The only one missing was Draven, who was likely guarding the Aether's family.

She smiled as she recalled the tanzanite ring she wore. *"Thanks, gang."*

Their nods of respect were gratifying.

Trevor was humbled by those filtering through the door. There were quite a few he recognized as the victims from Loman O'Connor's reign of terror, and he was happy to see they weren't as gaunt as they'd been when he'd helped rescue them last year.

"What's the meaning of this?" Councilman Glen blustered.

"These are character witnesses for my son. Having been subjected to your rigged trial in the past, I thought I'd give him a fighting chance."

A few members of the head table exchanged nervous glances.

"Your son violated Authority code and conduct, Blane, as have *you* on multiple occasions," Councilwoman Cynthia Doyle said with an arch look. "The apple doesn't fall far from the tree, I see."

"Resorting to age-old clichés, Cynthia?" Ben taunted. "Are you upset I never called you back after our last night—"

"Enough." Councilman Louis Garcia banged a gavel. "I move that we accept the witnesses and continue. Objections?"

Three raised their hands, but the majority were for allowing character witnesses for Trevor.

He sighed in relief.

"I'm not finished," Soleil stated, head held high. "I want to press charges against those who agreed with my abduction and attempted murder at the hands of Agnes Vector and her daughter, Denillia. And I want answers as to why."

Trevor had never seen her so fierce. The sight stole his breath, and he wanted to jump up and clap on her behalf. She hadn't looked his way since he'd ordered Damian to stop her, and the realization Trevor had hurt her deeply was difficult to bear. At his hands, she'd suffered. Physically, mentally, and emotionally. It gutted him, and the first chance he got, he intended to set the record straight with a profound apology. He only hoped she had it in her heart to forgive him.

"Denied. Take a seat, Ms. Stephens, or you'll be escorted from this chamber." Melvin Glen avoided looking at the Aether, but when the room temperature dropped again, he quickly added, "Respectfully, of course, and under Authority protection."

Soleil huffed out a breath. "You're saying it's okay for your council members to take unconscionable action against those of us not special or skilled enough to sit on this bench?" Her hands rested on her hips, and she glared her fury. "We're all at the whim of your games? Our lives are forfeit if you decide to bang your little mallet and declare it so?"

A collective murmur flew through the crowd behind him.

"Go, Dalli!"

Again, she ignored him, refusing to respond or glance in his direction.

"Captain Ellis, escort Ms. Stephens from the room," Glen ordered.

Although the head of the Red Guard approached, she made no move to touch Soleil. She seemed to hover protectively, prepared to defend her should the need arise.

"Councilman Glen, I'm positive that's not the best course of action for anyone involved," Damian said, and the unmistakable threat was in his tone. "But, in an effort of fairness and good faith, Soleil will shelve her rightful complaint until after Mr. Blane's trial."

"I don't wish to be handled, Damian," she said coolly.

Trevor grinned. Here was the woman he'd come to love. When it mattered, she wouldn't let a slight stand.

"Not handled, Soleil," Damian replied with a warm smile. "You'll have your day in court, my dear. Those who wished you harm will be held accountable." He looked at Agnes, then Melvin. *"Count on it."*

Somewhat appeased, Soleil nodded and marched back to her seat. The entire time, she refused to glance Trevor's way.

"Dalli?"

"Not now."

"I'm sorry, sweetheart."

"Not now."

"But—"

"You insulted my intelligence, Trevor. You said I'd make it worse."

"I also said it was because you don't know the Authority like we do. It was never an insult to your intelligence, Dalli. I didn't want you to interfere and put yourself front and center."

"Because you're ashamed of me."

"No!"

"You think I'm a backwoods witch with no worldly experience."

"Not backwoods, but perhaps a little innocent to the ways of the world."

She glared at him, and his heart sank. Forgiveness would be a long time coming.

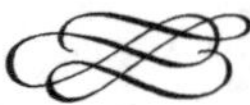

CHAPTER 27

Soleil was happy to see there were fair council members on the bench. Agnes Vector wasn't allowed to resume her position with them and was forced to wait in the galley for her turn to speak. From the looks of it, she and her daughter were at odds, but everyone knew looks could be deceiving. Soleil didn't trust them not to be cooking things up behind the scenes.

For every person who spoke against Trevor, three more testified on his behalf. She was gratified at the amount of people who valued him for his previously held gifts. It showed he had a kind heart, even if he was stupid on occasion.

"I heard that, Dalli."

"You were meant to."

He hid a smile behind his hand, but from her angle, she saw the gesture.

While the trial was in progress, she learned how the tanzanite's telepathic connection worked. One had to be thinking of a person to communicate. Earlier, when she considered the Sentinels as a whole, they all heard her and responded in kind. Her link to Trevor was different and much more challenging to block, but in her anger, she'd been able to. The key was emotional distance. The less invested she was, the greater the block.

Councilwoman Florence Carter held up a hand. "I believe we've heard enough."

Throughout the trial, those whose lives Trevor had saved spoke in glowing terms. Those whose family member or loved one he'd seen fit to destroy were harsh with their criticisms. They desired to witness his ultimate demise.

In his lifetime, Trevor Blane had made a multitude of enemies.

It gave Soleil pause. If he could no longer protect himself with his abilities, he was a sitting duck. Anyone seeking revenge would find it easy to achieve. Damian had done him irreparable harm by removing his magic.

"I agree." Councilwoman Arwa Macari and Talutah Ishtasapa said in unison. They acknowledged each other with a nod, and Councilwoman Macari gestured for Councilwoman Ishtasapa to continue.

"With the list of witnesses in favor of Mr. Blane, this trial could go on indefinitely. Let us assume there are many positive attributes the young man possesses and move on. We need to hear the testimony of Councilwoman Vector and her daughter, Denillia, before we make a ruling," Talutah said.

"All in agreement?" Councilman Garcia asked.

As one, the remaining members nodded.

"Councilwoman Vector, you have the floor," he said.

Agnes went on ad nauseam about how she'd strived to be Trevor's mentor, yet he'd continually ignored her advice to run his own game. She then admitted to the scheme, encouraging him to fall in love with Deni to break his heart and return him to his true purpose of Death Dealer. The crowd gasped at her callousness, and Soleil's rage brewed and bubbled beneath the surface when it became apparent the rest of the Authority found nothing wrong with her machinations.

"This is bullshit!" Soleil spat.

All eyes turned to her. Some, like Agnes, Melvin, and Deni, were gloating. Others were annoyed by her interruption, but many seemed to share her opinion, nodding their agreement. Trevor was the most difficult to read, merely watching her with a detached air. It was as if he'd retreated into himself so the proceedings didn't touch him.

"You've had your say, girl. It's our turn now," Agnes declared.

Soleil sneered her hatred for the woman and the con game she was playing. "Your turn to railroad him?"

Councilman Robert Knowles leaned forward. "Ms. Stephens, please refrain from commenting, or you'll be required to leave. Your objections are noted."

"What about *my* objections?" Alastair Thorne rose and took his time tugging down his cuffs. "I have plenty."

Knowles's mouth thinned, but he didn't reply.

Turning toward Spring, Alastair held out his hand, then smiled when she delivered a folder into his keeping. "Thank you, child."

"This is highly irregular, Mr. Thorne," Councilman Phillip Reed said, not unkindly. He'd been listening intently to the entire farce and had refrained from commenting until that moment. "If you're to present evidence for this trial, it should be done through proper channels, sir."

Alastair's demeanor remained businesslike, yet Soleil had the distinct impression he respected the other man. "Agreed, Councilman. However, this information just came to light moments before our arrival."

With a glance along the table, Reed nodded and held out his hand. "Please present your case."

After taking a moment to straighten his tie, Alastair walked through the gate and approached, waving a manila envelope. "In here, you'll find documentation proving collusion between Melvin Glen and Agnes Vector. They hold shares in fifteen prominent pharmaceutical companies around the globe." He opened the file and handed out copies to everyone on the bench. "Note the gross earnings their investments have made this year alone."

Councilwoman Cynthia Doyle's eyes flared wide, and she glared toward Agnes.

"On this second document"—he waved a hand and a paper settled before each of them—"you can see the communication between the two, discussing the need to shut down the Rainforest restoration project of Spring Thorne and Soleil Stephens at *any* cost."

Frowns darkened faces, but the Authority held their peace as they allowed Alastair to continue.

"Prior to Ms. Stephens's *sanctioned* abduction, there were four attempts on her life."

Trevor jumped to his feet and spun to face her. "Four, Dalli? *Four?* What the actual fuck?"

"Mr. Blane, if you'll suppress your incredulousness, I'll explain." Alastair nodded toward his seat. "Please."

Sinking down, Trev glanced back at her. *"Four?"* he mouthed.

She grimaced. Yes, there had been a few oddball circumstances, like the pit viper in her greenhouse, but she hadn't realized they were murder attempts. At the time, she'd assumed it was some idiot's pet that had escaped. As for the broken water pipes and electrical shorts at her shop, it was an old building.

Black rage clouded Trevor's face, and he turned his attention on Agnes, shooting her a look of promised retribution.

"And your niece, Mr. Thorne? How many attempts on her life?"

"None before yesterday. But she's not as easily accessible as Ms. Stephens." His cold stare focused on the true villains in the room. "My head of security has had Agnes Vector and Melvin

Glen under surveillance since the explosion at Spring's greenhouse. Not only did they perpetrate the attack on her person, but they also destroyed years' worth of work meant to repopulate plants that, if restored, could heal the masses without the need for high-priced, ineffectual drugs sold by their partners."

"You have no proof—"

"Actually, Ms. Vector, I do," he said succinctly. "Plenty." His grin resembled a cat with a canary in its mouth, predatory and self-satisfied. "Two years ago, when my dear cousin Evelyn Thorne and Simon Blane were attacked, the Aether asked me to look into the disappearance of one Deni Adams from Trevor Blane's life. Only Deni Adams doesn't exist. She never did." Alastair shifted his focus to Denillia. "On paper, anyway. Denillia Jones does, however. And surprise of surprises, she works as a spy for the Witches' Council, recommended by none other than Agnes Vector and Melvin Glen. He happens to be her father, for those of you unaware."

Trevor's brows shot to his hairline, and his mouth opened, making it obvious he knew nothing of the connection to Melvin until that moment.

"Until recently, I'd been unable to prove the connection or that Deni and Denillia were the same person. But I kept detailed records on her movements." He waved a hand, and another sheaf of papers appeared before the Authority panel. "Her most recent activity was today when she assisted you in the abduction of Soleil Stephens and the magical manipulation of a lethal Death Dealer."

His voice had chilled, losing its conversational tone. "The perfume bottle remains were recovered at the scene and analyzed. Not only did they contain fingerprints for you and your daughter, Agnes, but the spell was reverse-engineered along with the contents."

"Manipulation of Trevor Blane was *sanctioned*, Mr. Thorne, or did you miss that part of this hearing?" Agnes retorted with a sneer.

"Manipulation to keep him as your hired assassin, yes. Did that include compelling him to murder a woman he loves? One he'd be heartbroken to lose when the spell wore off?"

"He doesn't love her!" Deni bound to her feet and fixed Trevor with a look of longing, one that begged forgiveness for her sins. "He loves me. Tell them, darling. Tell them how you intended to propose. Tell them she means *nothing* to you."

An odd look crossed his face, and he stood. The air was sucked from Soleil's lungs when his expression altered to one of adoration as he stared at Deni. But as he opened his mouth, prepared to reply in the affirmative, Damian touched his arm, sending Trevor reeling backward and crashing into the rail.

Soleil crawled over those seated to help him, but hatred transformed his countenance the second he spotted her. One thought danced through his mind and into hers.

Obliterate.

Trevor leaped over the railing and headed straight for Soleil, arms outstretched and reaching for her neck.

She stumbled in her shock, unprepared for a second attack. Yes, Damian had removed his powers, but that didn't mean Trev wasn't strong enough to hurt her. But the question keeping her glued to the spot was *how?*

Through their tanzanite ring connection, the Sentinels registered his intent, taking action to stop him. They weren't as fast as he was, and for the second time that day, Trevor's hands closed around her throat. She didn't try to plead with him as she had before. It was no use. The spell was clouding his mind.

Closing her eyes against the blazing hate in his, she pressed her palm over his heart.

"I love you, Trevor," she whispered in her mind. "*I forgive you. Forgive yourself.*"

Her world went black on her last thought.
The Death Dealer had completed his mission.

CHAPTER 28

The instant the fight left Soleil and her soul abandoned her body, the compulsion to kill left Trevor. As he stared down at her pale, still face, with its single teardrop trailing toward her hairline, horror filled him.

"Soleil?" He touched her bruised throat, feeling for a pulse. Unable to find one, he linked his fingers and began chest compressions. "Don't give up, Dalli! Don't give up!"

But she had, and she was gone.

He could feel the absence of their link and her soul.

Each press of his joined hands wrung a sob from him.

"Come back, Dalli," he begged. "Please come back to me."

He was a mindless machine as he performed CPR, attempting to blow air through her crushed trachea and declaring his love for her with each breath. Part of her had to hear him, right? He hadn't possessed the power to decimate her soul, and if she transitioned to the Otherworld, part of her had to be aware of what was happening on this plane.

"You must move, Mr. Blane," Jordon Brothers urged softly. "I can't treat her if you don't move, sir."

Rough arms dragged Trev away, and he fought like a madman to return to her side.

"Dalli!" he cried.

A glowing light extended from Jordon's palms to the entire column of Soleil's neck as he tried to repair the damage Trevor had inflicted.

Ceasing to struggle, Trev stared at his hands, disbelieving of the devastation they'd caused.

Red Guards rushed him, but his Sentinel teammates formed a line, blocking them from reaching him for an arrest. With his back to the wall and arms resting on his raised knees, he stared at Soleil's unmoving form through a curtain of moisture.

"Trevor."

Hearing Mattie next to him, he turned his head, but his unseeing gaze remained locked on Soleil.

"Trevor, you need to ask your friends to stand down." Her statement was kind and filled with compassion. "It will be worse for everyone if they don't."

"Stand down," he croaked. Mainly because he didn't care what the fuck happened to him now. If the Authority decided to end his life, it would be a blessing. There was no recovering from what he'd done.

Amid angry protests but no physical scuffles, the Red Guard dragged him to his feet and shackled his arms. A sympathetic look from Brooke Ellis made him want to vomit. He didn't deserve any kindness. He was a stone-cold killer.

"What's going to happen to him?" Simon demanded to know. "Dad? Where are they taking him?"

"For reprogramming." Ben's voice was rough, and his pallor gray. *"If* they decide he can be rehabilitated."

From his father's grim statement, it wasn't likely the Authority would favor reprogramming over an end-of-existence sentence. The truth, they both knew, was Death Dealers were expendable. They were too dangerous not to be.

"That's ridiculous! Trev!" Simon fought the crowd to get to him, shoving his way through the Red Guard. Knowing what he was capable of, the fainter-hearted ones stepped back to allow his brother access.

"It's okay, Si." Trevor's throat ached with all the words he wanted to say but couldn't. "Tell"—he inhaled deeply—"tell her family… I didn't mean it. I loved her, and the monster who did that to her wasn't me. Tell them, okay?"

Simon nodded jerkily as he cast a desperate glance Damian's way.

The Aether was granite-faced, giving nothing away as he coolly observed them.

Trevor choked back his need to beg forgiveness. It wasn't due to someone like him. A man who possessed a black hole of a soul, constantly consuming and destroying everything within reach.

"If they can't bring her back, Si, make sure they rule against reprogramming, okay? I don't want to live in a world without her." When his brother would've protested, he cut him off. "If it were Evelyn, you'd feel the same."

"She could pull through, Trev."

"She could, but she's lost to me either way now."

Damian would never let him close to her again, should Trevor manage to escape the Authority's brand of justice. But the truth was, he'd murdered an innocent in front of a roomful of witnesses, and his days were numbered.

"You're the best brother a person could have, Trev," Simon said through his apparent grief. "Thank you for all you've done to ensure I had a normal life."

"I've done one thing right, at least." They pressed their foreheads together in their shared understanding. "I love you, little brother."

"I love you, too, big brother."

Trevor cleared his throat and growled, "Now get the fuck out of here and get home to Evelyn. Fuck this place and all in it."

Simon's mouth twisted into a semblance of a smile, but it never reached his eyes. "I can do that."

"Don't look back. Ever. Remember Lot's wife."

"That's a bedtime story to scare kids and the self-righteous pricks of the world."

"That's a true story born of a very talented Death Dealer," Brooke said from behind them. "We need to go, Mr. Blane."

Trevor let his gaze linger on Soleil one final time. Her coloring leaned toward gray, and he wished he hadn't looked. The sight of her lifeless body was a commotio cordis blow to his heart, and he bent double in his agony.

"Trev!"

When Simon would've assisted him, Brooke stepped in his path. "I'm sorry, sir. You've said your goodbyes."

"But—"

Trevor slowly straightened and used his forearm to swipe at the dampness on his cheeks. "I want to speak to my father first. Will you allow me to do that? Please, Ms. Ellis?"

"Make it quick."

She gestured Ben over. Her generosity earned her a reprimanding look from the Council, but she lifted her chin in defiance. Trevor frowned as he watched her. Either she knew something they didn't, or she felt terrible for the trouble they'd caused him. Both would see her called on the carpet and punished if she didn't do her job to the fullest.

Feeling he owed her a warning, he said, "Don't risk anything on my account, Brooke. They don't fuck around when it comes to disobedience."

"I'm well aware, Mr. Blane. But I'll run my command as I see fit. You have two minutes. Don't waste it."

She stepped back to allow him privacy.

His father eyed everyone as if he wanted to explode their brains in one fell swoop as he closed the distance between them.

"Don't let them fuck with my head, Dad. Please."

"I'm not going to take your life, Trevor."

"I've never asked you for anything, but I'm asking now." He cleared his throat. "I've seen what their rehabilitation is like. Seen how others return. Saw how you did." Trev swallowed hard. "It's no better than a lobotomy. I don't want that."

"You'll still be alive," Ben snapped.

"But at what cost?" he asked softly. "She's gone. You and I both know they aren't bringing her back. Not without help from the Goddess. And if there's nothing in it for her, why would she?"

He hated the begging in his voice, but his father was the only one with the power to end his suffering.

"If I take your life, I take your soul, Trevor." The tortured expression in his father's eyes was reminiscent of when their mother died, and he was forced to endure Ben's explanation of why. "I can't do that, son. You need the chance to be reborn if you can. To live a normal existence. And what do I tell Simon?"

The truth was a punch to the head.

There would be no swaying him. Not if he thought he had to answer to Trevor's brother.

"Yeah, okay. Thanks anyway." As he shifted to tell Brooke he was done, his father embraced him. "I love you, Trevor. If there was any other—"

Trev jerked away. "Don't say you love me when you can't be bothered to show it, Benjamin," he replied coldly. "We both know there's only room in your heart for one son, and it's not me. It never was." To Brooke, he said, "I'm done here."

As they led his eldest away, Ben fought the urge to demand they come back. To grant Trevor his last request. Denying his son anything, especially when he was tortured by what he'd been compelled to do, was unbearable. But he wouldn't go against his promise to Gloria. Since her death, he'd been a shell of his former self. His primary reason for remaining on this plane was the care of his sons, although they weren't aware of it. He'd do whatever it took to make their lives better, fuller. Remove any strife from their path if it was within his power to.

Resigned to his current course of action, Ben met the Aether's obsidian eyes. The man always peered into his soul and pulled the best out of him, even when Ben believed he had nothing left to give. This time, he would do whatever Damian demanded because the stakes were higher than ever. He also needed to break Deni's hold over Trevor. If it meant killing a roomful of Authority members, so be it.

Ben jumped into action as soon as his son cleared the doorway and his back was to the room. Knowing it was now or never, he rushed to Soleil's side. Pressing one palm to her chest and the other to his, he drew out the spark he'd stolen from her the first time he'd healed her. With great care, he infused it back inside her, bonding it to her cells.

Soleil woke, gasping and choking as she sucked in a breath. Her eyes flew wide as they locked with his, and her hands flew to her throat to feel for damage.

He ignored the disbelieving exclamations of those around them and smiled down at her. "Welcome back, child. We have work to do."

"What? How?" Her focus left him to dart around the room. "Where's Trevor?"

"He's been detained." He touched a finger to her third eye, transferring all that had transpired while she lingered in another realm awaiting recall. Leaning in, he asked in a hushed voice, "What was the keyword Denillia used to trigger Trevor?"

"I don't know."

"You do. Think hard. You heard their thoughts." When she shook her head, he helped her to sit and conjured a cup of water for her to drink. "Sip it slowly."

She did as ordered, leaning into him. Instinctively understanding his desire for secrecy, she lowered her voice and said, "I didn't hear anything, but he looked odd after her speech, didn't he? It happened the last time, too."

"You share a link with him, hon. What was he thinking?"

"Obliterate." She appeared tormented. Lips compressed, she shook her head. "That's it. Both times."

"Okay. But if you can recall anything either said aloud, please let me know immediately." He helped Soleil to her feet, giving her added energy as he led her to Damian. "Get her out of here and somewhere safe, Dethridge. Somewhere those three will never find her."

"Consider it done, Ben. And thank you for your fast thinking both times."

"Yeah, well, I suspected if Denillia tried her magical hypnosis once, she'd try it again. I felt it was better to secure Soleil's essence the first time."

She looked between them, confusion on her pretty face. "I don't understand."

Ben smiled at her, hoping she'd be Trevor's perfect mate when all was said and done. His son needed someone grounded and sweet like her. Although different in looks, she reminded him of his Gloria, and to a degree, he suspected her calming energy was what appealed to Trevor more than anything else. It helped that the girl had spunk. His son wouldn't abide a pushover.

"Let's just say I anticipated the second attack," Ben told her. "In case Trevor's magic restored itself, I wanted to ensure your beautiful light wasn't snuffed out for good."

Gratitude was reflected in her eyes, and a wide, warm smile curled her lips. "I adore you, Benjamin Blane."

"I'm glad someone does." He hadn't meant his comment to sound all woe-is-me, but nevertheless, it did. Compassion transformed her face as she cupped his jaw. "Be good to Trevor, hon. Can you do that?"

She winced.

"He wasn't himself, you know. And whatever it takes, I'm going to break her spell," he said.

"We both will," Damian assured them.

Soleil touched her throat. Her haunted expression caused his stomach to clench and anger to fill his soul. Today's events had instilled a fear of Trevor inside her. Ben only hoped a future without incident might put that fear to rest.

"It's my turn to face the Authority's punishment. Avoid Trevor until we resolve all this, okay?" he urged.

She nodded, and her sadness damned near broke his heart.

Looking at Damian for reassurance, he addressed her again, "All will be well, Soleil Stephens. Have faith in this wily ol' Death Dealer, my dear. I still have a few tricks in my hat."

CHAPTER 29

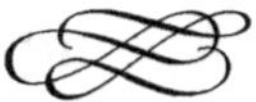

Twenty-seven hours passed, with Trevor counting every fucking minute of it. Isolated as he was, he had no idea what happened to Soleil, but he assumed it wasn't good since no one came to tell him differently. During the time he was imprisoned, he had nothing but time to think. He sure as hell couldn't sleep. Whenever he dozed off, the nightmare of Soleil's horror-filled face, with blood-vessel-ruptured eyes, filled his mind. Countless times, he'd screamed himself awake.

"Dalli?"

The empty echo of nothingness was his reply. He wasn't sure if distance was a factor in their link. If maybe she was still alive, but on her island, too far away for him to reach. But he kept trying.

"If a part of you remains anywhere out there, please know I'm sorry. To the very depths of my soul, I'm sorry."

Nothing.

"As much as I hate the idea of you with anyone else, my wish for you —if you're still alive—is to have the best life. For you to meet someone who will cherish you and appreciate your love of romance novels."

Silence.

"Someone who will help you pot your precious plants and restore the earth to its original splendor."

He felt like he was cracking up, but he needed to say the words if there was even a single chance she might hear them.

"You are beautiful, Dalli. Not just physically—which you are—but deep down where it matters. Truly lovely."

Trevor rolled on his side and stared at the white cinderblock wall. The Authority's reprogramming crew would be coming for him soon. When they tied him to their table, and their specialists took turns frying his brain, they'd withdraw his memories for good. A handful of Death Dealers, like his father, had been able to regenerate what was damaged in the frontal lobes, eventually recalling their past. But with Trevor's magic gone, it was unlikely he could.

He frowned into the void.

Why alter his mind if he was powerless? What could they possibly gain?

It begged the question: *would they even bother?*

Surely they'd have come for him by now.

Were they setting up for his demise? Why not just send another Death Dealer to get the job done?

"I'm driving myself fucking crazy," he muttered as he gripped his hair and tugged. "What the fuck does any of this shit matter?"

An outer door clanged, and the Aether entered, followed by Alexander Castor and Alastair Thorne. The latter of which seemed green around his elegantly clad gills. He'd heard somewhere Alastair hated enclosed spaces due to capture and confinement by his greatest enemies during the Witches' War years before. His entering what equated to the Authority's dungeon spoke volumes of his commitment to Damian Dethridge and their bond of friendship.

The courteous thing would be standing and greeting them, but he couldn't. Their grim expressions indicated bad news, and the only reason for their presence would be to inform Trev of Soleil's passing. He shook his head and covered his face with his arms.

"Please don't tell me you couldn't save her," he rasped. "Please, no."

"We're here to escort you to the continuation of your trial, Blane," Damian said. There was no inflection in his voice. Nothing to indicate what he thought of Trevor's fate or if he even cared if there should be one.

"Why do I need to be there? What the fuck difference does it make?"

"Why are all the Blane men so quick to give up? Are they genetically defective or something?" Castor asked in a loud aside. "You'd think they'd have a little more gumption."

A murderous rage consumed Trevor, and he surged off the rock-like mattress toward the opening of his cell. The glass partition was the only thing saving the Traveler's life. "You never quit, do you, Castor?"

"I never do. Not like some."

"I wasn't referring to life. I was referring to your smartass mouth."

That mouth quirked mockingly. "Some say it's my greatest asset, next to my stunning good looks."

"I say it's going to get you killed one day, asshole."

Alastair snorted and shot a dry look toward Castor before returning his focus to Trevor. "You wouldn't be wrong, son. I've thought the same many a' time."

"Stuff it, Al," Alexander replied without heat. To Trevor, he said, "Well, pull up your big-girl diapers, Baby Blane, and join the winner's circle."

"I've got your big-girl diapers right here, ass—"

"*Enough!*"

Damian's voice was akin to God's, echoing around the prison

yet causing stillness with the command. Even his two best buddies took heed and straightened.

"You look like roadkill, Mr. Blane," he said. "Al will assist you in making yourself presentable. You have exactly five minutes." Like a king making a decree and expecting it to be obeyed to the last letter, the Aether nodded and pivoted to leave.

"Wait! Why do I have to enter that bloody cell?" Alastair demanded.

Trev would swear the man's voice held an edge of panic.

"Because Trevor and Castor are little better than animals and would kill each other for sport. You're the only one I trust, Al."

Alastair cast an uneasy glance at the cell.

"Dethridge." There was deep meaning in the two syllables he uttered.

"It's okay, Mr. Thorne," Trev said, unable to see another person suffer on his behalf. "Conjure a suit and hand it through the hatch to your right. I can get myself ready."

Cool sapphire eyes assessed him, summing him up in a single sweep from head to toe. In a flash of white light, a cream-colored two-piece suit with a white button-down shirt appeared in Alastair's outstretched arms. He bent it double to hand it through the opening.

"What size shoes, son?"

"Twelve and a half."

Next, Alastair conjured tan leather shoes, dark brown socks, and a pocket square the exact color of Soleil's eyes when they were glowing with happiness.

For an entire moment, with the arrival of the men, Trev forgot she was gone. The memories all flooded back with a single hammer-like blow to his heart.

"These should complete the look nicely." Alastair set them on the dropdown tray in the center of the hatch, oblivious to Trevor's immediate pain.

He wanted to demand the other man change the color, but the

words remained locked behind a tight lump in his throat. If Trev choked on them, it was nothing more than Karma.

Alastair's eyes were twinkling when Trevor's gaze met his. "Problem?"

Still unable to speak, Trev frowned and shook his head.

"Good. I'll turn around and give you privacy to change."

HALL B WAS PACKED WHEN TREVOR AND HIS ENTOURAGE ENTERED. After a quick sweeping glance at the Authority members' table, he let his gaze travel over the assembled Lookie-loos. Once again, Damian's Sentinels lined the back wall, and they all nodded or smiled at him with varying degrees of encouragement.

Why?

He didn't receive an answer, not that he expected one. Access to their unified link was broken when his ring had been removed and turned over to Damian after the farce of a first trial.

Brooke Ellis stood at attention by the fence, and her eagle eyes missed nothing as more observers filed into the room. Finally, the main doors swung shut, and she relaxed her guard. And as the final person found their seat, Trevor's last hope of Soleil's survival was destroyed. Regardless of her feelings about him or his attack, she'd be present if she was alive. Her sense of right and wrong would demand it.

With dead eyes, he faced forward, uncaring of today's outcome.

From his peripheral, he was aware of Damian's approach.

"I can't believe you're still willing to support me in all this." Trev stared straight ahead. "But thank you."

"You're one of my team, Blane. I don't abandon friends."

"How can you consider me anything but an enemy after...

after…" The building burn from his tears forced him to blink them away.

"Soleil is alive and well, and I should've led with that information when I arrived at your cell. I apologize for my oversight."

Trev sighed under the weight of his relief and rested his forehead on his folded arms. "Thank you," he said feelingly. Apparently he'd been wrong and had scared her to the extent of avoidance. That information didn't ease his suffering. After the long minute it took to compose himself, he straightened. "Will you give her a message for me?"

"You can give it to her yourself after this."

"I doubt she wants to hear from me."

Damian viewed him through twinkling eyes. "Her sisters practically had to sit on her to keep her away today, Trevor."

Hope blossomed in Trev's chest. "But why… Oh. Right."

Until he spontaneously stopped trying to kill her, she was safer away from him.

"That, yes." Damian replied to Trevor's unspoken thought. "But more importantly, the goal was to keep her safe from Agnes Vector and her black widow of a daughter."

"Black widow?" Deni hadn't revealed she'd been married. But then again, she wasn't the poster child for honesty. Their entire relationship was an epic lie.

Damian's mouth tightened into a thin line. "Count yourself lucky to have escaped her marriage noose. Four others weren't as fortunate."

Acid seared Trev's insides as he met Deni's calculating dark eyes across the chamber.

"How many of those did I unknowingly kill on her behalf?" he asked hoarsely.

"Only one."

"*Christ!*"

"He doesn't weigh into what the magical community does, and with good reason. Some of those with power are godless."

Damian rose as the Council filed in. He handed Trevor a tanzanite signet ring, following it with a pair of earpieces. "Put these in."

"What are they?" He hurried to comply.

"The best your father and I could figure, they implanted a sleeper term, and when spoken directly to you, it wakes up your inner killer."

Trevor stared at him, incredulous. "I'm their Manchurian Candidate?"

"I believe so, yes."

He swayed on his feet as the far-reaching implications occurred to him. "You need to put me down, Dethridge."

"Nonsense. The earpieces act as filters. Nothing she says will be able to penetrate the device. Her mother or Melvin either."

"What if there are other agents able to activate me?"

"I have a good idea what wording they crafted as their call to action. Today, I hope they prove me correct."

Trevor swallowed hard. Damian was playing fast and loose with people's lives, and he didn't know why. As the Aether, he could've and should've easily stopped Trev from harming Soleil, and yet he didn't. Why, when he continually swore he wouldn't let anything happen to her?

The Aether plucked the fears from Trevor's mind. "I'm not, you know. Playing fast and loose with people's lives, that is. I trust in the ability of those around us to stop you should the need arise. Without your power, they can easily subdue you."

"They didn't the last time. Neither did you, for that matter."

Damian opened his mouth and closed it, as if he wanted to speak but feared revealing what he shouldn't. Finally, he said, "All will be well, Blane. Trust the process, and remember what I said about knowing too many details about the future. Things happen for a reason.""I wish I had your confidence, Dethridge."

Brooke Ellis stepped forward and held up her hand for silence. "The trial of Trevor Blane will now reconvene!"

CHAPTER 30

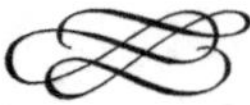

Soleil was going stir-crazy.

She'd been cut off from Trevor for two solid days and had no idea how his trial was progressing. No one saw fit to inform her of the details. She figured she had two choices: continue to sit and stew like a turnip or defy the Aether and attend the hearing.

The first made her itchy, and the second made her nerves raw. Who in their right mind would defy Damian? But she wasn't in her right mind.

"Sure, and why don't ya just go, then?"

From her spot by the floor-to-ceiling windows, she glanced over to see Ronan O'Connor watching her from the entryway with those disturbing silver eyes of his. His arms were crossed over his brawny chest, and he acted as if his suggestion wouldn't land them both in trouble. Her for going, and him for allowing it after he'd promised to keep her safe.

"I was just asking myself the same thing," she said with a rueful smile.

His grin made his already arrestingly handsome face heart-stopping in its beauty, and she sucked in a breath.

"Stop scattering the girl's wits to the wind, ya scut," Dubheasa O'Malley scolded with an elbow to his ribs.

"I'm doin' nothing of the kind," he denied with a panty-melting smile for his mate. "But to kin you're *éad* is heartwarming, to be sure."

Flinging her long black locks over her shoulder, she snapped, "Feck off." Yet there was affection in her tone, solidifying Soleil's guess that they were teasing.

As bonded Guardians assigned by the Goddesses Isis and Anu, Ronan and Dubheasa were a formidable team. Damian entrusted them to watch over Viv and his children, and his trust hadn't been misplaced. Soleil had been added to their list of charges, which led to her feelings of uselessness.

Dubheasa strode to her side in her standard no-nonsense fashion and rested her hands on curvy hips as she studied Soleil's face with keen emerald eyes. "The oversized *wean* is right. You should go and be done with all your worrying."

Ronan growled, and Dubheasa chuckled her triumph at having scored a direct hit. Her eyes flew wide as his arms encircled her and he buried his face against her throat.

"I take exception to ya callin' me a baby, I do," he told his mate with a laughing glance and wink for Soleil. "Will ya be excusing us, then, love? I'm after showing my darlin' Dove my oversized—"

Dubheasa slapped her palm over his mouth with a gasping laugh. "Ronan O'Connor! You'll be watching your tongue, or I'll remove it from your head!"

He peeled back her hand and kissed her knuckles.

"Oh, I'll be watching my tongue soon enough," he assured her.

Feeling like a naughty voyeur, Soleil blushed in the face of Ronan's sexual banter. "Yeah, on that note, I'm heading out. If you two come up for air anytime soon, let my sister know where I've gone."

His molten silver eyes held approval. "Take no prisoners, love."

"Give 'em hell," Dubheasa added with a husky laugh.

Soleil squinted at them consideringly. "Why do I feel egging me on was your intent all along?"

"Because you're clever," Vivian said from behind them, surprising a squeak from her.

"You, too, sister dear?"

"Me, too." Viv handed her a piece of paper. "Damian said to use this spell, and it'll deposit you right outside the doors of Hall B, where the trial is being held."

She cut her sister a dry look. "He knew I was done waiting, huh?"

"I think he suspected, at the very least." Viv tucked a wisp of Soleil's unruly hair behind her ear. "Be careful, though. I don't trust those bastards."

Her ice-blue eyes held worry, and her uncanny resemblance to their mother brought a tidal wave of wistfulness.

Soleil hugged her, giving her an extra tight squeeze. "Promise! I'm learning to be less naive by the day."

"You're too good, Lei. Of all of us, you have the purest heart."

"I don't know about that," she protested with a skeptical laugh. "I feel hatred like anyone else. More so for Deni and Agnes Vector."

"Rightfully so," Viv assured her with a scowl. "Go on, now."

Stepping out onto the terrace, Soleil inhaled deeply. All hell had broken loose the last time she was at the Dethridge estate. It was also the first time she'd seen Trevor. To say she was smitten at first sight wasn't a stretch. Hell, she'd been obsessed with him since the beginning, and nothing had changed.

For the millionth time, she mentally debated whether she should go to the trial again. Twice in twenty-four hours, Trevor tried to murder her. Not his fault, but she was feeling a little gun-shy. Again and again, she'd wracked her brain, trying to recall the exact words Deni had uttered to set him off, but they wouldn't come. What if it happened again? What if he succeeded in snuffing her out of existence for good?

Soleil didn't want to fear him, but she was beginning to. Had she become one of those brainwashed women who suffered abuse but stayed with their attacker? Trevor had never hurt her in any way before. Even at his worst, he'd been courteous and tried to put her needs first. What did it say about her that she was considering a long-term commitment to a man who was programmed to kill her?

She hung her head.

"You should go, Aunt Soleil," Sabrina said as she approached.

Soleil desperately wanted to ask her niece what she saw for their future, but she lacked the courage. What if it wasn't what she wanted to hear? What if Trevor was right and their relationship was destined to end in her early demise?

Sabrina's pixie face transformed with her smile. "You should go, Aunt Soleil," she repeated.

"Really?"

"Really, really."

Kneeling, she gazed into Sabrina's fathomless eyes. "You're a blessing to this family, Sabrina Dethridge. Whether you have the gift of sight or not, you're a treasure to us. You know that, right?"

"I know." Sabrina lifted her hands and used her palms to frame Soleil's face. "Uncle Trevor is waiting for you. And you aren't *nothing*."

"Nothing?"

With a sly smile, her niece dropped her arms. "Will you let Papa know I didn't tell you the future? I found another way."

Frowning, Soleil watched her skip away. Their conversation was odd, and there were keywords scattered within it. She only had to decode what the Oracle meant. Rising to her feet, she glanced down at herself and gasped. During her musings, she hadn't taken any pains to dress for the day. Her outfit would only be considered fashionable if she lived in the swamps and never saw another human being for the remainder of her days.

Smoothing her hands down her waist and hips, she visualized a smart, cream-colored pantsuit with flared leg bottoms and filmy, see-through sleeves. She paired it with strappy, low-heeled sandals and a tan leather belt. For her hair, she swept it into a high ponytail, leaving wispy curls at her temples and along the nape of her neck. Trevor hadn't cared for her super-sleek appearance the last time she'd tried to dress up, and rightfully after seeing Deni. This time, Soleil softened her look. Her makeup was subtle but classy as she checked her appearance in the reflection of the terrace doors.

She was ready.

Or so she told herself.

Inhaling deeply, she read through Damian's elegant scrawl.

"From here to Hall B, I'll swiftly go,

protected from those who would do me harm.

Through time and wards, my body traverses,

And portals I'll pass, avoiding all curses."

"Simple and effective. Seems he covered all bases," she murmured. "Here goes nothing—"

The paper fluttered from her hand as the truth registered.

Nothing.

Deni worked the word in whenever she spoke directly to Trevor!

Running onto the lawn to pick up the spell, Soleil conjured a vial and squatted. With her free hand, she curled her fingers into a ball and envisioned the grass roots doing the same to protect itself. When she'd uncovered the soil, she used the jar to scoop it up.

Solidifying her resolve, she shook the container in her hand and said,

"By the magic of this sacred dirt,
Let silence befall and words not assert.
With this spell, Denillia's voice is confined
With my power, this soil shall bind."

"Simple and effective," Vivian said with a grin, repeating Soleil's earlier comment.

"Oh!" She gave a nervous laugh. "I didn't know anyone was watching me."

"I wanted to be sure you didn't have a problem with Damian's spell. It inspired you to use one of your own in dealing with the panty stain tormenting Trevor."

"Viv!" But she wasn't as shocked by her classy sister's remark as she pretended. Indeed, she loved Vivian's spitefulness.

"Pfft. Don't act like you weren't thinking the same thing. She's a waste of space."

The clicking of Vivian's heels on the stone terrace was as light and rhythmic as her seductive walk. Soleil found it easy to see why men would think her sister attractive. A small flame of jealousy flared to life inside her, but she snuffed it out. Viv and Damian were forever; Trevor had told her he believed she was beautiful. Her sisters held no attraction for him.

"Why the strange look?" Viv asked in her standard, gentle-probing way.

"I was thinking about how drop-dead gorgeous my sisters are and how many times I've felt like the ugly duckling in a room full of swans."

Viv's expression turned to one of dismay. "Soleil!"

She held up a hand. "It's okay, sister. I don't resent any of you."

With a concerted frown, Viv clapped her hands together and spread them body-width apart. Between them, a full-length mirror formed, and she propped it up against one of the four-foot-high planters dotting the terrace.

"Come here, Lei, please." The instant Soleil joined her, Viv entwined their fingers. Lifting their joined hands to the sky, she said, "Goddess, grant her the power of objectivity."

An electrical surge ran throughout Soleil's body, and she meeped in surprise. "What the hell?"

"Shh. Look."

When she turned her attention to the two women in the mirror, she didn't recognize the chestnut-haired bombshell at first. But the moment she did, she gasped and moved closer, touching the glass.

"That's me?"

"It is," Viv assured her. "This is how anyone with two eyes views you, sister."

"But I'm not overweight or frumpy."

"You never were. Full-figured doesn't equate to not being sexy, Lei. It doesn't equate to not being gorgeous." Viv's smile was luminous. "Yes, people's preferences differ, and that's a great thing. It would be boring as hell if we all looked the same, wouldn't it? But your differences don't make you any less attractive than the rest of us. To some, I'm scrawny, and Josie dresses too slutty. There are those who would view Taryn as unattractive with her tattoos and piercings, but we all know she's bewitchingly beautiful like Josie is beguiling and sex on a stick."

"I don't know what to say." And she didn't. Vivian had given her a gift. The gift of self-confidence she never truly had.

"I'm ashamed we all missed seeing how you viewed yourself. We could've boosted your confidence years ago."

"Maybe it was a good thing you didn't." With a melancholy smile, Soleil met Viv's loving blue gaze in the mirror. "My head might've grown to match my bust size."

"You'd be well within your rights." Viv's focus dipped to the cleavage displayed above Soleil's V-neck. "That bosom is fucking impressive as hell!"

They shared a laugh. Their love of historical novels was mutual.

"Remind me to loan you Kate Bateman's latest release," Soleil said.

"Too late. I already own it." Viv waved a hand to disappear the mirror. "Get going, or you'll miss the hearing. Oh, and take a few extra charmed vials of dirt with you. Damian texted before I came out here to check on you. He and Trevor believe the Villainous Vectors may have pulled a Manchurian Candidate, setting Trev up for failure."

"I'm going to murder that bitch."

"Bitch singular?" Viv asked with a laugh.

"Okay, those *bitches*, but Deni gets it first," Soleil promised.

CHAPTER 31

Trevor's link to Soleil sparked to life.

"Dalli."

Shutting his eyes and thanking the Goddess for small favors, he expelled a breath in relief.

She entered the hall and didn't stop walking until she reached the front row of spectators. With a cajoling smile for the unknown man in the aisle seat, she asked, "Do you mind if I have this seat? That's my boyfriend, and—"

Every man in the row stood and offered their spot with a warm smile. Each eager to be the one to assist her.

When her gaze locked with Trevor's, her smile grew tight.

"It appears you're a femme fatale, after all."

Her gaze dropped as if she were wary and undesiring of his attention. Perhaps she was. Her suffering at his hands was significant. Only the fence separated them, and his need to haul her across the bar and into his lap was strong. If the situation had been any different and his programmed threat to her any less, he would've, to reassure them both nothing had changed and whatever they had between them was still viable.

"Thanks for the spell, Damian," she said in a low voice, casting a fleeting glance toward the high table. "I've created one of my own." Opening her hand, she displayed three small vials of what looked to be dirt. "Will you toss them at Asshat Agnes, Devil Deni, or Melvin the Malevolent if they even *think* the word 'nothing'?"

"It would be my utmost delight," he replied. His gaze sharpened as he studied the containers in his hand. "This is dirt from my estate."

"Is that a problem?"

"It may be slightly more powerful than you expected."

Her worried gaze dropped to the objects Damian cradled. "Should I modify them?"

"Not at all. But if you're certain you can live with the consequences of your actions, I'm happy to assist."

"Why does that sound dire?" Trev asked with a downward twist of his lips. "And why do I want you to save us all the time and chuck them across the room now?"

"Because you're as bloodthirsty as your mate," Damian replied dryly. "Soleil, my dear, please take a seat. The trial is about to resume."

Trevor once again locked gazes with her. "Thank you for coming. There's so much I want to say, Dalli. And I hope you're willing to listen. *After.*"

"I'm willing."

Beneath her sweet smile lurked uncertainty. The urge to sweep her up and teleport away was chipping away at his restraint, but resolving the issues at hand was paramount. After another twenty minutes, it became apparent why his instinct to grab her and run had become an insidious need to act immediately.

"Sentencing will now commence," Councilwoman Maria Aguilar intoned.

As one, the Council rose and joined hands.

"Wait." Damian's commanding voice jolted them from the trance they'd entered. "It's imperative you consider one final fact."

"What's that, Aether?" Councilman Doyle asked with arched brows.

"Trevor Blane's power is no more. I suggest you consider the possibility that you're sentencing a mortal to a magical being's punishment should you find him guilty."

"What's this?" Agnes bound to her feet.

Damian unfurled the fingers holding the vials. "I removed his magic the first time your daughter used compulsion against him."

"Give it back!" Melvin demanded, casting a panicked look around. "He's essential for… er, uh… well, his power is essential for a Death Dealer, should the Council decide to reconstitute him."

"Reconstitute him?" Damian climbed to his feet and rested his knuckles on the table, leaning forward. "What an interesting term, Mr. Glen. Why should you be concerned with their wish to reconstitute his power, I wonder? How does it benefit you?'

The Aether's voice deepened, becoming as smooth and seductive as a siren's. Nearly the entire collective of individuals present stared at him, eyes glazed. The exceptions were the Sentinels, Soleil, and him. Trev sought Fintan across the distance.

"What the fuck is he doing, Fin?"

Fintan didn't reply, remaining hyper-vigilant and focused on the Aether.

"They're sharing a power, cher," Draven responded in the Seer's stead.

Soleil shifted, turning her head to watch Fintan. *"How is that possible? I thought Fintan was a Seer. Is he a Siren, too?"*

Trevor glanced at her over his shoulder. *"If he is, I didn't know about it. We'll ask Damian when this is over."*

"He has work to do." Agnes was cagey and acted like Damian's questions were equivalent to having teeth pulled without lidocaine. "We need him."

"What work?" the Aether asked. Although his coaxing tone hadn't changed, tension lined his shoulders, and Trevor felt the subtle shift in his energy.

It appeared Agnes and cohorts intended to use Trevor's gifts for their own nefarious reasons, and Damian was doing his damnedest to reveal what those were. As the explanations fell from forked tongues, Trev grew angry on behalf of Soleil and himself.

In the last months of his relationship with Deni, they'd triggered him three separate times to destroy their enemies. Mindlessly killing and obliterating souls, who may have been innocents like Soliel, while retaining no memory of the act. Their machinations made him sick. The heat of embarrassment for his gullibility crept up his neck. Unable to meet questioning gazes directed at him, he stared over the head of the Authority, focusing his attention on the emblem embedded there. The day he stepped foot on these grounds was the day he'd been damned. Except for Soleil, nothing he touched was good, but he'd also tainted their relationship.

Touching Damian's wrist, he said, "Enough."

"We need to get to the bottom of their crimes."

"You do. But their crimes are mine, with what they forced me to do. I'm ready for sentencing." He swallowed hard. Removing his ring, he cut off his link to the Sentinels, then purposefully blocked Soleil. "Convince the Authority to take my life, Dethridge. Please." He didn't care that his low-voiced plea came out ragged. He didn't possess the constitution for reprogramming, nor could he live with what he'd done.

"What about Soleil?" Damian asked softly.

"You can ease the sting of my passing. She hasn't known me long enough for it to affect her long-term. And I'm sure, after two attempted murders by me, she's wary of a relationship anyway."

"You have it all figured out, don't you?"

Disappointment was present in the Aether's tone, and Trevor shot him a sharp glance.

"What do you expect of me, Dethridge?"

"I expect you not to roll over and let them win." Those disturbing obsidian eyes narrowed. "But perhaps it's too much to ask of *you*."

"It's too much to ask of anyone. I've murdered people. Do you get that? Do you get that my soul is blackened by their actions?"

"I do. Do you?"

"What the fuck is that supposed to mean?" Trev demanded.

"You said it yourself. *Their actions*. Not yours."

"But I was their tool. A mindless fucking tool."

"Mindless, yes. You were *hypnotized*." Damian shifted, presenting his back to the panel, uncaring that they were all waiting for him to continue with questioning. "What if it had been Soleil? What if she had your ability and had been compelled to kill without knowledge or consent? Should she, in turn, be put to death for those crimes she had no ability to prevent?"

"Of course not!"

"Then what makes you special, Blane? What makes you unforgivable?"

"I'm tired," Trevor confessed. "So fucking tired. Of fighting them, of death, of the goddamned curse related to my touch. All of it."

"Live over two hundred years under the taint of your mother's killing spree, and come talk to me again," Damian said coldly. "You've done your job, and only to those who deserved it. The exception was the fault of Agnes Vector and her hoard of evildoers. Not you, Trevor." His tone had softened, as had his forbidding expression. "Forgive yourself."

"I need to know who their victims were. To make restitution, if I can."

They sat in silence for an uncomfortable few minutes before Damian spoke again. "And Soleil? What is your intent?"

"To leave her in peace."

"You're a bloody fool," Damian muttered.

"Maybe, but I'm not bringing my ugly into her world."

As Soleil watched the whispered exchange between Trevor and Damian, she experienced a sinking sensation in her stomach. Once the confessions began from the opposing team, Trevor shut down, refusing to glance her way. His profile had hardened with each loathsome detail revealed.

He blamed himself.

When he severed their link, she was sure of it.

Her desire to jump up and defend him was strong. She wanted to hold his head to her breast and stroke his luxurious hair until he understood he was worthy to be loved. But she'd encountered his impenetrable wall before, and there was no breeching or scaling it when he was in this mood.

Deni began speaking. "Damian is *noth—*"

Had Soleil been any less prepared, the sinister twat would've succeeded in flipping Trevor's kill switch. But her reaction to Deni was instinctual, and she sent one of the vials on the defendant's table flying in the other woman's direction the instant she opened her mouth to speak. The glass smacked Deni in the chest and shattered on impact. Dirt particles danced in the air before her, then formed a bony hand. It grew in size, elongating its skeletal fingers, until it was triple human size. The sight shocked everyone silent.

For a moment, Soleil took great delight in Deni's terror, and as the woman opened her mouth to scream, the hand fisted and plunged inside. Her shriek was choked off as the air left her lungs. The magic expanded, and the soil tripled in quantity, pouring out her mouth, nose, and eye sockets. She began to gag and claw at her throat and, in doing so, sucked in the ever-growing mound of dirt.

There shouldn't have been that much. Not enough to suffocate her, only the right amount to keep her from speaking. Yet the earth magic had a life of its own. When Deni fell to the floor, her pallor gray and blood vessels bursted in her eyes, those same eyes, although those of a deceased woman, were accusing.

Soleil covered her mouth to hold back her cry of horror. She needn't have. Any sound she might've made wouldn't have been heard over the grief-stricken shrieks of Melvin and the outpouring of complaints from Agnes.

Damian rose and cautiously approached Soleil as if she were a wild mustang ready to bolt. And perhaps she was because she feared the Authority's wrath for inadvertently causing Deni's death.

"She murdered my daughter! Before witnesses," Agnes charged. "Red Guard, arrest her! I want her to stand trial." No tears poured from her, only demands.

Lifting her gaze to meet Trevor's, Soleil saw grimness with an underlying compassion.

"It's no small thing to take a life," Damian said in a carrying voice as he wrapped an arm around her. "But Soleil Stephens saved two others by stopping Denillia's plan."

"What plan?" Councilwoman Doyle stared at them. Worry tightened the skin around her mouth, deepening the lines. "What just happened?"

"Join hands, please."

"This is highly irregular, Aether. Even for you," Councilman Reed stated, frowning his displeasure.

"I intend to show you what my future would be had my sister-in-law not stepped in. I ask again, please join hands."

Those along the table complied with the Aether's directive,

keeping a wary eye on Soleil as the Red Guard removed Deni's lifeless body from the room.

Damian squeezed Soleil's shoulder and motioned her to sit in his abandoned chair. With a wary glance around the room, she crossed to the table and sat. Trevor made no move to touch her or offer any comfort. He'd shut down, and the knowledge he'd blocked her hurt. For as tough as she could be and had been during multiple murder attempts against her, she was feeling an overwhelming urge to cry.

"Don't stress it, Dalli." Trevor's voice was low and gruff when he eventually spoke. He was sweating it enough for both of them. "She deserved what she got. Damian was right. You saved two people tonight. You should be proud of the fact and hold on to it when things become too much."

"I've never taken a life before."

"Your reaction was self-defense. You saw a threat, and you ended it."

She nodded, thoroughly miserable.

Leaning in, he kissed her temple. "You're incredible. Never forget it."

It sounded like he was saying goodbye, and Soleil wanted to cling to him. Wanted to hold on so tightly he'd never be able to live without her. But she couldn't be the only one fighting to keep a relationship alive. Especially when the other person wouldn't.

CHAPTER 32

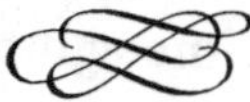

Trevor understood Soleil's misery all too well. He'd been in a similar state after his first kill, sickened by what he'd done and throwing up in a bathroom stall after a hearty congratulations by Agnes Vector. Looking back, he had to wonder if his victim had deserved it at all. Or any of the ones who followed.

Yes, there were those like Loman O'Connor and Morcant Thywyll who had required putting down and more, but Trevor wanted every single one of his previous assignments re-examined. If any were undeserving, he intended to find out and make restitution. Or at least have Damian make it on his behalf if the Authority ruled against him.

As he waited for the Aether to make his point and show the council members Deni's intent, Trevor considered the two remaining vials of dirt on the table before them. With a sleight of hand taught to him by Draven Masters, he pocketed one of the two.

Agnes Vector and Melvin Glen wouldn't live out the rest of their natural-born days. Of that, he was certain. If Trev had to go out of this world as a murderer, so be it. When the time came for him to stand in the Otherworld's waiting room and the scales tipped one way or another, he hoped their deaths were in his plus column. The duo was evil, and he didn't intend to give them another shot at hurting Soleil.

Trevor studied her stoic profile. Inside, in the private reaches of his mind where he could appreciate the ironies of life, he smiled. Was it such a short time ago that he thought her plain? It hardly seemed possible when she'd become so incredibly beautiful to him.

Her updo wasn't perfectly coiffed, and she'd left some of her waves to frame her face and fall down her graceful neck. With her subtle makeup, she was a stunner. The perfect mate for him.

Although he wanted to tell her, he couldn't. If things went against him, as he suspected, people needed to believe he didn't hold her in the highest of regards. His enemies were watching. At the very least, he could remove the threat of retaliation against her.

"Now, do you understand?" Damian was saying.

Eight of the remaining eleven council members nodded. Three appeared disturbed and volleyed concerned glances between the defendant's table and the Aether.

"Denillia was acting on her mother's behalf in most instances," Melvin Glen confessed when pressed. Sweat poured profusely down his face, and he repeatedly sent Trevor wary looks, no doubt fearing immediate retaliation.

Justice wouldn't be swift, but it would happen. If Trev couldn't do it, he'd find someone who wasn't hindered.

"Trevor Blane, please rise," Councilman Reed said.

Soleil's tormented eyes met Trevor's as he stood, and he opened his mind to her one last time.

"It's okay, Dalli. No matter what the outcome, you're going to be safe."

Seeming to be dismissive, she looked away, and his heart

thumped painfully in his chest. As much as he probably earned her scorn, he didn't want her to hate him.

"I don't care about my welfare, you idiot. I'm worried about yours."

He released a breath he hadn't been aware of holding. *"You should always care about yourself first, sweetheart. Especially in instances like this."*

"Is that why you stole one of the vials?"

Trevor fought a grin. *"You know it."*

"I hope you use it on that warthog, Agnes Vector."

"If I've never said it, I'm saying it now. I appreciate the fuck out of your savage tendencies. You're the perfect Death Dealer mate."

She spared him a glance but was quick to look away, understanding the need for their surreptitious conversation. *"But not yours?"*

"It can't be mine, Dalli. We have no future. If the Authority doesn't recall or end my life, the threat of Agnes's pre-programmed trigger lies between us. I won't take the risk."

"Shouldn't that be my call to make, Trev? It's my life at stake, after all.."

"No, because I'd have to live with the devastation. I won't do that. I can't."

A short, barely perceptible nod indicated her understanding, but he sensed she disagreed. The heaviness of grief clogged his throat, and though he sensed some of it was hers, he knew the bulk of it belonged to him.

For a distraction, he tuned into what Damian was saying.

"Again, I ask you to consider that Mr. Blane's powers were removed," he argued.

"But they can be restored by you," Councilwoman Doyle countered.

"Actually, they can't." With an elegant shrug of his shoulders, Damian cast her a faux sheepish smile. "I didn't keep them for myself. I used his abilities against him to obliterate the magic itself. I swear on my soul, I cannot restore Trevor Blane's powers."

To a man or woman, the Authority was stunned by the Aether's statement.

Trevor cast him a sharp look, wishing like hell he hadn't given up his tanzanite ring so he knew what was going through the man's clever mind. If one spark of Trevor's power remained, it would regenerate, making a liar of Damian. The Authority would call him to task.

Soleil's delight tickled his mind, and Trevor glanced down at her with a frown.

"It's not technically a lie." Her full, cherry-colored lips curled ever so distractingly, and he had to concentrate on her next comment. *"He's unable to restore your power, but if, as you suspect, a spark remains, you can regenerate it yourself."*

Christ almighty! He hadn't even considered it! The act of leaving any of his magic behind was reckless on Damian's part. What if Trev used it to hurt Soleil?

"We're going to find that trigger or eliminate the threat, babe," she telegraphed. *"Count on it."*

"We'll need time to examine and consider this new information," Councilwoman Ishtasapa said among the nods of her peers. "We will reconvene in one hour."

"As you wish," Damian replied with a slight bow of his head. "However, I would take it as a personal favor if you ruled in favor of allowing him to remain on my team. Abilities or no, he's a valued member and friend."

The implication was clear. The Aether wouldn't be happy if they decided Trevor needed to be put down like the rabid dog they believed him to be.

"And as for the matter of Ms. Stephens—"

All signs of affability left Damian when Councilman Pettigrew mentioned Soleil.

"Uh, yes... well, we... uh, that is to say..." Tom Pettigrew stammered in the face of the Aether's cold stare. "I find her actions to be in keeping with self-defense and an act of heroism in saving the Aether's life. All in favor?"

The entire Authority was quick to agree, with the exception of Agnes and Melvin.

"No! No!" Agnes surged to her feet, her skin darkening to that of a beet. "She needs to be held accountable! She murdered my daughter!"

"Our ruling stands, Councilwoman Vector," Knowles stated in chilly tones. "You and Councilman Glen will face an inquiry into your actions."

"But—"

He continued as if she'd never objected. "Actions in direct odds with those of this organization. Actions for profit, on your behalf."

Councilman Garcia banged his gavel. "This hearing is now adjourned and will recommence in exactly sixty minutes."

"WE FIND TREVOR BLANE TO BE A CONTRIBUTING MEMBER OF OUR society. However, in light of his behavior and the steps taken against innocents and mortals alike, we suggest rehabilitation, requiring six months of reconditioning," Councilwoman Florence Carter stated exactly sixty-two minutes later. "If he passes the battery of tests and the psych evaluation when that time is up, the Authority will work with the gods to restore his magic."

"However, should he fail, we will readdress the punishment. He is to be taken from this hall to an undisclosed location, where his immediate sentence begins," Councilwoman Aguilar added.

Fearing she understood what the readdressed punishment would entail, Soleil jumped to her feet. "No! This isn't right!"

Damian gestured downward for her to sit, but she ignored him.

"This is bullshit," she shouted. "Trevor has done nothing wrong. Nothing more than your corrupt council has demanded of him."

"Ms. Stephens, we ask that you sit down. Your personal wants or concerns are not relevant to this sentencing," Florence said. "Mr. Blane has gone rogue on more than one occasion." The elderly councilwoman frowned in his direction. "It has come to light that you've healed a mortal girl only this past week. Without permission, I might add. That will need to be reversed by another Death Dealer, of course." When Soleil would've objected, Florence held up her hand. "You've also taken the lives of others under the direction of the Aether, without sanction from the Authority. These things weighed heavily into our decision."

"Trevor Blane, do you understand our judgment and accept the consequences of your actions?" Councilman Garcia asked.

"I understand, but do not accept," he responded in a dull voice.

Sickened with dread, Soleil leaned forward and tugged on Damian's sleeve. "What does that mean? What—"

Councilwoman Mattie Price appeared stricken. "Trevor! Or, er, Mr. Blane, you understand by not accepting your punishment, you will be put to death, yes?"

Gasping for air, Soleil stared at the other woman in shock. *Death?*

His beautiful light extinguished forever?

"No, Trevor," she croaked. *"Please!"*

"I'm sorry, Dalli." His aching voice echoed in her head. *"It's time for you to leave."*

"Don't do this. Accept. Just accept, and in six months—"

Their connection ended with a sharp snap and a sizzle. His doing or the Authority, she didn't know.

"I understand, Councilwoman Price," he said aloud. "As my

last request, I ask that you not reverse my cancer treatment on Lily Stockton and that you allow Jordan Brothers to remove the last of the disease from her body."

After a rapid-fire discussion with the Council, Mattie agreed.

"Then I'm ready," Trevor said gravely.

Soleil reached for him, but he sidestepped, crossed to the center of the room, and bowed his head, prepared for whatever they intended.

"Damian, please! Don't let them do this," she begged.

"Captain Ellis, remove Ms. Stephens from these proceedings." Mattie's voice, although crisp, held an edge of pain, and Soleil met her troubled eyes. She didn't want Trevor to die, but she was bound by her duty to the Authority.

"Mattie, please!"

"It's his choice, Soleil," she said, not unkindly.

Brooke blocked her view and touched her arm. "Ms. Stephens, please don't resist. You'll create chaos the likes you can't imagine," she said in a quiet voice for Soleil's hearing alone. "The Aether and the Death Dealer will fight if you're forcefully removed. As I expect the line of Sentinels against the back wall will, too. One look at their expressions should tell you all you need to know."

"Will they do it right now?" Soleil asked her. "Will they kill Trevor here? I can't leave him if they intend to. I can't."

Her expression softened marginally. "No. He'll have three days to reconsider, and they'll put the question to him again. If he maintains his position, he'll be given three additional days to consider his options."

"And then?" Soleil feared her reply. In her heart, she knew Trevor's mind wouldn't change.

"Then he will be executed."

The air between them grew thick, or maybe she'd lost her ability to breathe as her worry expanded within her chest. Brooke also appeared sad at the prospect of his demise. Had they had a thing once upon a time, too? He'd never said, but he wasn't a monk prior to their brief association.

Soleil rose on her tiptoes to peer over the Captain's shoulder.

With his back to them, Trevor stood with his hands fisted by his sides, as if it were taking all his strength not to come to her.

Next, she sought Damian's reaction. His visage was stern, and his obsidian eyes held disappointment—*for her behavior!*

"Go," he ordered with a firm nod.

Tears blurred her vision as she shook her head. "I can't," she whispered. "I can't let this be his end. Our end."

Comforting arms wrapped around her, and she buried her face against the warm leather of Draven's duster. "I've got you, *cher*," he told her. To Brooke, he said, "I'll escort her out." When Soleil would've pulled away, he touched her temple. "Sleep."

The sensation of falling was halted by his strong arms, and the room grew dark as her conscious mind shut down.

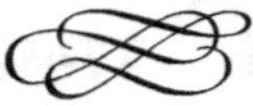

CHAPTER 33

"Ach! Why are you after being a stubborn eejit?" Fintan demanded. "Sure, and you've got a beautiful *cailín* awaitin' ya at home, but are ya happy for it? No!"

"The Authority's reconditioning means a magical lobotomy, Fin! It's not like I'll remember her when it's over." Trev pounded the glass wall with the side of his fist, viciously swearing when he received an electrical shock for his display of temper.

Those closest to him had gathered to convince him to reverse his decision. They refused to adhere to his wishes.

"But you'll be alive, ya gobshite. And your wet personality will still be the same, yeah?"

"Why did I ever consider you a friend when all you do is insult me?" Trev growled.

"Because before today, ya weren't acting the fool," Fintan snapped back.

"Fuck off."

Frustration drew the Seer's mouth down, and his sea-green eyes darkened with worry. "Trev, I'm as serious as I've never been before, I am. They're after killin' ya tomorrow if you don't change your mind at today's meetin'. Sure, and where there's life, they're's hope."

"My father came back changed, Fin. Dead inside." Trevor didn't know how to relay his concerns. Relay he didn't want that for himself. Didn't want to be half the man he was, always with one foot in a darker world.

"That wasn't from the reconstitution, son," Ben said on the heels of his comment. He occupied the adjoining cell. His trial hadn't gone well, and Ben was slated for the same punishment for his part in killing a Red Guard. "It was from the knowledge I failed my family. That I failed your mother and you boys. That I failed to protect you from the Authority."

"You were changed, though. And what happens when I fail to remember Soleil? How is she going to feel?"

"Happy you're alive?" Ben suggested. "You can rebuild what was lost. Your memories will return, eventually. I'll restore them."

"And you, Dad? What if your outcome is different this time around? What if they take pains to wipe your memory and lessen your abilities?"

Draven pushed away from the wall, uncrossed his arms from his chest, and straightened. "Then the rest of us will appeal to the Aether on your behalf, *mon ami*."

"It feels hopeless," Trev confessed.

"You didn't see her." Mattie shook her head as she frowned at him through the glass wall. "She was wrecked. That woman loves you and will continue to until her dying—"

"Don't talk about her death, please." He scrubbed his scalp with his fingertips, ruffling his unkempt hair.

"You get my point, Trev. You're sentencing her to hell right along with you." When he remained silent, Mattie sighed. "She wants to see you."

"No."

"Have you always been a stubborn ass, or is it a recent development?" she asked in a snippy voice.

"Always," Ben answered first. "I don't recall a time when he wasn't. He does what he believes is right every single time."

"I don't want this to be her last memory of me, okay?" Trevor hoped to shut them all the hell up. Dropping his head into his hands, he said, "Can you leave it alone? Please? Grant a dying man his wish."

"No."

He jerked upright and searched for the owner of that voice.

Soleil was right inside the doorway with her arms crossed and a pissy expression darkening her lovely face. His thirsty eyes drank in the sight of her even as his mind rejected the idea of her seeing him at his worst.

"I'm only allowed two minutes, so listen up, Trevor Blane." Her balled fists relocated to her hips, and she stared at him with a ferocity he fully appreciated. Nothing was more beautiful than Soleil when she was riled. "When I gave you my heart, I didn't realize you were a coward."

"What the hell—"

"I'm not finished." Cold fury pinched her mouth tight. "I've had five days to think about what I wanted to say, and it's this. You're a Grade-A coward. You won't fight for your right to live and our right to be together. You believe you're taking it on the chin and going to your great reward some hero, but you aren't."

"I never said I was a hero," he objected, stung by her assessment. "And they were never going to rule any other way. I'm not into having my brain fucked with. Thank you very much!"

"Oh, boo hoo! So what? You'll still be alive."

"But I won't be *me*, Dalli. Don't you get it? I won't be the guy you fell in love with." He needed her to understand.

"I fell in love with a false idol," she retorted. "With someone I believed was worthy. You're not him."

"Now you're just being mean!"

"Pfft." She glanced up at the camera mounted in the corner of the room, then at Mattie. "It's off?"

"Yes."

"Good." Soleil held up two small vials. "I know you think my ability to create potions is ridiculous and that what I sell in my shop is for fools, but—"

"I don't think that!"

"But I am good at what I do. I know exactly which plants do what and their effect when enhanced by magic." She stomped forward and held up one of the two small containers. "The one with the green cap is if you change your mind and decide I'm worth fighting for."

"You are!"

"We'll see." Holding up one with a red cap, she said, "This one is if you decide to go through with your stupid plan to die. It'll take away your pain and speed up the process. Remember, red, you're dead. Even your pea brain can retain that much."

Fintan laughed.

Trevor shot him the bird before facing Soleil again. "Dalli—"

"Shut up. I have thirty seconds left." Walking to the bench by the entrance, she bent and stuffed them underneath the seat. "Use the excuse that you need to tie your shoe or something when they come for you. Choose the vial that corresponds to your decision. Personally, I'm voting for you to get your head out of your ass and choose the green, but I won't hold out much hope."

Draven chuckled. "I'll help you forget him, *cher*. You and I—"

Trevor exploded with anger. "I swear to the Goddess, I will come back from the Otherworld and fuck you up, Draven Masters! See if I don't."

Soleil stepped up to Draven and kissed his cheek. "I'll need about a week to get over him."

His father chortled when she flipped Trevor the bird and headed for the door.

"Get back here, woman!" he shouted.

She kept walking.

"Dalli!"

The others filed out after her, and he released a guttural yell.

"Choose the green, son. She's a once-in-a-lifetime kind of woman. You'll never find her like again."

CHAPTER 34

Footsteps on the gravel path alerted Soleil to her visitor. Her gut clenched. Taking an extraordinarily long time, she debated teleporting to her room and hiding out for the foreseeable future. She didn't want to hear about Trevor's death at the hands of the Authority. Tears stung her eyes, and she blinked to dispel them.

After a few cleansing breaths, she firmed her resolve. Really, she should get it over with. The sooner she faced the truth, the sooner she could grieve. She almost scoffed at her ridiculous thoughts. It wasn't as if she hadn't been suffering since the trial. Since Trevor so stupidly agreed to take death over the rehabilitation program.

Placing her spade on the workbench, she eased her work gloves from her hands and turned to greet her visitor.

She blinked again. And again.

"No hug for your returning lover, Dalli?"

Dressed in formal Regency garb, Trevor looked like he was attending a ball. In his widespread arms, he held a garment bag tied up with a massive pink bow that should have looked absurd but was charming.

"Am I dreaming?" she asked past the lump in her throat.

He grinned. "No."

"Did you escape?"

"No."

"Then how are you here?"

"They released me." Walking to her favorite reading spot, he draped his present over the back of the bench and straightened to face her. "But I thought you should know, I picked the green vial."

Her heart hiccuped, and she pressed her fist against her chest. "You did?"

"Yeah. For you. For us. For our fighting chance."

"Why, when you hadn't before?"

"It was something my father said." Trevor approached and smoothed her wayward hair from her hot skin. "He reminded me you're a once-in-a-lifetime sort of woman."

Her heart began to pound, and his nearness had begun to short-circuit her brain's wiring. All she wanted to do was tackle him to the ground and kiss him for a month of Sundays, but she needed to understand what was happening and where they stood. "I am?"

"You are," he assured her with a loving smile. "I love you, Soleil."

"Okay, then."

His brows shot up. "That's it?"

She wasn't sure what he'd been expecting, so she said, "Clearly you made the right decision, so yes, that's it."

He kissed her. His touch was worshipful, and she tasted the sweet promise of a long life together. Drawing away, he rubbed his thumb across her swollen lower lip. "What would the potion have done had I taken it?"

"Knitted your memories back together to keep you from forgetting."

Closing his eyes, he pressed his forehead to hers. "Thank you."

"It was for purely selfish reasons," she admitted.

He chuckled and shook his head. "Which aligned with mine."

"I guess that makes us perfect mates."

"It does." His fingertips caressed her jaw. "May I ask you an important question?"

"I have a confession first," she blurted, oddly nervous now that he'd returned to her. The truth was, they'd known each other less than a month, and it had been a whirlwind romance if one could call it that. What if he decided she wasn't forever-mate material?

"What's your confession?"

"Both vials were the same potion."

He frowned and drew back to see her face. "You said the red-capped potion would've eased my pain and killed me faster."

Soleil scrunched her nose and went for broke. "I lied."

"What if I'd chosen death?" he asked, plainly confused by her plan.

"There may have been a little something extra in that vial that would've changed your mind."

Gaping, he dropped his arms and stepped away. "You were going to use magic to influence me?"

"No!"

His brows flew to his hairline, and his expression was pure disbelief.

She winced. "Okay, well, yes, but not in a bad way. Just to keep you alive and return you to me."

"It wasn't your call to make, Soleil." Expression dangerous, he presented his back and strode a few feet away, only to return and glare at her. "I'm not sure how I'm supposed to feel about it."

"I couldn't let you die," she argued, planting her hands on her hips. "Not for such a stupid reason."

"Did you have an idea what they'd planned?" he asked incredulously. "What reconstitution and reconditioning is like?"

"No, but Damian told me." Lifting her chin, she met his furious gaze. "Everything would've remained intact. That's what my potion does."

He shook his head in what she could only assume was disgust at her manipulation.

"I'm not sorry." Hugging herself, she closed her eyes and swallowed her misery as she tried to hang on to her righteous indignation. "I'm not sorry," she said again. "You didn't deserve to die, Trevor."

"It wasn't your call to make," he repeated slowly as if she were too dumb to comprehend.

Her anger over the entire situation and his inability to see her point boiled over. Hands trembling, she shoved his chest. "Go! Take your fancy get-up and whatever beautiful thing is in that bag, and go!"

"What the actual fuck?"

"I thought you were choosing to die, Trev. Of course I was going to do whatever it took to save you," she cried. "Not only for me but for *everyone* who loves you. Simon, Ben, Fintan, Draven, and Mattie. You have a family in all of them."

For the first time in her life, her greenhouse was no longer her sanctuary. It had become tainted by him. Because everywhere she looked, she could recall moments they shared. Yet those sweet memories were overcome by this confrontation. And his accusation hinted she wasn't any better than the Denillias of the world.

Chest heaving, Soleil ran.

"Dalli!"

She ran on, heart pounding double-time, making her incapable of hearing whether he was behind her or not.

"Soleil, *wait!*" His hand closed around her upper arm, halting her flight, and he swung her back toward him. "Stop running away from me, dammit!"

"If you think I'm going to stand here while you rain down accusations or insults on me, you can fuck all the way off, Trevor Blane!"

The sides of his mouth kicked up. Ducking down, he sandwiched her face between his warm palms. "I'm sorry."

"What?"

"I'm sorry. For a split second, your manipulation of me felt reminiscent of Deni."

Soleil had guessed correctly, and she was miserable for it. "It wasn't a manipulation of you. It wasn't anything other than to encourage you to choose life. And I'm not *her*." Glaring at him, she shook her head. "Not in looks, not in actions. If she's the type you're searching for, the kind of woman you want—"

Like one of Kate Bateman's heroes, Trevor wrapped an arm around her waist and hauled her against him. She gasped her surprise and secret delight when he palmed the back of her neck and lowered his head. In the next instant, he was kissing her into silence. When he pulled back, her focus remained on his mouth, and she moaned when he swiped his tongue across his lower lip.

"You're who I want, Dalli. Now and always."

"You're making me crazy, Mr. Blane," she muttered.

He chuckled and lifted her so he could bury his face in her cleavage. His sigh of contentment made her laugh.

"You were right, you know," he said as he reached behind her knee to wrap it around his waist. She followed suit with the other and linked her arms around his neck for good measure.

"I was?" Snuggling closer, she rested her face against his throat, needing to feel his heartbeat to know he was alive and well. She wanted to be sure she wasn't in the midst of some twisted dream and would wake up any second to find he wasn't there. "About what?"

"All Trevor's *are* assholes."

"See? I told you." She laughed and hugged him tighter, then loosened her hold to stare into his beloved face. "But I'm coming around to the name."

He grew serious as he gazed up at her. "Thank you for fighting for the both of us, Dalli. I wasn't strong enough."

"You were. When it came down to it, you changed your mind. Ben gave you the reason you needed."

"Maybe."

"Definitely." She toyed with a button on his formal coat and tails. "What's all this?"

He released her and bowed as if they were being formally introduced at a soiree. Lifting her hand, he bussed her knuckles, then cast her a roguish grin. "I needed a grand gesture."

She bit her lip to keep from giggling and nodded sagely.

"That's what's in the bag. A dress for you." The tips of his ears turned pink, but he met her gaze through his embarrassment. "I've come to court you properly, m'lady."

"But, sir! We can't go anywhere without my chaperone." Conjuring a fan, she waved it like a courtesan and batted her eyelashes. "We shouldn't be alone now, either. You'll destroy my reputation."

"You lied to me, Dalli."

Her stomach flipped, and she folded the fan, preparing to defend herself in light of his about-face. "I already apologized for that. I—"

"Not that. At our first, er, joining."

"Our first... Ah!" She bit her lip to hide a grin. "How so?"

"You were no virgin. Your reputation was already in ruins," he charged.

"Why, sir! Are you besmirching my good name?"

"I've already besmirched it," he replied dryly.

Unable to keep up the pretense, she laughed and dropped the fan to the ground. "You did indeed. Do you want to do some more besmirching? I know a splendid little alcove..."

"Why, Ms. Stephens! You're a practiced flirt!"

"I'm getting there."

His laugh was pure wicked delight. "Lead the way, Dalli. I'm going to besmirch the hell out of you."

"You say the sweetest things!"

"And I intend to continue for the rest of our lives."

She giggled as she drew him down on top of her.

"Commence with the besmirching, good sir," she purred with the bawdy laugh he greatly appreciated.

EPILOGUE

ONE WEEK LATER

amian traversed the hallway to Agnes's living room, taking his time to view the pictures on her walls. Some were of her, Melvin, and their children as a family unit; others were single shots of Deni or Agnes. No one appeared particularly happy the way one assumed they would if they'd had a healthy, loving home life. He almost felt sorry for Denillia. Almost. Perhaps he would've had she not attempted to trigger Trevor into attacking him.

Foolish girl.

Soleil's earth magic, mixed with the enchanted soil from his estate, had given an extra boost to the spell. She'd only meant to stuff dirt in Deni's mouth to prevent her from speaking, but his added power had amped up the charm one thousandfold. It was something she never could've foreseen, as he told her time and again when her guilt flared up.

With Beastie's assistance, he'd been able to see into the past to the day Agnes and Melvin had brainwashed Trevor. Their plan to weaponize him was genius. But deep in his subconscious, he recognized their sinister intent and avoided them whenever possible. As a failsafe, they persuaded Deni to seduce him and used her to activate their Death Dealer assassin whenever needed.

But that plan, too, had faced opposition.

With each passing day, Trevor's discontentment with her and his life grew, until the dastardly trio was forced to concoct a new plan. One to break his heart. The general idea was if he were disillusioned, he'd be uncaring and wouldn't examine his assignments too closely. And to a degree, it worked well for them.

They erred in sending Trevor after Soleil. While awaiting the kill order, he'd fallen in love. Although it hadn't quite stopped him from trying to carry out his mission once activated, it *had* lost Agnes and Melvin a valuable tool, their daughter, and soon, their lives.

Damian sensed her presence before she spoke and shifted to face her.

"Ms. Vector."

"*Councilwoman* Vector to you, Aether," she replied in a haughty voice. "You still report to me."

Like hell!

He merely smiled at her posturing.

Lifting her chin in the air, she sniffed her displeasure, but he also felt her fear. Right about now, she'd be wondering why he was here, worrying he intended to retaliate.

"I was surprised when you sent a note to say you'd be coming by." She cast a telling glance behind him before quickly looking away.

"Mr. Glen," Damian said smoothly without turning. "Why don't you come out where I can see you, hmm? I'm not particularly fond of people standing behind me. Especially backstabbers, such as yourself."

A rapid shuffling of feet announced Melvin's clumsy charge, and Damian shifted out of the way, implementing a force field. At the same time, he lifted his arm and swept the other man into the wall with a tornadic blast of air. With a death groan, Melvin slunk to the floor.

"Not the greeting I'd hoped for, but definitely the one I expected." Shifting his ire to Agnes, Damian shook his head. "How did you hope to pull that off?"

Considering his unlimited power and the compassionate man he was raised to be, he found her terrified reaction distasteful. Yet, getting his point across was necessary. If their magical community perceived him as weak, it would invite attacks against his person and, ultimately, his family. He had no desire to have another Morcant situation on his hands.

A crafty expression crossed her face, and she smoothed her hair back toward its bun. The lie forming upon her lips made his skin itch as he awaited her response.

"It was Mel's idea," she finally said. "He never thought things through."

Like with her daughter, she showed no concern for Melvin's demise. But then, cold-hearted snakes were only out for themselves, and Agnes Vector was the worst sort of reptile.

"I see."

And he did.

All of it.

Damian doubted she knew half of what he was capable of. "Why don't we discuss what I came for?"

"Of course."

Head held high, she minced toward the open sitting area.

Rather than watch her pathetic attempt at a seductive walk, he studied the layout of her house. The room they entered was an ocean of white, with neutral textured items tossed about. Instead of appearing light and airy, it leaned toward sterile and oppressive.

He despised it.

Not because it was in direct contrast to the warmth of his home but because it lacked joy. Despite the belief that material objects held no life, they contained trace amounts of an occupant's energy. If Damian touched a lamp, he would sense immediately if there had been love in this household.

He kept his hands to his sides, preferring not to be subjected to the negative vibes he suspected of coursing through this place on an average day.

Agnes settled on the white velvet sofa and cast him what she assumed was a flirty glance from under her lashes as she patted the seat next to her.

His stomach revolted, and he suppressed a shudder of revulsion.

"What did you wish to see me about?" she asked stiffly when he ignored her overtures to examine the family portrait over the mantle.

If one looked closely, they could see the coldness in their eyes.

"You have a son. Where is he?"

"Away at college." She waved a hand in dismissal. "He's worthless. Like his father."

And the Mother of the Year Award goes to...

"That's convenient, I suppose," Damian murmured.

Facing her, he raised a brow. While his back was to her, she'd unfastened the top two buttons of her blouse, exposing a great deal of cleavage.

"To anyone else, you're not an unattractive woman on the outside, Agnes," he said with a cool smile. "But my gifts allow me to see you in a far different light. The darker the soul, the uglier the package. You possess the visage of the devil's spawn."

Her jaw dropped in shock, and he tasted sweet satisfaction. But he hadn't come here to be cruel, merely to get answers.

"Now, enough games." He held up a hand to stop her from interrupting. "Before you try to convince me otherwise, be aware I already know the answer to whatever I ask. I'm simply testing you." Cocking his head, he studied her as if she were an alien species. "It's always interesting when someone tries to lie to me. I like to puzzle out if they truly believe what they're spouting or seek to convince me they're blameless."

"I'm not blameless."

"No. You're, not," Damian said silkily. Closing the distance but maintaining a healthy space between them, he clasped his hands behind his back. "Confess."

The enchanted word worked its magic as she regurgitated the barest facts of all her crimes. One hour later, she ran out of breath, and her energy was depleted.

"Was money so important to you?" He waved a hand to encompass her palatial mansion. "With so many in need, why wasn't this adequate for your needs? Why wasn't your family enough to feed the emptiness in your soul?"

"I don't know."

Those were the first honest words she'd spoken of her own free will, and a fluttering sense of sadness rose between them. Hers, for not appreciating what she had, and his, for anyone incapable of understanding there was more to life than the collection of material possessions.

"Many people have suffered and died because you wanted more than your fair share, Agnes. Good people who might have benefited from the medical gifts the earth provides. Benefits no manufactured pill can provide." He purposefully hardened his features, and the room's temperature dropped to freezing. Taking satisfaction in her shiver, he said, "You'll write the names of those involved. Mortal or magical, I care not. They will face justice."

"Why do you care about one frumpy earth witch so damned much?" she cried, realizing she wasn't getting out of this room alive.

"Frumpy?" He laughed, incredulous. "You see an overweight woman who enjoys toiling in the dirt. Those who love her recognize she holds a thousand times more beauty than you and your daughter combined." Damian gave Agnes a pitying look. "You'll never understand her worth because you are worthless. Soleil brings love and laughter wherever she goes. Her heart is solid gold." He rocked back on his heels and shook his head. "And that richness of soul is priceless. Far more valuable than all you hold sacred."

"Thank you, Damian."

His watchful gaze remained locked on his prey, but he smiled for Trevor, who stepped up behind Agnes, dropping his cloaking spell.

"I assume Soleil heard through your connection?" Damian asked him.

"She did."

"Excellent. And now, I'll leave you to do what you do best, Blane."

When Trevor's hand clamped down on Agnes's shoulder, locking her in place, Damian addressed the other hidden occupants in the room. "I trust Mr. Blane's loyalty will no longer be in question, Councilwoman Carter?"

"We understand his value to our organization," she replied as she revealed the group.

"Excellent. Then consider this a promise fulfilled. Thank you for granting his freedom in exchange for this one last mission."

"Last mission? No one—"

The Aether came to the forefront and stared the group into submission. "Trevor Blane no longer works for you. Nor will his brother, Simon, take his place."

"You don't make the rules Aether," Councilman Reed stammered.

"He doesn't, but I do." Golden lights, like a starburst of fireflies, exploded beside him, and the Goddess Isis appeared, touching Damian's arm to show her favor. "The entire Blane family will retain their powers and be answerable to the Aether and to me."

As one, the Council bowed their heads, acknowledging her rule.

"Trevor has another destiny ahead of him. One to help his future bride, and to write entertaining novels for future generations."

"Books? Me?" Trevor choked out a laugh, but the instant he saw her kohl-lined eyes narrow and irritation transform her exotic countenance, he changed his tune. "I—uh, sure. Yeah. I'm good with that if it's what you want."

Damian smirked, earning a deadly glare from the Death Dealer. "Oh, if looks could kill," he murmured.

"I'm working on adding that ability to my repertoire," Trevor retorted.

Isis laughed.

"Trust me, child, the muse will strike soon enough." She tapped her chin as if pondering. "Nine months and three years, if I'm not mistaken."

She was *never* mistaken.

"Nine—" Trevor shut his eyes and groaned. "Soleil's pregnant, isn't she?"

"My understanding was that you had one helluva reunion." Damian snorted at the horror dawning on his face. "*Dalli* bragged to her sisters, and Viv tells me everything."

"I'm going to kill her," Trevor muttered.

Unable to help himself and prepared to take delight in the other man's adverse reaction, Damian said, "Welcome to the family, *Uncle* Trevor."

He wasn't disappointed.

Damian grinned. "I hope *now* you understand why things happened in the order they did."

EXACTLY NINE MONTHS AND THREE HOURS LATER, TREVOR AND Soleil welcomed their first of three sons into the world. The instant Damon Simon Blane was placed in his arms, Trev felt their father-son connection click into place, and he had a deeper understanding of his own father's love.

Tears stung his eyes as he gazed lovingly down at the squalling, red-faced infant he held. "He has your temper, Dalli."

"My temper?" Her laugh turned into a groan, and she pressed a hand to her swollen abdomen. "Ouch!"

"Here, hold him, and I'll heal you," he offered, settling Damon against her. "I suspect he's already hungry."

The second their son touched her, he turned his face up to meet her eyes and latch on to her breast. His color returned to normal as he sighed his contentment.

"I called it." Trev trailed a finger over one perfect, creamy globe, and sighed. "I'm going to have to fight him for these, aren't I?"

"You've had them all to yourself since you and I hooked up. I think you can share for a bit."

"You could bottle feed him," he said, not at all serious.

As expected, she grinned. "Get to healing, please. His abnormally large head was beyond painful." She gave him an arch look. "He gets *that* from you!"

Trev peeled back the swaddling to check Damon's package.

"Not *that* head." She flicked his ear. "The other one."

"Rude."

"I get to be. I was in labor for half the day."

Spreading her robe, Trevor placed his palms flat on her abdomen, tuning into his regenerated Death Dealer magic to knit any tears, calm inflammation, and help her body restore itself to pre-pregnancy health.

"Better?"

She beamed her gratitude. "Much. Thank you."

Scooting to sit beside her, he wrapped an arm around her

shoulders and gazed down at their nursing son. "No, Dalli. Thank you. You've given me a precious gift. One I never dreamed I could have because of what I am."

"Yours is an antiquated view." She scowled. "I mean, I appreciate the sentiment after all that work. But having the little woman provide you with a strapping son then thanking her is—"

He shut her up with a kiss, quickly forgetting himself as she dug her fingers into his hair and took charge. When they parted, he grinned at the stunned expression on her glowing face. Their passion would always be off the charts, and he was a happier person for it.

"I wasn't thanking you in the way you assumed," he said, tenderly stroking her jaw, then tucking a lock of her burnt-chestnut hair behind her ear. "By the way, I don't think you've ever looked more beautiful."

She blushed.

Her skin color reminded him of a Keira Garden Rose's center —the perfect shade of pink and one he'd always associated with her.

He touched his nose to hers. "It was for the tough love you gave me at the Authority prison and for making me remember what was important."

"Oh, Trev."

"I believed I was cursed, and you helped me see it was only my fear getting in the way of my happiness. Thank you for allowing me to believe in good again."

Her chocolaty eyes were brimming with tears, seemingly at direct odds with her luminous smile. "I love you."

He grinned. "I love you, too, Soleil Dalliance Stephens."

"I have a confession."

But he already knew what she intended to say.

"I'm not a dalliance sort of girl," she blurted.

Lifting her left hand, he dropped a kiss on her engagement ring. "I know."

Thank you for taking the time to read **The Death Dealer**! I hope you enjoyed Trevor and Soleil's story. Up next is **The Seer**, with Fintan Sullivan and Taryn Stephens. Keep reading for a glimpse of their story.

To stay current on information regarding this series along with my future book release, please subscribe to my newsletter. https://www.tmcromer.com/newsletter/

THE SEER

Fintan Sullivan hated his gift. He always had. Having the sight was a fecking bitch, and he'd prefer not to deal with it if he didn't have to. Mainly, it was why he avoided anyone outside the Authority.

But when the Aether called, you came running.

He sighed heavily as he checked the number and walked up the path to the old Victorian house with the black wrought-iron fence. Already, he despised the place. Its overall vibe screamed old. Not as old as some of the estates he'd seen in Europe or even his own family's Irish home, but old enough that a few spirits likely lingered in the American mausoleum in front of him.

Also, his ultimate demise lay on the other side of the wooden door with its stained glass.

And her name was Taryn Stephens.

The visions had told him as much.

"Feckin' second sight," he muttered.

From behind him, his attention was caught by the slapping of shoe soles against the walkway. He glanced over his shoulder and frowned.

"Draven? Sure, and what are you doing here, man?"

"When the Aether calls, you come running."

Fintan snorted. "Yeah, and didn't I have a similar conversation with meself just minutes ago?"

"Why are you standin' out here, *cher*? Why not in there?" Draven possessed a raspy leftover-from-old-Louisiana accent, the only true hint of his heritage since he never spoke of his past.

"Fate, visions, and my ultimate demise."

One side of Draven's mouth kicked up, and humor lit his warm whiskey eyes. "Sounds like a woman."

"It is."

"Why am I not surprised?"

"What the feck are ya meanin'?" Fintan demanded, not really irate but definitely stalling for time. If it required getting into a heated debate rather than walking through that bleeding door, he'd do it. He was Irish, and his people preferred fighting to exploring their inner feelings.

"You'll not get a rise out of me, *cher*. I've been summoned."

"I hate it when you do that, I do," he grumbled.

"What?"

"*That.* Skirt a volatile situation as easily as ya do, ya scut!"

Draven laughed, and the sound was pure magic. Low and throaty, but leaving one in no doubt his amusement was real. "You're tryin' to fight me so you don't have to deal with one petite female? She doesn't seem threatenin' to me."

"You'll be after tellin' me why, ya will. And how do you know Taryn?" Fintan was truly angry this time. He may not want her for himself, but he sure as feck didn't want to see her hook up with Draven.

Dark-blond brows drawn together in confusion, his friend

shook his head. "Give in now, Fintan. You're obviously head over heels."

"I didn't say I *didn't* care about her. Just that I don't *want* to care about her."

"She's your *ultimate demise?*"

"Aye."

Draven clapped him on the back and grinned. "What a way to go, *cher*! What a way to go!"

"Sure, and I never got a clear vision of the future with her," he mumbled as he scratched his chest and stared at the offending door.

"What's all this?" A gravely male voice asked from behind them.

Fintan didn't need to turn around. He'd known five minutes ago Trevor Blane would be joining their group. Next would be Alexander Castor, then Creed Calder. Only Jordan Brothers would be late to this pointless meeting of the Aether's.

"Our man Fintan is stallin' for time. He doesn't want to face what's on the other side of that door." Draven smirked triumphantly when Trevor chuckled.

Fintan never wanted to plant another person a facer as badly as he did his long-time friend.

He didn't dignify Draven's response with a reply. Instead, charging for the fecking door.

PREORDER THE SEER TODAY!
tmcromer.com

BOOKS BY T.M. CROMER

Get your printable list here:

www.tmcromer.com/printable-booklist

PARANORMAL ROMANCE

The Sentinels of Magic Series:

THE AETHER

THE DEATH DEALER

THE SEER

The Thorne Witches Series:

SUMMER MAGIC

AUTUMN MAGIC

WINTER MAGIC

SPRING MAGIC

REKINDLED MAGIC

LONG LOST MAGIC

FOREVER MAGIC

ESSENTIAL MAGIC

MOONLIT MAGIC

ENCHANTED MAGIC

CELESTIAL MAGIC

EVERLASTING MAGIC

CAPTIVATING MAGIC

The Thorne Witches: Happily Ever Afters Series:

ENDURING MAGIC

BOUNDLESS MAGIC

The Unlucky Charms Series:

PINTS & POTIONS

WHISKEY & WITCHES

BEER & BROOMSTICKS

COCKTAILS & CAULDRONS

WINE & WARLOCKS

HIGHBALLS & HEXES